A Double-Minded Man

What others say about Bill Prickett

Bill Prickett is a friend and a hero. He and I were both former leaders in the early "ex-gay" movement, and since leaving those programs far behind, Bill has become a major voice for love, inclusion, and forgiveness. For several years, he and I worked together in a support group of people who'd been involved in the programs, many with lasting wounds.

Bill has what's known as a way with words, and they come from a deep and caring part of his soul. He is also a wonderful storyteller, as I think you'll soon see.

—Michael Bussee, former "ex-gay" leader and an original founder of Exodus International

Around the same time I was leading the Courage ministry in the UK, Bill was doing similar work in the States. Our respective groups promised to help people change their sexual orientation. Eventually, we both realized the ineffectuality of such efforts, beyond simple behavioral modification. I took Courage to a fully affirming ministry for gay Christian people, refuting the "ex-gay" proposition.

I met Bill years later as part of an alliance of former leaders confronting the teachings of these "ex-gay" groups. I value him as a friend as well as a persistent voice in speaking the truth about the harm these programs and procedures inflict, particularly on young people. This must-read book combines Bill's own experiences with more than thirty years of research in an uplifting story of hope.

—Jeremy Marks, founder of Courage, UK

I've known Bill for several years and have seen him work tirelessly to expose the grim reality of the "ex-gay" movement. If anyone can write a novel that depicts the experience of a man compelled to comply with the expectations of those who claim God wants gay people to change their stripes, it's Bill.

—Yvette Cantu Schneider, former policy analyst at Family Research Council and former director of Women's Ministry at Exodus and author of *Never Not Broken: A Journey of Unbridled Transformation*

Since his exit from "ex-gay" ministry more than thirty years ago, Bill Prickett has been speaking out against conversion therapy programs. *A Double-Minded Man* accurately and poignantly captures the mental conflict and struggle many of us faced on our quest to reconcile our faith with our biology and longing for unconditional love and acceptance. Bill uses his insight and decades-long experience in conservative Christian culture to bring a not-so-uncommon story to life.

—Tim Rymel, MEd, former outreach director of Love in Action and author of *Rethinking Everything: When Faith and Reality Don't Make Sense.*

I'm the mother of a gay son and interact daily with parents of LGBTQ kids. The idea of conversion therapy—that someone refuses to accept my child as he is, and would insist that he change—is offensive to me.

For years, I've valued the tireless work Bill Prickett does to inform and educate about these spurious programs. He has spoken to our moms' group, and I've watched him interact with those who've been harmed by these ministries.

His writing is a valuable resource to both LGBTQ people and their loved ones. I hope this book, written in a fiction format, will be a another tool to enlighten people about the insidious nature of so-called "ex-gay" treatments.

—Liz Dyer, founder of Serendipitydodah—home of the Mama Bears, a private Facebook group for moms of LGBT kids, with more than 6,000 members

Other Books by Bill Prickett

Sow the Wind, Reap the Whirlwind

"An emotional roller coaster. Parts had me openly crying as I turned the pages. I love the characters." —KJ

"What a great read! I wondered if the author went to the same churches I have attended!" —MC

"Brilliant, talented, witty, life-giving." —JW

"The author manages to touch on many of the challenges that faced the church in the seventies and continue to confront faithful people in the new century. The issues are rather skillfully woven into the storyline with optimism and faith, and without becoming excessively preachy." —JAT

"Although set against the backdrop of the social changes of the 1970s, this novel and the issues it portrays are as contemporary as the evening news. While painting robust and multidimensional characters and guiding us through a captivating plot, the author keeps us thinking about the 'big questions' of religion without being bogged down. It's a fascinating, topical, and character-driven reading experience. —DT

"I don't consider myself a religious person, so I wasn't sure what to expect from a book with the church as an integral part of the storyline. Was I pleasantly surprised!" —LK

The Mind Set on the Flesh

"A clear, flowing story. Prickett's real life experience with these characters is evident in his descriptions. They are believable and have personalities that allow you empathize and care for them." —PK

"The story is approachable, and the characters are uncomfortably recognizable. I enjoyed the way the author dips deeply, exploring their strengths, weaknesses, and motivations. I enthusiastically recommend this book to friends and family." —KS

"Riveting and challenging. As an avid reader, I found this was one book I could not put down." —SL

A Time to Every Purpose

"I was quickly drawn into the plot. Its touches on [many] topics: AIDS, disillusionment, suicide, abandonment, and hatred cloaked as religion, all topped by a sassy drag queen angel…woven into a message of hope and gratitude. I still cannot figure out how the author did it. I guess that's one reason it's so good." —KS

"The book starts out like a cross between *It's A Wonderful Life* and *A Christmas Carol*, with a heaping helping of *Touched By An Angel*. But what Prickett does is take this framework and make something new and wonderful from it. It's engaging, historically accurate, compelling, immersive, and above all, FUN. You'll enjoy the journey!" —JH

"It is a beautifully written and hopeful story we can all learn from. The author does a fabulous job of showing how the past instructs our present and future. We influence each other either positively or negatively depending on our attitude toward those we come into contact with every day." —DM

"Bill Prickett weaves a story filled with compassion, hope, and humor. This was a fantastic book. It really touched me." —TJ

"Another great book by Bill Prickett." —ED

A DOUBLE-MINDED MAN

A Novel *by* Bill Prickett

A Double-Minded Man

Printed in the United States of America

Cover Design: Melissa K. Thomas

Headshot by Cynthia Hammond Photography, LLC

Luminare Press
442 Charnelton St.
Eugene, OR 97401
www.luminarepress.com

ISBN: 978-1-64388-193-5
LCCN: 2019911961

To the brave survivors of these harmful "ex-gay" programs.
I acknowledge your wounds.
Your perseverance and courage inspire me.

To those who couldn't endure the soul-crushing message.
My heart grieves your death, so my commitment is to honor
your life by trying to prevent others from being hurt.

To other "ex-gay" leaders who walked away,
then stood up and spoke out. Many of you are my friends.
All of you are my heroes.

Finally, to my patient husband.
You didn't suffer the trauma of this religious abuse
(Thank God!), but you've seen the detrimental impact it had
on my life. And still you love me, for better or for worse.

First Person, *Imperfect.*

My name is Nate Truett. I'm five-ten and weigh around one-sixty. I don't think it's self-deprecating when I admit that I'm not classically handsome—you know, high cheekbones, square jaw line, deep dimples, cleft chin, and thick, wavy hair. My face has light freckles across my nose and cheeks that have lightened over time to almost unnoticeable. My ears and nose seem proportional to the size of my head and perform their function as intended. Girls never swooned when I entered a room, but they've called me "cute," which I took as a compliment. I'm told my exceptional feature—what people first notice—is my eyes; they are large and blue, with long lashes. My aunt used to say they were "too pretty" for a boy, which I assume was also a compliment. I wish my hair had stayed the light blond color of my childhood; however, as I got older, it washed out to brownish blond. These days, it's also mixed with generous amounts of well-earned gray.

Yes, I know this is an unorthodox way to begin a book, but there's "method to my madness." I recently read an entire novel written in first person—*I, me, my.* It was enjoyable; the main character was relatable though I had no clue what he looked like. Well, this is *my* story. I'm the one telling it, in first person, and didn't want you to have that same experience. (I suppose I could have sneaked it in, using one of those subtle literary devices—describing what I see in a mirror or having another character talk about my appearance—but that seemed contrived.)

As I write this, I'm far enough past forty to *think* I have the maturity and perspective to tell what happened with as much honest detachment as possible when talking about my own life. More than a decade has passed since the events related here began, so I at least have the advantage of reflective hindsight. Thankfully, I also have personal journals, a discipline I began in high school. They've provided an unvarnished snapshot of my emotions and musings during those times, minus my ego's attempts to retroactively improve my history.

I moved from my hometown of Memphis to Birmingham, Alabama, to attend Evangelical Presbyterian College of the South, where I'd received a full academic scholarship. EPCS was one of three schools operated by the National Association of Evangelical Presbyterian Churches, a group of churches too small to be called a denomination but too vocal to remain attached to our previous organization. In the early sixties, ministers from about eighty churches, primarily in the South, grew concerned about the "rising onslaught of biblical compromise and moral relativism" in the denomination, so they broke away to form our renegade association. My father and my grandfather were two of those ministers. That's my ecclesiastical ancestry—a legacy difficult to ignore and impossible to live up to.

I earned a Bachelor of Science in marriage and family counseling, with a concentration in theology and an emphasis on biblical counseling. It seemed an ideal symbiotic combination—I liked helping people and wanted to serve the church, without being a pastor. (A *great* disappointment to my father.) Plus, for years, I struggled with "hidden desires" and lived in fear that someone would discover my secret. I think I unconsciously hoped counseling others might also help me eradicate those sinful attractions. After college, I completed my master's degree along with the state requirements to become a licensed marriage and family therapist.

For the sake of structure, I've divided the book into three parts, titled with biblical text. (That seemed ironically appropriate.) However, when all these things were happening…*to* me and *around* me…they didn't fit into those precise designations.

They still don't!

How nice it'd be if this were like one of those cheesy after-school specials in which everyone learns valuable life lessons, all the loose ends get wrapped up, and everyone lives happily ever after.

Real life doesn't work that way, does it?

Mom always told me that everything happens for a reason. I'm not sure I believe that now, but here's what I do know: one *seemingly* random encounter, and everything changed. Parts of myself I'd refused to acknowledge were exposed. Then fear and religious dogma prevailed over reason, and I made decisions that would reshape my life, moving me out of the protective insulation of my religious environment and catapulting me into a community on the cusp of seismic change.

I know we all do things we regret later: that's part of being human. But looking back, I see nagging questions that *should* have been answered. Confusion was ignored, not confronted. I dismissed inconsistencies in what I was being told was right and true.

A decade later, and I'm still healing from the damage—to my life, my core beliefs, my very soul. People I cared about were hurt, friendships were lost, and lives were damaged.

One person is dead.

How do I reconcile my role in all this devastation?

Please know that I didn't intentionally, or even consciously, set out to harm anyone. Including myself. But that doesn't change the tragic outcome. I trusted those who were untrustworthy. I believed lies when my own heart told me the truth.

I don't offer this account of the events as an excuse. It wasn't as if I were an unwilling pawn, under the spell of a Svengali master. I take full responsibility for my actions, the beliefs that motivated them, and the consequences. I've dedicated my life to making amends, though I'm aware there are those who can never forgive me. I struggle to forgive myself. At the very least, I hope others can learn from my mistakes.

Finally, just so you know, the more "carnal" elements of my story (Yes, there *are* carnal parts!) have been toned down. I can't avoid including them because, although a couple constituted those bad decisions I've mentioned earlier, one was consequential and life altering. Nonetheless, my strict Southern and religious upbringing remains an incessant voice of restraint. In other words, I'm a bit of a prude. If you're reading this for salacious content, you will likely be disappointed.

Let's begin in January of 1982…

Part I

The Things Hidden in the Darkness

One

"Why not take off your coat and stay awhile?"

The question came from Miss Gert, my administrative assistant, standing in the open doorway, holding a copy of my morning appointments in one hand and my coffee mug in the other. I forced a weak smile as I stood, removed my coat, and held it close to me, like Linus's security blanket.

The intrusion startled me, interrupting the moody refrains of Anne Murray's "You Needed Me" still reverberating in my head.

You gave me strength to stand alone again
To face the world out on my own again

I'd stayed in the warm car, listening to the entire song—partly because I like it but mostly to avoid going into my office. Then I took extra time to compose myself after the wet, flowing emotions the lyrics had brought up.

"Who does the counselor go to when he needs to talk with someone?" she asked.

I didn't see it as a question with an expected answer. Which was good, since answering would require admitting that I wanted, or needed, to talk.

Which I don't.

She put the mug on the coaster and placed the schedule next to my phone. Her morning routine. Today she patted me, maternally, on the arm. "I baked a raisin-cinnamon coffee cake to welcome you back. I'll bring some in and refill your mug. I also have a stack of mail that accumulated while you were away."

Grace Presbyterian Church had hired me a few months out of college as director of congregational care, a position the church had created. I met the qualifications with my degree in marriage and family counseling, combined with theological education. I assumed that my last name, and the pastoral pedigree that came from my grandfather's and father's prominence in the denomination, helped the church make its decision. My primary responsibility was counseling church members, but the role also included personal contact with those who were homebound, hospitalized, or in nursing homes. After two years on staff, the results, and my competency, were evident. The counseling load increased, and I had developed education and training programs and implemented the *ASSISTeam*—volunteers trained to handle short-term counseling with couples and parents, matters of faith, and other life issues. I had built solid relationships with other groups around the county, resulting in a steady increase of outside clients from referrals.

That's when I came up with the idea for Arms of Grace Counseling Center. It would serve as an extension and expansion of our congregational care ministry and as an outreach to the community—for those who might never come into the church offices for counseling. It took weeks of meetings and presentations, but the Board of Elders agreed, naming me the executive director—a title that sounded loftier than it was, given that the staff consisted of me and a receptionist, who would also function as my administrative assistant.

Mrs. Gertrude Carmichael—*Miss Gert*—had been on staff with Grace Presbyterian Church, in one capacity or another, since before I was born. She retired, then her husband died, so she offered her time and skills and was "assigned" to help me. Of course I knew who she was; everyone at church knew, and *loved*, Miss Gert. Nonetheless, I had voiced my objections to the Board of Elders, and privately to Dr. Shannon, our senior pastor. My primary resistance wasn't technically related to her age, which I guessed was pushing seventy, though I'd never be so bold as to ask. I was concerned about her adaptability to such a new, innovative venture. Would she be supportive and flexible as we discovered how we should operate? Was she equipped to manage the many details of day-to-day operations, freeing me to concentrate on seeing clients, promoting the center, and forging referral relationships?

She was a petite woman, not more than five feet tall, and I could not imagine her providing much of an obstacle to those who might try to barge in without an appointment. Her hair was mostly white, worn short around her face, and her sense of fashion seemed tied to a different era. She projected the image of a doting grandmother, not a receptionist.

It didn't take long though for her to prove me wrong. On everything! Her organizational skills were astounding, particularly evident in those early days. The church agreed to headquarter Arms of Grace in the old office wing after the ministerial staff had relocated to the new education building. We had sufficient parking, and a separate entrance, which offered a sense of privacy. A heavy wooden double door, with vertical panes of translucent glass on either side, opened to an ample waiting area. The imposing receptionist desk blocked direct access to the counseling offices and conference room. On the tables throughout the room lay copies of Christian publications and informational literature about the services we provided along with pamphlets on various subjects: *Discerning God's Will*, *Raising Godly Children*, *Signs of a Healthy Marriage*, *Overcoming Fear and Anxiety*, *Handling Doubts*, and *Facing Serious Illness*. We purchased most from a Christian publisher, but I'd written several of them myself. The literature rack also featured copies of a slick, full-color flyer about the church.

Once we opened, Miss Gert showed that she had the necessary compassion to greet those who came to see us, often in times of great distress, and the essential discretion to maintain confidentiality. She had an exhaustive knowledge of the membership, complete with first-hand, inside information about marriages, divorces, children, internal conflicts, and touchy or taboo subjects. Her outgoing personality made everyone feel welcome, yet—when necessary—she could be formidable. I had seen her stand up to the insistent and the belligerent and do so with a rare mix of poise, politeness, and tenacity.

In short, Gert Carmichael was indispensable.

"Things going OK around here?" I asked her.

"Not too bad. Of course, people have been wondering when you'd be back, and Millie Garmin got a bit testy when she couldn't get her niece an appointment right away. Well, I let her know *toot sweet* that it wasn't like you'd been on vacation or..."

The pause spoke volumes. She was unsure how to finish the sentence.

"You were missed, if that's what you mean, Brother Truett?"

It wasn't.

In the beginning, I'd asked her to call me Nate.

"Ministers deserve a show of respect," she replied with demure defiance. "Folks who come here won't hear me disrespecting you with such familiarity."

Since I wasn't technically a minister, and not fond of titles, I tried several times to dissuade the designation, thinking that after she had gotten to know me...after we had worked together for a while...she'd relent. All I got was a polite nod—her way of informing me that I was wasting my time.

"Things got a bit busy during the holidays," she informed. I must have displayed a look of concern, and she held up her hand. "Don't worry. I did referrals to the ASSISTeam and pastoral staff. Even Dr. Shannon pitched in. I was able to push most of your regulars, and they'll show up on your schedule for the next few weeks, so today should be light." She moved to where I was sitting, took the coat from my arms, and hung it on the back of my door. "Though I'm still not sure you should be here. It's hasn't even been—"

The phone rang, interrupting what was sure to be an uncomfortable conversation. "Arms of Grace Counseling Center," she answered in her most professional voice. "How may I help you?"

"That was Pastor Shannon," she informed when the call ended. "He's at home but heading to the hospital. He'd like to see you this afternoon, if you feel up to it, he said. Let me know, and I'll call to confirm."

I let out a puff of air and picked up the coffee mug. It was all the answer I could muster.

"Your first appointment isn't due for a while." She turned to leave as I sat down at my desk. "Brother Truett," she said in a soft voice. "I'm real sorry about your loss. We all loved her." Her voice cracked, but without waiting for a reply, she closed the door.

Widower.

It was not an identity that resonated with me. *About* me.

Until two months ago, when it became my reality.

It felt like wearing someone else's clothes—those of an older man, with gray hair and grandchildren, recollecting memories of all those years together with his wife.

I'm twenty-eight years old. We were only married for five years.

Maybe coming to work today was a mistake. Perhaps I should've taken Mom's, and everyone's, advice and waited a while longer.

I'd determined after Leigh's death that I would return to work as soon as possible. At some level, I think I had something to prove. After all, I should be an example, demonstrating how faith prevailed during the time of crisis. So here I was, trying to resume a normal routine, though nothing about my life felt "normal" these days.

I stared bleary-eyed at my schedule, unmotivated. I'd need maximum amounts of caffeine today. Right on cue, Miss Gert walked in with a carafe and an oversized slice of her homemade apple-cinnamon cake.

That's not going to help with my growing waistline, I concluded, taking a small bite.

The coffee tasted wonderful; I welcomed the warmth as much as I needed the caffeine. As I picked at the cake, I glanced at the mail on the credenza, though I lacked the energy...or motivation...to begin opening it. I couldn't handle more sympathy—cards or otherwise. I looked at the schedule Miss Gert had left on the desk. More accurately, I stared through it, taking slow draws from my coffee.

The room was quiet, part of the intended design. My design. We had the walls double insulated to mask outside noises—people talking in the next room, or more accurately, the fear of people in the next room hearing, could disrupt a counseling session.

I was on my third cup of coffee when my first appointment arrived. Ready or not, the day had begun.

The promised "light day" escalated quickly.

My return to work apparently signaled people to drop in, unannounced and unscheduled. A young woman had to meet with me *today* to discuss God's will in asking her boss for a promotion. One guy in the church's college group wanted my "godly counsel" on whether he should date a lapsed Catholic girl he had met at school. A woman who'd been close to my wife wanted me to pray with her about the tedious process of adoption.

There were several short chats with church members who came to welcome me back and offer condolences. Most were sincere, accompanied by sharing fond memories of my wife. I listened with an intentional, practiced smile.

Eulogy, the sequel.

None of these visits took long, but each exacted time and energy. Miss Gert would rescue me with a reminder that someone was waiting. My appointments included one regular client, an intake for a "rebellious" teenager sent to me by her exasperated parents, and a young man adjusting to his new job, in a new city, while his girlfriend back home was "moving on" without him. There was also a couple seeking to avert an impending divorce.

I'd not even had time to finish part of a sandwich; each time I'd exit my office from an appointment, someone was waiting. By two o'clock, I was wound tight and felt the initial hint of a tension headache. The pain was at the point of causing me to drop my plans to work out—one of my New Year's resolutions—when the intercom buzzed.

"Mrs. Briggs is on line one. She wants to know if you can see her right away."

Teresa Briggs was a counselor's dream, if you charged a hundred dollars an hour. Which we didn't! A middle-aged, wealthy woman, she complained with a multitude of problems, all stemming from an unconscious desire for sympathy. Her husband had long since stopped caring, so she sought it from whomever she could find. I'd been "counseling" her, off and on, for three years.

It was an easy choice.

"Please tell her I have another appointment. See if next week is acceptable."

Off to the gym!

IN THE PAST, I'D KEPT IN DECENT SHAPE BY PLAYING TENNIS AND with a less-than-consistent jogging routine. Admittedly, I'd put on some weight in the past year. I refused to beat myself up about it because...well, it had been a monumentally crappy year. As Leigh grew sicker, my diet consisted of too many fast food meals, unhealthy snacks at all hours of the night, and way too much stress eating. Plus, in those final six months, a complete lack of exercise. Once Mom arrived, and stayed after the funeral, there was an abundance...and over-indulgence...of comfort foods. I wouldn't have considered myself fat, though I did see the formation of "love handles."

So I purchased a gym membership at a large facility near the church that boasted aerobic classes, an indoor track, twelve racquetball courts, separate whirlpools for men and women, a pro shop, and a juice and snack bar. While our church had a Family Life Center that housed a room with fitness equipment, I preferred to embark on this odyssey of good health without church members and staff watching.

"The pastor came by," Miss Gert informed when I pushed through the doors. "But had a meeting downtown and couldn't stay."

"Was he upset I wasn't here?" I propped my elbows on the waist-high counter of the receptionist desk.

"Not at all," she said, looking up from her files. "I explained how your day had filled up and that you didn't even have time to eat lunch." She moved in close, lowering her voice like she was sharing a secret. "Your last appointment rescheduled, so you *could* go home early and get some rest."

"That sounds great, but I'm gonna tackle all that mail that's been piling up. Plus, I have tons of thank-you notes to write."

"If you concentrate on writing the notes, I'll address the envelopes." She handed me a pink piece of paper. WHILE YOU WERE OUT was printed in big letters at the top.

I glanced down to see Susan Bradley's name and office telephone number printed in Miss Gert's flawless handwriting.

"I'll call her later," I muttered as I entered my office and hung up my coat. I stood, fixated on the credenza across the room.

It's just mail, I reminded myself, hoping to inspire some courage, or force my legs to move in that direction.

Once I started opening them, and reading them, it would invite the memories back to the surface. And everything else as well. I would need to write sweet, personal notes of gratitude when what I felt was anything but gratitude. I was sad and angry. And alone.

For more than a year, I watched my wife suffer through the treatments, the pain, and the sickness that accompanied her cervical cancer. Getting worse. Fading away. Through all of it, she exhibited those qualities associated with the brave folks in inspirational Lifetime movies: faith, strength, humor, courage, and positivity. Until that day she informed me, "I can't do this anymore." The surgery, the chemotherapy, and the radiation had not worked. Her body was tired, and she needed rest.

Two months later, just before Halloween, she was gone.

In the weeks after she had died, I patiently endured Mom's ever-present, sometimes incessant, ministrations. Proper Southern etiquette and Christian deportment—my mom was staying with me, so I couldn't avoid compliance—required that I cordially greet guests who dropped by to express their condolences, offer their support, or pray with me. I listened to countless expressions of love, augmented with stories of what she'd done and the impact she'd had. I kindly deflected invitations to get me out of the house for a movie, a racquetball match, a walk in the park, or lunch.

I carried out my daily activities with perfunctory obligation. Even my favorite holidays, Thanksgiving and Christmas, passed as nothing more than another day, different only because of the food and festive activities, which I also declined.

Who wants a morose mix of Scrooge, Grinch, and Eeyore at their Christmas party?

Despite Mom's chagrin, I watched lots of TV, more for distraction than entertainment, caring little about the activities on the flickering screen. At night, sleep required my headphones and cassettes of my favorite hymns to drown out the endless turbulence inside my mind.

My training and experience recognized these symptoms as grief and depression.

Time heals all wounds had been repeated to me so many times, by so many people. Each time, I coerced a civil "thank you," though my mind screamed, *Shut up!*

God is my strength, I affirmed to myself today. Leigh repeated this throughout her illness. It seemed to bring her such peace. She would insist I say it aloud with her, aware that my faith was not as strong as hers.

Resisting the urge to begin with the innocuous mail, I reached for the shoebox of cards Mom had collected from those who'd sent flowers or donated to Leigh's requested charity—Magic City Women's Shelter, where she volunteered, using her degree in elementary education to set up a tutoring program for the children who couldn't attend school. There were several piles, organized and labeled. The stack of sympathy cards, from groups, organizations, and individuals I worked with throughout the city, was the biggest.

The intercom rescued me from writer's cramp. "Miss Bradley is on line two," Miss Gert informed. "Says you *better* take her call."

"SUZ," I SAID IN THE CONTRIVED CHEERFULNESS THAT MARKED most of my casual interactions in recent weeks. "Why aren't you here helping me open all this mail?"

"Sounds like more fun than I'm having. I've been working on a report to the Finance Committee all day," she groaned. "I could take you to dinner as a consolation prize. It's time you clock out, kiddo."

It was almost five o'clock; before answering Susan's call, I'd insisted Miss Gert go home, as there was nothing more she could do until I finished writing the notes.

"How was your first day back?"

"Not bad," I replied. "It's been busy. Had some scheduled appointments, and two drop-ins. Several folks came in to welcome me back." Knowing she questioned my returning to work right now, I inserted, "Oh, and I even hit the gym this afternoon."

"Such a good boy, keeping that New Year's resolution."

Susan Bradley and I met on our first day at college; we were both trying to register for the Monday-Wednesday-Friday morning "Introduction to the Old Testament" class, a required course for all freshmen. The school's simple registration system laid out a predetermined number of index cards, printed with the class, the times, and the professor. If there was a prerequisite before taking the class, that was included. All you had to do was show your student ID, sign a list, and pick up the card. You were registered.

However, if there were no cards left, the class was full. Keep looking. The school offered most required classes at various times and days, and by several professors.

"I need that," I'd objected when she picked up the last card.

"We all do," she replied, clutching the card close to her chest. The mandated nametag identified her as *Susan*, from Little Rock. She was short, though I think girls preferred the term "petite." Her red hair, with bangs cut above her eyebrows and loose curls around her head, gave a fuller frame to her thin face. As she talked, her hair moved and bounced, unlike most hairdos I'd seen around campus and at church—the ones that sat on their heads like a domed structure, held inert with a coat of shellac.

"But that's the last one," I explained, in case she didn't understand how the system worked. "Making the class full."

"So *that's* what it means when there are no cards left?" Her tone was condescending, and for added effect, she slapped her palm against her forehead. "There are lots of other choices."

I shut my eyes and took in a measured breath through my mouth, which I let out through pursed lips. "I figured taking Old Testament first thing in the morning, after several cups of coffee, would help me stay awake."

Susan turned to the woman sitting on the other side of the table. "He didn't mean that, professor. I'm sure your class is stimulating and informative."

I was mortified. Had I just insulted the professor who would decide my fate?

They both laughed. Then I read the nametag around the woman's neck: *Volunteer Janet.*

"You are too easy, kiddo." She checked out my nametag. "So, Nathaniel from Memphis, we seem to be at a stalemate."

"Whatever." I threw my backpack over my shoulder, ready to move to the next table to get away from her. "And it's Nate."

"It's also offered on Tuesday and Thursdays." This was Volunteer Janet, being helpful.

"Yeah," I replied, forcing a politeness. "I have English Comp at that time."

Volunteer Janet was persistent. Taking out a printed sheet from a manila folder, she perused through it. "What about eleven, on Monday, Wednesday, and Friday?"

I checked the schedule I'd recorded in my spiral notebook as I had gotten class cards. "I have P.E."

"Tell you what," Susan interjected. "Take this one, but you owe me lunch after registration."

I regarded her, and her intentions, with suspicion. "Lunch is provided in the cafeteria." Again, I wondered if she was aware. "And it's free," I added.

She slipped the card in the pocket of my shirt and walked away. After two or three steps, she looked back over her shoulder. "See you outside the lunchroom Friday, at one-fifteen...*Nathaniel.*" She blew me a kiss and was then lost in the crowded room.

She's very forward, I concluded.

"Nathaniel, are you listening to me?"

"Yes," I responded, drawn back to our conversation.

"So, buy you dinner? It's your first day back at work. I'm sure you haven't stopped to eat."

She was correct. I'd been concentrating on the tedious task of being repetitively grateful. In cursive.

"It sound great, but there's still so much work to do here. Rain check?"

We set a tentative lunch for next week. "I'm gonna hold you to that," she reminded me as we ended the call.

SHORTLY AFTER SUSAN AND I MET—ON THAT FATEFUL DAY AT registration—we did have lunch. I was relieved to discover it was not a date. We discussed the usual things: hometown, parents, high school, and class schedules. Our inherent differences surfaced when the conversation turned to career plans. I was surprised at her intentions to go into the ministry since our association didn't allow women to serve in such leadership roles. My face must have signaled my thoughts.

"Maybe I can change them," she said with defiant confidence.

For the next hour, we discussed the Bible, Paul's writing, and the church. We also veered off to social issues such as the war in Vietnam and women's liberation. We disagreed on most everything! The only conservative thing about her was her outfit, which was in keeping with the school's dress code.

For the next two years, we had several classes together and often studied together. Her coarse language could offend me, but she was witty, smart, and incredibly insightful. We became one another's confidant. I would listen as she ranted about the sexism of our association, and was her shoulder to cry on when an upperclassman dumped her. In return, I talked to her about being overwhelmed by my class load and my part-time job as youth minister at a rural church in Gadsden, about thirty minutes north of Birmingham. She listened when I was discouraged or in those times at which I struggled with decisions—what she deemed "too much inside my own head." I talked to her about switching my concentration from Christian education to counseling. Susan was my sounding board. Of all the people I knew, I could count on her to be honest with me, often to the point of merciless. In her words: "Don't come to me if you want someone who'll bullshit you."

At the end of our sophomore year, she told me she was transferring to Birmingham-Southern, a liberal arts Methodist college on the other side of town. From what I knew of the school, the operative word was *liberal*. She'd realized there might never be a pastoral role for her in our denomination. "I'm so pissed at male chauvinism at this school. Even when it's cloaked in Scripture, it's demeaning."

I tried to convince her to stay, but she'd made up her mind. "I know what I'm called to do, and I do not believe God made a mistake. I have to pursue this, so I'll go somewhere where having a vagina is not an issue."

We continued to talk on the phone, and got together for lunch or dinner. Then I met Leigh in my junior year, and she captured much of my time. Susan wanted to meet Leigh, so we scheduled dinner. I was stunned when she arrived, fifteen minutes late. Her hair, which had once been short, wavy, and red, was now long, straight, and black. It reminded me of Morticia Adams, an observation I did *not* say aloud. If we'd passed one another on the street, I would not have recognized her. I expressed concern at how thin she looked; she appeared sick. "I'm fine. I eat organic, with very little meat and almost no sweets," was her explanation. Her face had almost no makeup, and she wore large, black-rimmed glasses that slipped down her nose when she talked. Which was a lot. And with fervency and volume.

She showed great interest in Leigh, asking how we'd met and about her training to be an elementary school teacher. For the most part, I was the spectator as they got to know one another. When I did enter the conversation, we fell into the routine of old times: we disagreed. It was infuriating. I left with the conclusion she was a raving, opinionated, left-wing liberal feminist with aspirations for domination. Leigh thought Susan was "brash, but interesting."

When Susan went to seminary out of state, we lost touch. I'd been at Grace for a couple of years, still in the position of director of congregational care, when out of the blue, the church's receptionist buzzed my phone to say, "I have a Susan Bradley on the line for you. She says you went to college together."

I learned she'd returned to Birmingham and was on the ministerial staff at Forestdale Methodist Church, a medium-sized congregation in a very affluent section of Birmingham's Southside with a reputation for social activism and liberal teaching that attracted a huge college crowd, along with the artistic types who lived in that area. It didn't take long to reveal our differences had only increased. We were cordial, but when the call ended, I determined it was the end of my friendship with Susan.

I had been wrong! From the time we'd found out about Leigh's cancer until the funeral, Susan had been there for her, and for me. She brought food, took Leigh to doctor visits, sat with her during chemo, and even cleaned the house. Her compassion, like her theology, was liberal.

"I SAW YOUR CAR IN THE PARKING LOT."

There was no mistaking that resonant voice.

"Sorry we missed one another today, but I wanted to stop by before heading home and welcome you back."

"Thanks, Pastor. It's good to be back. I needed to be here more than anyone who came in today."

Dr. David Shannon was Grace's senior pastor, only the third man to hold that title. He'd taken the position in 1967, when the church was still relatively small. Under his leadership, helped by remarkable growth in the city, the church had become the second largest in the association. Fortunately, the elders who founded the church in the late forties had had the foresight to buy a large parcel of land, so expansion—which would be cost prohibitive—had not been constrained by the burgeoning development of the city of Homewood, just south of Birmingham.

He had a PhD from Westminster Theological Seminary and served as an adjunct professor at EPCS—Evangelical Presbyterian College of the South, my alma mater—and a nationally renowned preacher and speaker. His Sunday morning sermons aired live on the local ABC station and also around the country on a Christian radio network. There were plans to broadcast the entire worship service nationally on TV as well.

He took a chair facing my desk. "You're working late."

I looked at my watch; it was after six. I motioned to the stacks of mail. "Catching up."

"This can't be an easy time, Nate," he offered with visible concern. "Nor will it get easier in the coming days. God is sufficient, and He is our strength, but with your training, you know that you can't rush the grieving or the healing."

He spoke from personal experience. His son, a police officer, had been killed in the line of duty the year I came to work for the church. Nonetheless, talking about Leigh's death was still difficult, so I just nodded my agreement.

"Is there anything you need, son?"

He'd never called me that before, and I fought getting choked up. "The church has been so thoughtful. Every time I think the supply of food will slow down, another Sunday school class comes by with more. The fridge stays full. I reckon at some point I'll have to learn to cook."

Dr. Shannon was a firm but fair boss. He listened to my thoughts, concerns, and ideas, which was helpful when we were starting Arms of Grace. Nothing seemed to ruffle or stress him out. I'd never seen him angry or heard him yell. His demeanor was always professional, detached, and somewhat formal. Cordial, but not chummy. Even though he was busy, talking to him never felt rushed, as though he had other things to do.

"Claire wanted me to invite you over to dinner. When you feel up to it. She likes being a mother hen."

"That's so kind. Tell her I would love that. I'll have Miss Gert call and set it up." Rather than rely solely on my memory, I made myself a note on the pad I kept by my phone.

He stood, and as I moved around the desk, he embraced me in a strong hug.

Another first.

THE SECOND WEEK OF JANUARY, BIRMINGHAM HAD A FREAK, unexpected snow and ice storm, after temperatures had hovered near zero for weeks. More than a foot of snow, which then froze, paralyzed the city.

Grace Presbyterian opened our Family Life Center as a shelter for people who were without power or for those who'd been stranded on the roads. All staff who could get there "camped out" in various Sunday school rooms for five days to help with the duties of keeping the kids entertained, cooking meals, offering Bible studies to those interested, singing songs...whatever necessary to help people through the crisis. Once it was over, the pastor encouraged us to take the next two days off to rest.

I went home, slept for ten hours, then had lots of coffee. With the two uninterrupted days, I decided it was time to tackle a task I'd been putting off for weeks: cleaning out Leigh's things. Mom and Suz had been nudging me since Thanksgiving. I wasn't ready then.

Was I ready now?

I expressed the collision of emotions in my journal. Just after sunrise, I visited her grave, where I tearfully shared my plan.

My emotions were erratic. Moods could shift without warning and at breakneck speed. Anger. Joy. Nostalgia. Sadness. Such as when I came across the small ceramic bell I'd given her for our first Christmas together. I gave myself permission to cry for exactly five minutes. Then I continued.

Throughout the process was an ever-present temptation to detach and distance myself from what I was doing.

This is not another house-cleaning project. Stay present. In the moment. Embrace the memories and the emotions.

The small dining room—little more than an extension of the kitchen—was my sorting station. Our combined life—her presence in my life—was reduced to a series of pragmatic decisions: Should I keep it? Give it away? Trash it?

I hated being dispassionate about things that mattered. About *someone* who mattered.

Worse, as I discarded so many items, the question came: *Now, where do I fit here?*

A HOT BOWL OF OATMEAL WAS ON THE COUNTER; I STIRRED TO cool it enough to eat. The phone startled me. "How's the cleaning project going?" It was Susan.

"How did you know—"

"I talked to Charlotte yesterday. She told me you were packing up Leigh Anne's stuff. I can come over and lend a hand."

"That's very...Wait, what? You talked to my mom?"

I might have been too tired to wrap my brain around that one. Mom had expressed her admiration for the way Susan had cared for me and Leigh, but when did they start talking to one another? I could imagine, in horror, Mom's reaction to some of Susan's liberal beliefs, profanity, and sacrilegious tendencies.

"Yes, of course. She likes to know how you're doing and assumes you won't tell the truth."

"I'm stunned. You two are like...polar opposites"

"We both care about you. Besides, she's a hoot. Yes, she presents all prim and proper and old-school on the outside, but she can read a person in short order after meeting them. Guess it's her training as a real estate agent and all those years being a pastor's wife. I think in a past life she could have been a psychic fortuneteller."

I had no response to that.

"So can I help?"

"Too late," I answered, "I finished last night."

"How are you handling it all?"

I paused and heard myself let out a breath. "Some of it was emotional. But I'm glad I did it."

"Are you remembering to eat?"

"Talking to my mother has you channeling her." I suppressed a snicker.

"You didn't answer the question."

"I'm having breakfast now. And I promise to stop and eat lunch later, so you don't have to call to check on me."

"Am I being a pest?" She sounded hurt.

"No, of course not. I was kidding. I appreciate that you're here for me."

Susan was coming over Friday morning, before work, and would take boxes and bags to the women's ministry. All Leigh's jewelry had gone to her sister in Huntsville. Just before Leigh died, she had made me promise to leave her wedding rings on for burial and to put my wedding band in with her as well.

"If not," she said, "You'll keep it on out of love and loyalty, which will prevent you from moving on with your life."

"What's wrong with that?"

She ignored my objection and made me promise.

There was still a picture of her in my office, but I'd relegated all our wedding photos to an antique steamer trunk I'd gotten after my father had died.

"I want you to go on," she'd pleaded.

Her words had echoed in my head all day as I cleaned, pushing me as I'd resisted every one of those "practical" determinations of what to keep and what to discard.

I glanced over my shoulder at the boxes and bags in the dining room.

This is me...going on.

Two

This afternoon's workout was not very serious; I'd used coming to the gym to escape a ladies luncheon at church, so I wasn't putting forth much energy. It had only been a few weeks, but it was intimidating trying to use those shiny metal machines with the confusing names. Dip bar. Hack squat. Lateral pulldown. Leg adduction. Most days, I thought I belonged in the room with the dumbbells, a name that better described my trying to maneuver the routine.

As I strained to pull the overhead press bar down to my waist, I glanced over at the free weight section of the room and saw someone who personified the type of body I would have ordered, had the decision been up to me. *That* man deserved admiration for the artful crafting of his physique.

An ache in my shoulders reminded me that I had the bar halfway down and was concentrating on his physique, not the machine. I relaxed and sent the bar upward, and the weights downward, with a loud clank. On instinct, I peeked over to see if the guy had heard the clangor. He had, and then nodded his head in my direction, a slight smile etched across his face.

Flustered, I returned the gesture, then continued my routine. But several times I cast a glance in his direction. Twice he caught me, so I looked elsewhere, hoping that he couldn't see me blush from over there.

"'Scuse me." The voice interrupted my thoughts. "Are you finished?"

A woman stood by the machine. I'd become lost in my thoughts and was no longer working anything other than my imagination.

"Sorry," I said, grabbing my towel. I glanced back at the weight room but didn't see him.

My favorite part of working out was sitting in the whirlpool afterward. Being encompassed by the swirls of hot water and steam was as comforting to an aching muscle as a mother's kiss to a skinned knee. Due to my flexible schedule, I was there when most men my age were still at their nine-to-five jobs, and the place was not crowded. After several luxurious minutes, my mind relaxed with my body, and I almost dozed off. When the water level rose, indicating the entrance of another weary afternoon athlete, I opened my eyes. And they probably bulged out like a surprised cartoon character. The guy I'd noticed earlier in the weight room, now stark naked, was standing knee-deep in the tub, not more than two feet away from me. Embarrassment rushed through me. He smiled, but not like he was amused at my reaction.

Did he think I was staring?

I nodded to acknowledge him and then relaxed back into the tranquil caress of the heated currents. But imprinted on my memory was the vivid image of his naked body. I was surprised at the details I could remember. Even my quick glance had confirmed, up close, how well-crafted his chest was. As he held himself on the side of the spa, his biceps flexed, and the veins in his arms streaked down his arm. At that moment, I understood, up close and personal, what the term "washboard" stomach meant.

Whenever possible, I avoided being naked in the presence of others, but he didn't appear bothered.

With that body, why would he be?

"The water's a little hot today," he said, obviously to me, as we were alone.

It would be rude not to talk with him.

He was propped against the side of the tub, with both legs in the water, but everything—*everything!*—else exposed. When I looked up, he smiled. It encompassed his whole face, revealing cavernous dimples on either side and causing the corners of his eyes to crinkle.

If he weren't naked in front of me, that smile would be the feature that I'd most remember about him.

"It feels good on my calf," he continued. "I hurt it playing racquetball last night; got a ball slammed into it. Left this big bruise." He pointed to a round blue area on his left leg. His voice was not the bass voice of a radio newscaster. It was very informal. His manner of speech was friendly and easy on the ears.

"You play racquetball?" I asked. "I picked it up a few years ago. Spent years perfecting my tennis skills, and now this indoor fad is drawing everyone away. I had to give in."

"We'll have to play sometime," he suggested.

"I wouldn't offer much competition."

"To get better, you have to play above your level."

An elderly man joined our ranks, and I excused myself so I'd be on time for my next appointment. "I look forward to seeing you again," I said as I exited.

Good grief, I thought. *I hope he doesn't take that the wrong way.*

I DISTINCTLY REMEMBER THE FIRST TIME I ADMITTED TO HAVING *those* desires. It was in high school, at our church's annual summer youth retreat—the one where I learned to journal. That year, we had a well-known author and youth leader as our teacher, and he spent the week talking to us about "the power of journaling," showing us that many of the biblical stories were personal records...journals... of one person's perspective of what was happening: times of sorrow, pain, confusion, or joy.

At the opening session, he gave us all spiral notebooks and encouraged us to write in them during the scheduled "quiet times" throughout the retreat. He emphasized two primary elements: personal honesty and staying in the present. Over and over he taught: "Be real and write in the now."

In those initial entries, I confessed that I "noticed" other boys, particularly those with muscular physiques. I liked looking at them in the locker room or at the pool, where I'd linger on their chest, stomach, or arms. I was young and sheltered, so there wasn't an adequate vocabulary to my admitted feelings, but it didn't take long for others to fill in the blanks, giving a name…many names, actually…to my feelings.

My father referenced it in his sermons. *Abomination. Sodomite. Unnatural.*

It was on the news and in magazines. *Gay. Pervert.*

Guys at school told jokes. *Queer. Fag.*

My journal became the sole outlet for examining the desires and expressing all my questions: *Where did the feelings come from? Why do I have them? Am I the only one?*

And the one most repeated: *How could I make them go away?*

As a Christian boy, determined to be a faithful disciple of Jesus, I prayed every night to have this sin excised. Every morning, I expected to wake up freed of this "thorn in my flesh." However, over time, I acknowledged the feelings were not going away, so I rationalized my fascination as innocent envy of those better built than I. Then I achieved a "neutral coexistence," likening it to someone allergic to peanuts: they might *want* to eat peanut butter, but they refrain, knowing it would make them sick.

I made a sincere oath: I could never eat peanuts!

But while my rationale and discipline served me well in the waking world, in my dreams, the desires emerged with a vengeance. Promises were not binding, self-control was abandoned, consequences were not considered. "Peanuts" were on the menu, and I consumed them without restraint. The guilt I'd feel was oppressive, leading to repentance and renewed perseverance to overcome. Hours of prayer, reinforced with intensive Bible study, occupied my time and energy.

In my senior year of high school, I "felt the call" to the ministry. The church, and the Bible, placed high moral standards on God's servants. Even though college had strict rules, living away from my parents offered me freedom and autonomy, and it presented new challenges for those old feelings. The campus was apparently a magnet for good-looking guys seeking to serve God. And distract me. My roommate, with his well-developed body, never wore a shirt in our dorm room. Being on the tennis team provided an outlet for pent-up energy, until we got to the showers. I worried those long-suppressed desires would become stronger than my ability to control them.

In my junior year, I met and began dating Leigh. We fell in love and decided to get married a year later—the summer before her senior year. My marriage vows were sacred and eternal, so those long-renounced desires were to be ignored. Matter closed! I maintained the prevailing hope that once I could experience sexual fulfillment righteously with my wife, normal feelings would eventually supersede the unnatural desires.

Throughout the years, I'd kept my promise and never acted on the feelings. Attractive men who stirred up those desires also reminded me of that vow. The guys could be admired, then I'd renew my resolve and plunge myself back into intensive Bible study, memorization, and prayer. Their manly allure would soon be relegated to nothing more than a pleasant afterthought.

Except for that guy from the gym. The *naked* guy in the hot tub. He refused to fade.

Why couldn't I stop thinking of him?

For reasons I refused to acknowledge, I adjusted the time of my workouts to the afternoon. However, I never saw the handsome, naked guy from the whirlpool. I also knew that referring to him…remembering him…in that way only reinforced the mental image. And triggered a new barrage of guilt's recrimination.

Maybe he doesn't work out on a regular basis, I rationalized.

The flawless details of his body dismissed that possibility!

More likely he comes in at another time.

Today, because of back-to-back meetings, my usual workout

time had been impossible, so I came around six o'clock, after my last appointment.

"How's it going?"

I was pushing up the bar on the bench press machine when the greeting came. I bent my head backward and saw *him*. He was wearing a pair of sweat pants, cut off at the knees, and a T-shirt that came down just below his navel. His stomach was wet from perspiration.

I didn't see him working out.

I grunted as I lowered the bars and swung around to a seated position on the bench. "Pretty good," I answered, gasping like an elephant in labor. "Who doesn't love grunting and sweating in a room full of strangers?"

"But the end results are worth the price," he retorted. "How ya' doing on racquetball?"

"To tell the truth, I haven't played since we talked. I might have scared everyone off."

"That good?" he questioned with a raised eyebrow.

"Self-preservation is more like it. I can be dangerous."

"I thrive on danger. Wanna play?"

I forced my mind to stay on racquetball.

"When?" I mumbled through my huffing.

"How 'bout now? You got time?"

I was probably wasting time on my haphazard workout, so at least I'd get some exercise. "Sure."

"By the way, my name's Alex." He extended his hand. "Trey to my friends."

Does seeing him naked in the hot tub, and since then in my dreams, qualify me as a friend?

Thankfully he answered by saying, "Please, call me Trey."

"Trey?" I questioned with genuine curiosity, taking his handshake.

"Well, my full name is Alexander Bastien Stavros, the third. Third...Trey." He held up three fingers. "It's a family legacy," he explained.

"Trey it is," I replied, mirroring his three-finger gesture. "Stavros, like the—?"

"Stavros Hot Dogs. Another family legacy. My grandfather started it back in the forties."

"I love them. There was one near the college campus, and we'd go there for lunch." When he didn't reply, I worried I might have embarrassed him by bringing up his connection to the well-known restaurants. "I'm Nate. And just so we're even, it's Nathaniel Stanton Truett. No number at the end."

He seemed to be thinking. The gaze made me uncomfortable, though his intense dark eyes were captivating. "Nice to meet you… *Nathaniel*."

Only two people—my mom and Susan—used my full first name, though it appeared that short list had just grown to three. Three…Trey.

I stood and retrieved my towel. "Let me go get my racket."

"It'll be fun."

"Said the Japanese as they headed for Pearl Harbor," I remarked, turning toward the locker room.

Afterward, we got juice in the downstairs snack bar. "You are fast as hell, and have a killer backhand."

"Right," I replied with exaggerated sarcasm. We were both sweating; I was panting from my humiliating display of athletic prowess.

He fixed his gaze on me as he sipped his orange juice. The simple act of raising the bottle to his lips caused his biceps to noticeably flex. "Your tennis background has given you the skills necessary to be a great player. Keep at it, and you'll soon be beating the pants off me."

Don't go there!

"Wanna try it again tomorrow night?" he asked. "I have a standing reservation for the courts, but my usual partner canceled."

Drat, that's church night.

"Can't tomorrow. How about Thursday?"

He cut his eyes upward for a second, giving the suggestion some thought. "That should be OK. Let me give you my home number so you can call me tomorrow evening. By then I'll know my Thursday schedule." He tore a rag-strip of paper from a flyer on the bulletin board and borrowed a pen from me. "If I'm not home, Gennie will take the message."

Gennie?

We said our good-byes, and he exited to the showers. I returned home to shower, risking a smelly car over seeing him naked again.

Lead us not into temptation.

But it wasn't so easy to restrain temptation. That night, when personal convictions couldn't assert control and while conscious resolve rested, long-forgotten specters overpowered my dreams, tapping into suppressed desires that would not be ignored. This incarnation involved a naked Trey—working out, playing racquetball, entering the hot tub.

It had been years since such activities had invaded my sleep. In the past, it had been like watching frames of an old home movie. A few flickers, then gone. This was different. More vivid.

It felt *real.*

In the morning came the all-too-familiar guilt. And an accompanying wet mess in my underwear.

"Is this an intake?" I asked Miss Gert after skimming through my afternoon appointments.

She walked to her desk, thumbed through file folders, and pulled one from the stack. "No, he's director of a ministry the church supports as part of our community missions. He was scheduled back in October, but since you were on leave, I moved the appointment. I think he wants to talk about what they do."

When I returned from the gym and lunch, a young man was in the waiting room. He sat upright in chairs not designed for long-term comfort, with his hands folded in his lap and his ankles crossed under the seat. Even as he turned his head to see me enter, his posture remained precise, and his gaze was expectant. Avoiding him would be impossible.

Did my workout run longer than planned?

A discreet glance at the clock gave the answer.

He's thirty minutes early.

"I'm Scot Nelson," he informed as he stood. The way he extended his hand, I wasn't sure if I was supposed to shake it or kiss his ring. "That's Scot, with one t."

"I'm Nate." His hand was soft and his grip, nonexistent. "Also with one t." He laughed, but it was more like a childish giggle.

"Let me get settled, and I'll be right with you."

From the frown and the pout that came over his face, you'd have thought I was sending him away instead of asking him to wait. Nonetheless, I hung up my jacket, took a couple of swigs of water from the jug in my small refrigerator, and briefly sat in silence before buzzing Miss Gert to send him in.

Scot with one t was dressed to the nines in a royal blue three-piece suit and shiny patent leather shoes. The fitted suit accentuated his thin build. He could pass for a sales associate in the men's department of an upscale clothing store. Or a televangelist. I estimated him to be five-two or five-three based on standing beside him. His light blond hair was neatly combed back with a curve that gave some height. Guessing his age would be difficult; his baby face was deceptive.

Moving gracefully into the room, he did a slow survey of his surroundings. "This is nice," he remarked, sitting in the area where I talked to clients. "Thank you for seeing me."

I took the chair across from him. "So tell me what brings you here today."

He reached in his side pocket and drew out a business card, which he handed me. "I'm the leader of a support group, and your church is a financial contributor."

That didn't answer my question.

Printed in large letters in the center of the card was *Whole-*

Hearted, and Scot's name and phone number were in the bottom corner. "So you're also a therapist?"

He had steel blue eyes, with near-white eyebrows that arched as he examined the room, and a smile like he was about to have his picture taken. "Oh, no." He was staring at a painting. If he hadn't continued, I might have assumed he was offering a critique of my office decor. "I founded the ministry." There was more animation now…more enthusiasm…in his enunciated response.

"That's great, but I'm not involved in the church's finances and budgeting—"

"I know," he interrupted, still smiling. "I met with the treasurer and one of the elders last year. They are very kind."

"Is this a group for recovering addicts, like AA?"

"We do use some of the concepts of a twelve-step program, but it's not AA."

Enough!

Time to end this game of Twenty Questions. "Tell me about your group."

"We minister to men who want to leave the gay lifestyle."

Years of training kicked in to prevent any outward reaction; it's inappropriate to telegraph reactions to the person talking. Silence could encourage more disclosure. But not always. Scot seemed fascinated—or amused, from the still-present smile on his face—with the bookcase behind my desk and apparently not in a hurry to provide more information.

Time slowed in the lull.

What does he want with me?

A long-forgotten anxiety engulfed my stomach with nausea, simultaneously causing my ears to ring and my mouth to go dry. If he spoke now, it might not be possible to hear over the pulse pounding in my ears.

Say something, my rattled brain screamed to my parched mouth.

"I've not heard…uhm, are there many such groups?"

He appeared to be in no hurry to answer, then looked at me,

smile intact. "We are seeing acceptance of homosexual behavior increasing. More boys and men are experimenting. The world is telling them that 'gay is okay.' The problem is growing, but praise God, the Holy Spirit is raising up groups like mine to stand against the attack of the devil."

His words were measured and deliberate, like he was reading a prepared statement.

"I see," my professional-self replied.

"Since your church supports the work we do, I wanted to meet. And talk. In person."

His cryptic responses were annoying. "Why?"

"In case you had any referrals."

"Referrals?" I hope he didn't hear the exhale of breath I'd fought to hold in.

"Yes, if you have young men—do you call them patients?—who are struggling with homosexual desires, our group is available as a resource. We can help them like we have helped so many others."

"Good to know." I stood to end our meeting. "Yes, I do like making suggestions to my *clients*." I held up his business card. "I'll put this in my Rolodex."

Once he'd left, I flopped down on the sofa and allowed my heart rate to normalize.

"Scot Nelson was here earlier and left this package for you."

The contents were in a plastic bag emblazoned with the name of Lighthouse, a local Christian bookstore.

"Hmmm," was my response as I picked up the wrapped bag from Miss Gert's desk and headed back to my office. Since he'd first come by, Scot had called several times, leaving messages with Miss Gert.

He's persistent.

There wasn't another appointment for about an hour, and I could return phone calls later. I cut open the shopping bag, which he'd sealed with enough tape to thwart a master criminal. Inside were two paperback books. One was titled *The Unhappy Gays*, written by a preacher I'd heard of: Dr. Tim LaHaye, who'd written several books on depression from a conservative Christian perspective. I put it in the bottom drawer of my desk, to read later, and to prevent my next client from seeing it on my desk. I'd never heard of the other author, Kent Philpott, but his book was *The Third Sex*, with a subtitle of *Six Homosexuals Tell Their Stories.* I skimmed through it. While the front cover identified them as *homosexuals*, the actual stories inside—related in an interview style—were about how these three men and three women had left the homosexual lifestyle.

Scot also included a spiral-bound booklet, with a simple cover and large lettering: *We gave Jesus our whole life, and we are Whole-Hearted.* Below, in smaller, italicized letters it read, *Gay men tell their personal stories of God's Transformation.* The table of contents listed twenty-six people, first name and last initial. I read them all. Some were emotional and dramatic. Each expressed a simple faith that brought powerful change in the desires and their behavior. They had all been able to do what I hadn't: overcome their impure homosexual desires.

What's their secret?

Up to that point, I'd more or less dismissed Scot. Maybe his ministry was doing good works, but it had little to do with me, like those parachurch organizations that had targeted ministries to truckers, or cowboys. For years, I'd acknowledged my inclinations but never considered them a *serious* problem. More of a persistent reminder of the weakness of my flesh. Like a gnat, buzzing around my head.

I had them under control.

In a moral rebuke, an image of Trey, naked in the hot tub, again popped in my head.

Could this group be the answer…finally!…for my struggle?

Three

When I arrived at the gym on Monday, Trey was waiting. "Ready for a rematch?"

"I'm never going to get that modeling career if you keep taking me away from those torturous machines."

"You're a model?"

How adorably gullible.

"For sure. I'm hoping to move from the *Before* to the *After* on those Weight Watcher ads."

I don't think he got my joke. Or wasn't amused. We agreed to one match, and then I'd do my workout. Once the game was over—I was defeated, again!—he walked with me up to the Nautilus room.

"What areas are you working on?" he questioned as I retrieved my exercise card from the file cabinet.

"Besides losing some weight, I'd like more definition in my arms and chest. I've given up on a flat stomach."

He lifted my shirt. "Stomachs are difficult. Combination of diet and lots of targeted work. If you want, I can help."

I was uncomfortable—and somewhat aroused—with him looking at my body, so I tugged my shirt back down and held it in place, an action that seemed to amuse him.

The Lord knoweth how to deliver the godly out of temptations.

"My private trainer?"

"I used to do it to earn extra money during college." He leaned close—the sweat from our game radiated off him—to read my card. "As far as your arms and chest, you just need to maximize what you're already doing. Work on smooth, slow movement. Do ten and then start over. Repetition is the key. I can add some exercises that'll concentrate on the stomach, plus some food tips. We'll see results pretty fast."

His use of the word "we" didn't escape my notice. He recommended three times a week for best results, but that seemed more ambitious than my schedule, perhaps my body, could manage. We agreed to Tuesdays and Thursdays, at four-thirty.

"We should also try and squeeze in some racquetball during the week as well," he informed with enthusiasm. "Jahlee and I play on Wednesdays, but any other day would work for me. It's a great way to get some cardio, burn calories, build muscles, and increase stamina."

Julie?

"I think you just like winning."

For years, my life had been routine. More like a rut. Other than walking to the education building for meetings with the pastor or elders, most of my activities were sedentary: attending meetings, studying, preparing reports, reading, listening to clients. Then I'd go home, eat, read, or watch TV.

Thus the weight gain.

I was excited to add The Gym to my schedule.

It's about getting in shape, not seeing Trey.

No torturer could ever have been so handsome and helpful. His success in developing his own body was both a motivation *and* a distraction. He showed me how I was using some machines improperly, then walked me through my exercises, forcing me to work slowly, methodically.

Besides being fun and energetic, he was attentive and caring. He called one Saturday, after a grueling workout, just to check on me. "If you're too sore, we can rein it back."

"I reckon it depends on how we define 'too sore.' Right now, my flabby, out-of-shape body would like to curl up in the fetal position and think up gruesome things to do to you in revenge."

"Sorry." His apology was accompanied with laughter. "Tylenol will help. Taking a brisk walk might loosen up the muscles. And we can always relax in the hot tub when we finish."

Like my dreams needed additional images of him naked!

"And by the way, you may be a little out of shape, but your body is *not* flabby. If we keep at it, I promise it will get better."

Again with the "we."

"I've been meaning to ask you a question."

"I'm an open book," he replied.

"As my personal trainer, shouldn't I be, you know, paying for your services?"

"No way! I'm doing this as a friend. It's fun having someone to work out with. How 'bout we meet up this evening? You can buy me a beer, and we'll call it even."

Spending the evening with him would be exciting, but I couldn't be seen at a bar. Because he still didn't know about my job, I needed a valid reason. "I really have to decline. I have shirts in the washer that will have to be ironed. Can't very well show up tomorrow in my smelly gray sweat suit, can I?"

"You work on Sundays?"

"Church," I clarified.

Silence.

"My father was a Presbyterian minister," I inserted, feeling the need to explain. "I've gone to church all my life."

It wasn't *all* the truth, but it was enough. For now.

"To each his own" he responded. "My folks are Greek Orthodox, but I haven't been to church in years. They've given up trying to convert me back into the fold."

"To each his own," I echoed.

I'll tell him the rest later.

"Hey, Mom. Just wanted to check in."

"The Lord must have prompted you to call." What I dubbed as her motherly-ness had intensified since Leigh's death. "I was praying for you last night and put in my day planner to check on you this evening."

"I appreciate the prayer. I'm doing OK these days."

"God is good. Our rock and our foundation."

"I need your expert advice. Do you have time?"

When I didn't hear anything, I suspected she was checking the thick binder where she recorded appointments with her real estate clients and meetings for church. My obsessive attention to detail and organization might not be hereditary since I'm adopted, but it could have passed from her by osmosis. "I got a showing in Cordova at three. Shouldn't take me thirty minutes to get there."

I'd thought out what to say. I hoped she'd be helpful and not shift into hyper-mom-mode.

"It seems...well, I got an unexpected letter, and check, in the mail. Apparently Leigh's school had life insurance on her. I didn't even know about it, but I'm the beneficiary. I'm thinking I'd like to..." One last breath to take me through my planned statement. "You know, combine it with the money Dad left me and use it to buy a house."

"Are you sure you're ready?" she asked. "It's not a buyer's market right now, and interest rates are up. Plus, that lovely apartment of yours holds so many memories."

Those memories are haunting me.

She should be able to understand. After Dad died, she'd sold our home and moved into a small "garden home" in Barlett, near the church in Memphis where Dad had been pastor.

"Yes, I *am* sure, and I'm ready. You always said that ownership is a good investment."

"Wouldn't be in the biz if I didn't. And I intend to help."

"You're a great real estate agent, Mom, but you can't drive down from Tennessee to show me homes on the market."

"Of course not, silly. Though I would, you know. Your father and I started a fund for you when you were young. One day, we hoped to give it to you and..." Her voice broke. "That account is available to help with the down payment."

"I think with the insurance money, and my own savings, I can manag—"

She huffed. "That area you live in...anywhere near your church... will cost you a pretty penny."

I couldn't argue with that. Just looking at the newspaper listings was startling, and way out of my price range. "I'm thinking of a condominium, in an area just outside Homewood. The drive to and from work wouldn't be bad, and the place would be mine."

"I'll check the directory and talk with an agent near you. Together we'll compile some places for you to see, and I can coordinate the entire process." My fears about her going full-on Mom were replaced with listening to her turn into Super Realtor.

She helped me determine a workable price range and cautioned about being too frugal or too extravagant. "If you spend too little, you end up with upgrades and repairs for years. But you don't wanna pay too much and be house poor, with no money for the expenses that come with homeownership. And before you begin looking, it'll save time if you decide what size house you want and what features are essential and what's optional."

Three bedrooms were top of my list—one for me, one for guests, and another for my study. A formal dining room was not important, but two bathrooms were essential, as were washer and dryer hookups. Having a pool in the complex would be nice, but not a must-have, since public swimming and my body consciousness were incompatible. I also wanted a private garage, if possible.

Within days, an envelope arrived in the mail with fliers for two local realtors. One was an older woman named Georgette Sanders, who reminded me of Aunt Bee, from Mayberry. The other was Jeff Heath, a very attractive young man who didn't look old enough to be out of high school much less have his own agency.

"I could've found my own agent," I told her when she called. "There are several women in our church."

"I talked to both of them and checked references. Besides, I didn't want you ending up with some predatory woman who uses her business to snare eligible bachelors. I've seen it too many times. You must always be on the alert for the wiles of the devil, son."

I glanced at the photo of the blond-haired, blue-eyed guy wearing the tight Polo shirt.

"Totally agree, Mom."

"OK IF WE SKIP OUR MATCH?"

We'd finished our workout and were hydrating before playing racquetball.

"One of my favorite old movies is playing tonight. I usually go with Jahlee, but that fell through. Wanna go with me? We could grab some food afterward."

Jolene?

"Sure, but I'm kinda sweaty." I was wearing a light blue T-shirt and motioned to my navy sweat pants. "I don't have anything else to change into."

"Who gives a shit? This is Birmingham, not Broadway."

He let me borrow his can of deodorant and, thankfully, didn't stand and watch as I removed my shirt to wash off my upper body. Then we jumped into his TransAm and headed to the interstate. "It's an older theater. Not great, but they have vintage movies during the week and classic science fiction films every Thursday."

"So we're seeing a science fiction movie?"

"Not just *any* science fiction movie. *The Day the Earth Stood Still*," he informed with much enthusiasm. "Have you seen it?"

A vacant stare was my answer.

"It's incredible. I guess I've seen it six or seven times. Michael Rennie and Patricia Neal. Oh, and Gort, the robot."

He was talking fast. "Uhm…Gort?"

"I won't give away anything, so we'll talk after you experience it."

On the drive to the east side of Birmingham, I learned Trey didn't just have an affinity for these movies; he had a vast knowledge of the stars and the stories. By the time we arrived, my expectations were high, to say the least.

After all, I wasn't just seeing a movie; I was having *an experience*.

"WHAT DO YOU DO? I MEAN, BESIDES THRASHING ME IN RACquetball and going to science fiction movies?"

We were sitting at a Shoney's near the theater, waiting for the waitress to acknowledge our existence. In the time we'd spent together, our conversations never veered much beyond ways to improve my workouts and playful banter during our matches.

"I manage a nonprofit legal firm."

"You're a lawyer?"

"No, I'm the office administrator, which means I supervise the staff. Everyone except our attorneys. What about you?"

It was not an unexpected question, and I was prepared to answer, giving me a chance to clear up the incomplete information I'd provided him earlier. However, our waitress slammed two glasses on the table and stood there, waiting for our response to her unvoiced question. Once we ordered, the conversation returned to the movie.

"It doesn't have the kind of special effects of *Star Wars*, and it's in black and white...which is a turn-off for many...but there's a certain quality I love about these old flicks. It's fascinating to watch them now. Many of the films of the fifties were propaganda tools, influenced by the paranoia of the Cold War during the McCarthy era."

My expression must have registered skepticism.

"It's true. Some studios intentionally designed the message of the films to fuel the concern of invasion by Communists, done in the guise of aliens from outer space, coming to destroy our world. *Earth versus the Flying Saucers* was a metaphor for the United States versus the evil Red Empire. Some, like *Invasion of the Body*

Snatchers, portrayed people who looked just like us who are out to destroy us. In other words, the enemy is among us. *Invaders from Mars* warned that our minds—our values—could be taken over by these dreaded creatures. And there was the consistent message that the government...particularly the military...was our savior, if we just submit to their wisdom and authority. *The Day the Earth Stood Still* is unique because the aliens were not the bad guys. They came to show us that we were doing bad things."

My fork was poised near my mouth. I was mesmerized. "That's heavy stuff."

"There's an important lesson for us today. The power of fear. Questioning those in power who dominate instead of govern. Don't let others define who we're supposed to fear, and hate."

"So inside your preppy exterior there's a rebel hippie, struggling to emerge?"

He laughed. "I can't see myself as a hippie, for sure. If I grew my hair much longer, the curls would start to look like Shirley Temple's. But yeah, I think there's at least an activist inside. How 'bout you?"

"Me? Definitely not an activist. I'm conformist, through and through."

"Your turn. What was your favorite movie growing up?"

"My parents wouldn't let me go to movies 'cause they thought it would be a bad influence. Teach me cuss words and rebellion."

"I'll be sure to watch my language," he said through his grin. "I take it you were raised in a strict home."

"Yes. As I told you, my dad was a minister; he died when I was in college. My childhood was idyllic in many ways, but once I got to high school, and then college, I realized how insular it had been. But we did watch *The Ten Commandments* every year, if that counts."

His face formed a frown. "I prefer Heston in *Planet of the Apes.*"

Another movie I'd not seen.

"You never snuck off to a movie without telling your parents?"

"Nope."

"A good, obedient boy."

Was he mocking me?

"So was I, most of the time." He gave a wink that eased my anxiety. He must have noticed I wasn't eating. "I'm talking too much. Am I boring you?"

"Far from it. I like listening to you." I was embarrassed at my response; it sounded like something a little girl with a crush would say.

"Because I love these movies, I know I can talk someone's ear off. *Earth versus the Flying Saucers* has special effects by Ray Harryhausen, one of the foremost artists specializing in stop-motion animation."

Again, he lost me.

"Have you seen those classic Christmas specials, like *Rudolph the Red-Nosed Reindeer* and *Santa Claus Is Coming to Town*?"

I remained silent, choosing not to disclose my father's total rejection of secularized Christmas and the materialism of Santa.

"Those are done with stop-action animation. That process originated in science fiction movies, and Harryhausen was one of the best. He did films like *7th Voyage of Sinbad* and last year's *Clash of the Titans*."

"If I'm gonna talk intelligently, I have lots of movies to catch up on."

"Well," he said, taking a sip of coffee, "maybe in addition to working out twice a week, we should add a classic movie on Thursday night."

"Does our exercise schedule interfere with managing a law firm?"

"I'm at work early, get my day started, and am able to leave in time for our sessions. There have been two or three times I go back to the office after we're done."

I'd done the same, so I offered, "We can always reschedule, or postpone, any time you need to."

The dialogue lulled while we waited on dessert.

"You've been working very hard and deserve to splurge," he'd replied when I questioned how my trainer, who knew I was trying to lose weight, could recommend something as decadent as strawberry pie.

"I've never heard of a nonprofit law firm."

"I work at Birmingham Center for Legal Services, and as the name says, we provide legal services to those in the metropolitan area who can't afford them."

I could identify with that. A primary reason for starting Grace Center was to make counseling available to those who couldn't pay the high prices of a professional therapist.

"What's your role? What does an office administrator do?"

"It's like an office manager, but broader. At first, I was the lone paralegal, but now we have five, plus three attorneys, and a host of others who work with us. I'm the supervisor of the paralegals and the staff. In addition to office administration, I oversee the firm's communications, making sure they're clear, accurate, and free of typos, grammatical errors, and other such nonsense. We interact with major law firms, other nonprofits, and large companies, so I never want us seen as less than professional. I also handle media relations—sending out press releases and arranging press conferences."

"Interesting," I responded, though most of that sounded dull and tedious.

"It can be. I like that it combines my training in law with my obsession for good grammar."

"You didn't want to be a lawyer?"

"No, much to the dismay of my father, who has his own corporate law firm. He envisioned my working at his firm and, one day, taking the reins to continue his dynasty."

I understand that.

"Why didn't you?"

"Not my path. I love my dad but would not enjoy practicing law like he does. My job doesn't pay as much, but isn't it better to do something you enjoy than something just to make money?" His shoulders rose as part of his question.

"I think so, yes."

"The idealist in me likes making a difference in the lives of people and in the world around me."

His good nature and lofty intentions accentuated his striking looks. I understood that sense of idealism and the desire to help mankind. And my father had also been less than thrilled that I wasn't following in his footsteps.

"Besides," he added. "I have all the money I need. Sharing the apartment with Gennie helps keep the expenses low. My car is paid for; it was a gift from my parents for my thirtieth birthday."

He'd talked about Gennie before. Earlier today, he mentioned someone named Jolie.

How many women is he dating?

"A car? We come from such different worlds. For my last birthday, my mother sent me...a tie."

"Hey, there's a lot to be said for a nice tie," he graciously replied. "It's kinda embarrassing, but my folks are, well, *rich*. And they like to be generous. They give to charities, and my dad's firm helps fund the Legal Aid Center. They can be extravagant, sometimes going overboard. When Papa—my grandfather—retired and sold the restaurants, he left my sister and me some money, which I've invested wisely. It gives me a regular dividend. Along with my salary at the firm, that pays for my basic needs as well as some of my...passions. Plus I'm frugal, so I don't run out of money before I run out of passion."

He nodded at me to confirm his statement. Or perhaps, expecting me to ask for specifics about those passions. Despite my curiosity, it was not a subject I intended to pursue.

Watch and pray, that ye enter not into temptation.

"And again, I'm doing all the talking. What do you do...for a living, I mean?"

"I'm a therapist."

He snickered. "A church-going shrink. You are full of surprises."

"A therapist, not a shrink. There's a difference."

There's also more, but that can wait.

Our conversation was again interrupted by the waitress, bringing the check. Trey insisted on paying, then noted the time. "I've got an early day tomorrow."

Four

I realized when I got home that I'd forgotten to call Susan, who'd left a message while I was in a session with an older man who'd recently received a prostate cancer diagnosis. She was a self-professed "night owl," so I wasn't concerned about waking her up. I was excited to tell her about my decision to buy a house.

"You just getting home from work?"

"No, I went to a movie and dinner with a friend."

She mumbled an indistinct response, then with sudden clarity: "I'm sorry…what did you say?"

I cradled the phone between my shoulder and neck, allowing me to get some cranberry juice from the refrigerator. "We saw a science fiction movie. It was interesting. Afterward, we went to Shoney's. I had a blast."

"Where did you two meet?"

"At the gym."

"And now you're going to movies and dinner together? Is this someone you like?"

"Of course I like him."

"It's a *him*?"

I was concentrating on pouring the juice to avoid spilling when it dawned on me. "You thought I was…that this was…that I was on a *date*?"

"You can't blame me. There was something in your voice when you talked about your evening. It was refreshing. Besides, I don't care if you're dating. Or who you date, for that matter."

I'd had a similar discussion with my mom, who was appalled at the idea of my dating so soon after Leigh's death. I assured her, and Susan, that I wasn't ready for that.

"Sounds like you had fun. It's great that you're getting out."

"His name is Trey. It's kinda nice having a friend who isn't part of the church. We don't talk about worship services, business meetings, or quirky church members. Don't get me wrong, I love what I do, as well as our staff and members. But when I'm around them, I'm always the minister. The counselor. Or Leigh's grieving husband. With him, it's different. It feels...*normal.* Does that sound crazy?"

"No, I totally get it. We all need those folks in our lives who don't relate to us through the lens of The High and Holy Clergy. They see just us, and we can be ourselves with them, without pretense. It's healthy. And liberating."

How will he relate to me when he finds out about my ministry?

"I'd like to be that kind of friend for you, Nathaniel."

"I know." My response was offhanded. I was pondering how and when to tell Trey, while trying to return the bottle to the refrigerator.

"I'm serious, dude." The emotion in her reply matched her declaration, catching me off guard. "We've known each other for many years. I think the fact that our beliefs are so divergent has kept us somewhat detached. Collegial and professional. You know me well enough to know it's not my style to say this, but I think divine providence brought us together. We were meant to be friends."

She was right. That did *not* sound like her.

Susan Bradley was complex, and contradictory, but *not* overly emotional or effusive. While adamant about her divine call into the ministry, she often spoke about God as unknowable and uninvolved in our daily lives. I wasn't sure if she believed the things she said or if she liked getting a reaction. Especially from male peers. At times, she was flippant and cynical, giving the impression that nothing mattered to her. Her liberal theology sometimes came across as irreverent, to the point of sacrilegious; nothing was off limits to challenge or criticize, especially traditional religious beliefs, including those I held to be true and immutable. If I asked her opinion, I had to be prepared for brutal honesty, often without the filters of decorum.

However, this was *not* one of her tirades, or pontifications, which I often tuned out. This not-usual admission was startling and demanded that I listen.

I can tell her about the house later.

"I love you like you were my own brother. I have such respect for you as a person. We don't agree on theology, but you are the kind of minister I aspire to be: dedicated, compassionate, selfless. Leigh Anne was worried that you would lose yourself in your work. I love…loved…her, and she wanted me to look after you because she knew how much I care for you. We both want you to be happy."

"Suz, I'm overwhelmed. I…yes, you're right, our friendship hasn't been all that close. But in this last year, I have come to rely on you more than anyone else. I could not have come through this without you."

"Dammit," she said. "Now that I've gotten all melancholy and weepy, I have to reapply my night cream. It's late, and I'm exhausted from dealing with the whims of men who are convinced they are hearing God. I need to get laid."

And with that, the Susan I'd known since college was back, though I would *never* view her the same way. In that moment, I realized she was my best friend.

Later, as I settled into bed and replayed the conversation, I agreed with Susan. I did need people, like her, who wanted what's best for me. I needed healthy friendships that made me a better person.

And because of my hidden feelings and unnatural desires, that could *not* be Trey.

I'd left Trey a message—a fabricated excuse—that I wouldn't be there for our workouts because my schedule was hectic. In truth, I was avoiding him. It was humiliating to admit, at my age, but the signs were undeniable: I had a crush. I found reasons to stand close to him, leaning in to watch how he operated a particular Nautilus machine. I liked the way his muscles flexed when he moved. I invited him to stay after our workouts, just to chat. When the phone rang, I hoped it was him. He had become this unattainable, forbidden fantasy—the incessant, pornographic participant in my dreams. If he found out, I would be mortified, so I had to admit that while he was helping me get physically healthy, he was not healthy for me *spiritually*.

My solution was to work out alone. Which helped. To a degree. There had been no more salacious dreams, which I blithely chalked up as a victory for my renewed devotion, though it could also have something to do with my new routine of masturbation at bedtime.

It's a choice between having a strong body or a stronger relationship with God.

I'd managed to keep up my avoidance for almost two weeks, but while getting ready for bed after a Saturday of workshops for our youth department, he called. "Just checkin' on you."

I offered a bland apology, reiterating the lie about my heavy client schedule.

"You'll be pleased to know that Jahlee clobbered me in racquetball yesterday."

"Somebody needed to knock you off your pedestal," I said with a snort.

"Wanna grab some lunch one afternoon? I can meet wherever, to make it easier on you."

"Let me look at the calendar when I get to my desk."

Another lie.

"Great, let me know. So see you on Monday?"

"My schedule is pretty busy."

"As your trainer, I will warn you that taking too much time off can be detrimental to the great progress you've made. As your friend, I miss working out with you."

I launched into my excuse, augmenting with an upcoming conference I would be teaching at church, detailing the research and preparation time I needed. Before I finished, he interrupted. "What's *really* going on, Nathaniel?"

It was disconcerting that he could see through my deception. The situation required a new tactic. "Between our workouts and playing racquetball, I feel like I'm monopolizing your time. You seemed so happy the other night when you talked about going to the movie with Gennie. I'm sure she'd love your being around more."

"Gennie? Sure, we always have fun. But we also give each other space for our different interests. She likes soap operas, and I go jogging. I enjoy reading, so she goes shopping. Sometimes, like last week, she drags me to a chick flick. It's a great arrangement."

"We're both very busy. I know that often you have to work after we finish. That doesn't seem right."

"Shouldn't that be my decision? I mean, I'm gonna work out anyway; might as well do it with someone I enjoy being around."

He likes being around me?

I'd assumed I was just the chubby guy he helped with workouts and an occasional racquetball opponent. We'd gone to dinner and a couple of movies, but I figured I was a stand-in for one of his girlfriends: Gennie or Julie.

"I appreciate what you've done for me. You've helped me learn the machines, and I'm making real progress. But I'm ready to do it on my own. It will take the pressure off us to keep to such a rigid schedule."

"I didn't realize I was putting pressure on you, or your schedule. I was only trying to help you with your fitness goals, which I assumed is what you wanted." He sounded annoyed. "I just wish you'd been upfront with me."

It's not going as I'd hoped.

"You've been great, Trey.

"Did I do something to upset you or offend you?"

"No. You are an amazing trainer, and I'm very grateful."

"I appreciate that, but I guess I thought we were more than just... well, that we were friends."

Friends?

"I do hope you'll continue your exercises. You're doing well. And if you ever need my advice, don't hesi—"

What am I doing?

"Please ignore everything I just said." I hadn't expected my own outburst, so I had to think a minute to explain. "I *do* want us to keep working out together. Without your help, I doubt I would keep at it. Before long, I'd go back to that soft, doughy body when we first met. Inevitably, I'd get fatter and fatter, and before long, I wouldn't even be able to leave my house, forever resigned to a lonely existence of watching bad daytime TV while eating ginormous bags of M&Ms and cases of Twinkies. When I die, they'll have to use a bulldozer to extract my body. Of course, you'll forever feel guilty, wondering what you could have done on this day when I tried to get out from under your expert tutelage."

There was silence for a moment, then the single response: "Wow."

"I just have so much going on right now. I'm overwhelmed, and my brain is kinda fried. I shouldn't have projected it on you."

"Can I do anything to help? I mean, you're the counselor, but if you need someone to listen, let me know. Fitness is more than how much you weigh or how much weight you can lift. It's physical *and* emotional."

Yeah, now I feel like a complete jerk.

"Just say we can get back to our schedule. I also miss spending time with you."

Get a grip! came the Warning Voice when my girlie crush became too evident.

"Rest up," he said. "And we'll get back to it on Monday."

"WASN'T SURE WHAT KIND OF BEER YOU LIKED." TREY BOUNDED into the room. "So I got my favorite."

He'd called earlier in the week, inviting me out for beer and pizza on Saturday night. I declined, using the excuse of having chores to accomplish rather than tell him I couldn't be seen drinking in public.

Without skipping a beat, he'd said, "Fine, I'll pick some up and come to your place. What would the world think about two good-looking guys like us, sitting at home alone on a Saturday night?"

Me...good looking?

"Where's Gennie?" I'd asked in a last-ditch attempt to deflect his invitation.

"Her mom's in town, and they're having dinner. Help me, Obi Wan."

Even I recognized that line from *Star Wars*.

He headed for the kitchen and placed the pizza on the counter. He opened two bottles, handing one to me and then looking around. I pointed to the cabinet next to the refrigerator, and he pulled out two plates. I took a large slice of pizza before heading to the den.

The room wasn't large enough for much furniture. The sofa sat in front of a half wall at the entry, with a well-worn coffee table. The TV was on the opposite full wall, and two mismatched chairs faced the middle of the room and served as a visual divider between the den and what Leigh designated the "breakfast nook."

"I almost didn't make it tonight," he huffed, moving to the chair nearest the sofa. "Gennie got home just before I left. Apparently, she and her mother had a fight, but she chose to take it out on me."

"Nothing serious I hope."

"Women can be so *feminine* sometimes. Tonight she threatened to move out."

"Maybe you should have stayed home with her."

"I didn't feel like listening to all her drivel. She'll get over it."

Now was as good a time as any to learn more about this mysterious relationship. "How long have you two been...I'm not sure if you're married or just living together?" I'd hoped to sound open-minded, considering what I believed about sex before marriage.

A mixture of expressions formed on his face. The first was surprise. "Married? Oh, hell no." Then he gave me a curious, almost confused look. "You do know I'm gay, don't you?"

My reaction must have answered his question.

"Oh God, you didn't. I just assumed that—"

I jumped to my feet. "Assumed what?" The ferocity of my voice surprised me. An array of emotions fueled my racing mind.

"Well mostly—" He maintained a controlled volume. "I *assumed* you knew."

Mostly?

Sudden weakness plunged me back onto the sofa.

Did I know?

My attention anchored to a small spot on the carpet. Though the silence was uncomfortable, I couldn't manage words, and I couldn't garner the courage to look up at him.

"I'd better leave." He stood, taking a step toward the door.

"Please don't," I muttered, glancing up.

He stopped, waiting for me to continue.

"Did you expect me to guess your sexual preference?" While my volume was now more controlled, there remained an inexplicable fury.

"It's not something I make a big deal about, but it's not something I hide. I just thought—"

"That I'm gay, too?" The anger increased, as did my decibel level.

"I'm sorry if you're offended." He returned to the chair.

"You should've told me," I whined.

"Look, Nathaniel. I like you. That's not a come-on, just a personal comment. I enjoy the time we spend together. I figured you'd picked up on the fact I was flirting with you." He gave me a shrug. "I misread the signals."

There were signals?

"Will this affect our friendship? I mean, even though this is Birmingham, people are more open-minded these days."

"Not where I come from." The response came before I thought.

"So the fact that I'm gay does make a difference?"

"Trey, give me a minute, please."

He did, though his gaze screamed his impatience. After a while, he asked, "Does me being gay bother you, or does it scare you?"

"Don't interrogate me like one of your witnesses. This is not one of those...those...what do you call it?"

"Deposition." His calmness was infuriating.

"Right, deposition. This is difficult for me. It's just that, well, there are things about me that you don't know."

"Then let's get it all out in the open. I was honest with you; now it's your turn."

"I told you I'm a counselor, which is true."

Did the moisture in my mouth evaporate?

I took a swig of the beer. I didn't care for the taste, but it wet my tongue enough to speak. Lifting the bottle, I noticed my hands were trembling like I'd never revealed my occupation, or like doing so might land me in jail. "It just wasn't *all* the truth." He leaned forward, waiting for my clarification. "I'm on staff at a church. A very conservative church."

His surprise was evident. "So," he uttered. "you're a minister. Like your dad. At least one of us followed in his father's footsteps."

"I'm not ordained though that's what he wanted for me. I *am* executive director for a Christian counseling center, sponsored by my church."

"Yeah, I can see the problem for you."

"Not to sound like I'm parroting your earlier statements: it's not something I make a big deal of, but I'm also not ashamed of what I do."

He let out a long breath. "I guess this *does* change things."

"I don't want it to," I blurted out. "Like you said, we can still be friends. But you told me about your personal life, and this is mine."

For a moment, he peered with his dark, probing eyes and then flashed his smile. "So I won't take you to singles' bars, and you won't try to get me married off."

"Something like that," I laughed. "I just have to be careful that people not, you know, misrepresent our friendship."

"What else?" he asked, his hands resting on his lap.

Confusion must have shown on my face.

"You said there were *things* about you that I didn't know. Being a minister is one thing. What else? Are you a spy with the CIA? Seeing somebody? Engaged?"

Oh, right. I did say that.

"No, not engaged. I *was* married. Le—, uh, my wife died a few months ago. I'm still adjusting to life without her."

He looked shocked, and then came that familiar display of sympathy. "Oh, geez. I'm so sorry."

"Thank you." I waved my hand to downplay his sympathy. "It's another thing I should have mentioned earlier but never found the right time. I've yet to find a smooth way to ease it into a casual conversation. And frankly, I enjoyed not being the young widower with you."

"No wonder you're stressed. I cannot even imagine what you must be going through. I hope you can accept my *interest* as the compliment it was intended to be." He went to the sink with his plate and beer can. "Want some help cleaning up?"

"You're leaving?"

"I think it's best. I've put my foot in my mouth and turned this into an awkward situation for both of us. Besides, you have to work tomorrow, right?"

I nodded at his reference to Sunday. We did the compulsory small talk, then he left.

But the dreams didn't.

Five

"Please know you're in our prayers, Mrs. DeLoach."

I'd finished an intake with Denise DeLoach, a Grace member who'd lost her husband of thirty-five years. She needed to talk, and I'd assign her to one of our ASSISTeam members. I also encouraged her to visit the church's grief support group.

"I'm sorry to burden you with this, Reverend Nate," she said as we walked to the reception area. "Knowing your own recent loss."

I assured her that objectivity came easier when dealing with others. Nonetheless, it was draining.

I returned to my desk, ready to write up my notes, when my intercom buzzed. "Brother Truett, Scot Nelson is on line two."

This can't be a coincidence.

"Good afternoon, Scot, with one t."

My greeting brought a repeat of his high-pitched giggle. "Did you get the books I dropped off, with the testimonies?"

"Yes, I did."

"Pretty inspiring, right?"

I couldn't disagree with him on that.

Trey's revelation about being gay was surprising, but admitting he was attracted to me was unnerving. It fueled the sexual dreams in which he was always prominent. My fantasies now attempted to move into the realm of possibility.

Could it happen?

My private admission of my infatuation with him made staying friends with him problematic.

I had hoped to talk with him more at our next workout, but he didn't show up. In fact, he hadn't shown up in two weeks. Sure, my reaction to his announcement had not been ideal, but he vanished without a word. Talk about rude and insensitive! I was angry and hurt that he'd chosen to shut me out. One night, I picked up the phone to call him but chickened out after I dialed the first few numbers. I told myself his no-show was God's way of giving me what I'd wanted...what I needed...all along. After all, Trey was a distraction, and a temptation, triggering the sin I was determined to conquer. My time and energy should be on my ministry, and working on my doctoral studies, which I'd put on hold when Leigh got sick.

"Would it be possible for me to attend a meeting?" I asked Scot. "You know, as an observer? I could learn about the group more directly. Of course, I'd understand if you think my presence would be disruptive."

"We have new people come to us every week. It would be our honor to have you visit. You will be impressed. Maybe after the meeting you can give me your expert observations."

"I'll have my secretary add it to my schedule. See you next week."

"WOULD YOU ALL JOIN ME AS WE OPEN IN PRAYER?"

Without waiting for a response, Scot launched into praying: "Lord Jesus, we are thankful for your presence with us today. By your sacrifice, you freed us from the bondage of sin. By your Spirit, you provide us with the power to overcome all temptation. Shine your light into the dark places of our lives. Search us, O God. Reveal our thoughts and our hearts. Amen."

Several sitting around me echoed with "amen."

Scot's group—which he referred to as the *Circle*—met in the basement fellowship hall of the Anointing Power Assembly of God in Woodlawn, an older suburb on Birmingham's east side. It was not an area of town I was familiar with, so it took me longer to find it than I'd anticipated. A small sign, similar to what my mom used for her real estate listings, identified the entrance. The cinder-block walls of the room didn't do much to protect from the cool April temperatures outside, so I was glad I'd worn a lightweight jacket. Propped on the ledge of a chalkboard on one wall was a large sign that read: *Whole-Hearted Ministry. Healing broken hearts, broken identities, and broken lives.* On a table were several Bibles, stacks of printed materials, and some books. There wasn't time to look at the titles, so I made a mental note to do that later.

Scot moved inside the circle of chairs. "Guys, before we begin, let me introduce a special guest." Walking to where I was sitting, he placed his hand on my shoulder. "This is my friend, Reverend Nate. He's a trained counselor, and I invited him to visit."

My recollection of how I came to attend was different, and I chose not to quibble about my title. Or our being friends.

"Nate is interested in learning about who we are, what we do and, more importantly, what God is doing in our lives. He understands our commitment to confidentiality, so please don't let his presence deter you from sharing. Oh, and his church is one of our financial supporters."

There was some applause and more "amens."

I acknowledged his introduction with a nod. When everyone grew silent, I noticed Scot was looking at me. Smiling, and waiting.

"Thank you, Scot. And all of you. I'm very glad to be here, and I look forward to learning from y'all."

"Now," he enjoined. "Let's stand, join hands, and repeat our Core Affirmation."

We all obeyed, and with fervor, they recited, "Therefore if any man be in Christ, he is a new creature: old things are passed away; behold, all things are become new."

I recognized that verse from Second Corinthians; it was one I often repeated to myself.

Does it work better for them than it does for me?

No one moved or let go. Looking around, I saw that everyone else was also looking around. There were grins and nods as they visually greeted each other. It was a varied group. Most looked young, a few possibly still in high school. There was one black guy and one who looked Asian.

"Today," Scot proclaimed loudly, "I affirm with the psalmist: 'Blessed are they that seek him with the whole heart.' Praise Jesus. Amen."

Hands released, and everyone sat down.

"Who wants to begin?"

A tall guy two chairs down from me stood. "Hello, my name is Barry, and I'm a new creation in Christ."

Barry talked about a life-long struggle with homosexual desires. He omitted sordid details, but inference was easy. In college, he tried to commit suicide; he had the scars on his wrist as testimony to his desperation, which he held out as evidence.

"A friend visited me in the hospital, shared with me about God's love and Jesus' sacrifice." He paused, getting his emotions in check. "I was saved and water baptized into this church—" He pointed up, obviously indicating the church that hosted the meetings. His volume was now strong and loud. "I got baptized with the Holy Spirit and made the decision to walk away from my homosexual lifestyle."

There was applause, accompanied by another round of enthusiastic "amens."

"I've been part of Whole-Hearted for almost two years. I am *convinced* that Scot, and this ministry, saved my life."

"Praise Jesus," Scot said, lifting one hand in the air.

When the additional applause subsided, Barry sat down.

"My name is…" The nervous young man looked around.

"It's OK not to give your name. We are here to support you."

"Uhm…I'm…I'm a new creature…thanks to Christ."

I recognized the structure as similar to a twelve-step program, but the group's members weren't admitting their weakness. When I asked about it, Scot explained, "We confess, in faith, the truth of God's Word. Faith is the substance of things hoped for, the evidence of things not seen," he quoted from the book of Hebrews. "We align our identity, and our words, with who God created us to be. We speak *His* truth, not our experience, nor our sin."

"My name is Matthew, and I'm a new creation in Christ,"

"How are things going at home?" Barry asked.

"My parents stay on my case. Dad is bent outta shape about me not going to school."

"Have you found a job yet?" A heavy-set guy sitting across the circle asked that question.

"We feel strongly that too much free time can lead to boredom," Scot clarified to me. "That is especially true in Matthew's case, where his parent's offer him little affirmation. The tendency is to go out and seek validation in the form of sexual activities."

"Is that part of the homosexual's problem?" I asked to no one in particular.

"There is no such thing as a homosexual," Barry interjected. "We are Christians who struggle with homosexual impulses."

"It *is* an important distinction," Scot pointed out. "If a person identifies as a homosexual, that kind of behavior becomes a self-fulfilling prophecy. It's the difference in committing a sin and adopting sin's identity. That's why our positive confession is so essential to our transformation."

"I committed sinful acts of homosexuality," one of the guys expounded, "but my sin doesn't get to define who I am."

When Matthew sat down, the Asian guy stood. "My name is Alton, and I'm a new creation in Christ. I had a pretty good week. My younger brother and I—"

"Gestures!" someone abruptly shouted. Alton's arms instantly dropped to his side.

On impulse, I looked at Scot.

"We hold one another accountable, and that includes feminine mannerisms and affectations: how we walk, how we talk—our pitch and inflections—how we use our hands, how we cross our legs. These grow out of sexual confusion, and to reclaim our masculinity, it's essential to *act* like men."

"I was your stereotypical sissy," Alton interjected. "My father was so embarrassed that he couldn't even be around me. He and my mother decided to send me to Prodigal Son. I was there for about a week, until...uh...there were some problems, so I had to leave. Then we found Whole-Hearted."

"Is Prodigal Son another support group?"

"It's a three-week residential camp operated by a group in Oklahoma," Scot answered.

I thanked Alton, but secretly wondered about the specifics of those "problems."

"My name is Eddie, and I'm a new creation in Christ." Tears rolled down his cheeks, and he hung his head.

This kid looked twelve years old. Short, thin, with a smooth face and a mop of brown hair. He was the personification of what Mom would describe as "ain't bigger than a minute."

"Did you slip up this week?" a group member asked.

He shuffled his feet and nodded.

"What happened this time?" Barry asked, sounding a bit exasperated.

"No triggers," Scot interjected, then turned to me. "While we want honesty in our confessions, we must refrain from carnal details that could cause our brothers to stumble."

"I needed money. For rent and groceries."

A cold chill went through me as I surmised what might be happening in Eddie's life.

As if Scot could see the machinations going on in my mind, he addressed Eddie. "Since this is Reverend Nate's first time here, could you give him a brief recap of your journey? If you feel comfortable."

The young man looked at me. "I was fifteen, and my mom caught me in bed with our pharmacist. They arrested him for statutory rape, and I got kicked out of the house. I was homeless and had to turn tricks to eat."

"That was your choice," Barry asserted. "No one *has* to be a whore."

Eddie spun around and yelled, "Kiss my ass, *Bartholomew*."

"Language, men. 'Let no unwholesome word proceed from your mouth, but only such a word as is good for edification according to the need of the moment, so that it will give grace to those who hear.'"

I was memorizing the book of Ephesians, so I recognized the source.

"Barry, let's not make judgments about those who've had different experiences than you did."

With a huff, Barry crossed his arms and spoke through tight lips. "I affirm you as a worthy child of God."

"And Eddie," Scot said. "We always want to remember that bad choices are not unavoidable. Let's not excuse sin as mandatory. We have the promise 'No temptation has overtaken you but such as is common to man; and God is faithful, who will not allow you to be tempted beyond what you are able, but with the temptation will provide the way of escape also, so that you will be able to endure it.' Would you like to continue?" Scot glanced over at Barry. "Without external commentary."

"I was messed up and strung out. Hustling paid the bills and bought me drugs. When I didn't have money, there was always someone willing to let me pay in trade."

I hadn't heard that term, but it wasn't difficult to discern the meaning.

"Some of the folks from Anointing visited those of us who lived under the viaduct. They had food, gave us Bibles, and invited us to church. I met Scot and told him my story. Now I'm trying to get my life together."

"I am *so* sorry all that happened to you," I offered Eddie.

Others shared the struggles of their respective weeks, and then around eight-thirty, Scot brought the meeting to a close. "Don't forget, men. We can do all things through Christ, who strengthens us. Go in the power of Jesus and with the peace of the Holy Ghost."

I stayed around and chatted. I saw Alton give Eddie a hug as the young man left, so I walked over. "Thank you for sharing, Alton. I learned so much tonight."

"We're a messed up bunch, ain't we?" he quipped.

"Well, from what I heard tonight, many of you have been through so much."

"To quote Stephen Sondheim, 'I'm still here.'"

I had no idea who that was, and before I could engage him more—to ask him about Prodigal Son—Scot informed us that he needed to lock up but invited me to join him at Burger King.

"THANK YOU FOR LETTING ME SIT IN TONIGHT. IT WAS INFORMATIVE." At the restaurant, I ordered an ice tea, and Scot got a large chocolate shake. We chose a booth in the back so we could talk. "Listening to the group, plus reading the testimonies you dropped off...it's all very impressive."

"This pattern is difficult to break, but by the power of the Word and the Holy Spirit, more than eighty percent of members who complete our *Wholeness* program are living in victory over the deeds of the flesh."

That *was* impressive.

Before I could respond, Scot patted himself on the chest. "In fact, you are looking at one."

No surprise there.

"You're gay?" I feigned politely.

"*Was!*" he corrected. "I was involved in the lifestyle for years. Spent my twenties and early thirties whoring all over New Orleans."

Thirties?

He's not as young as I had suspected.

"Once I came to Christ, I started searching for a way out. God planted the seeds of change, and this group...this ministry...is the fruit of the lessons I learned."

"I appreciate you telling me."

His hand flopped up, and with his fingers extended, he tapped his chest. "I give God the glory." He giggled, which caused me to wonder if anyone held *him* accountable for feminine affectations.

Then I checked myself for that pettiness.

"How long have you been...uhm, *straight*?"

He set his shake aside, crossed his arms on the table, and spoke with slow intensity. "Nate, I firmly believe we're all born straight. Circumstances, events, and people alter our perception, and the expression, of our God-given sexuality."

"So it's simply *behavioral*?" I kept my tone professional, knowing my many questions might come across as a challenge. Or skepticism. Coverage of this subject at my Christian college had been meager, but from my reading in psychology and sociology, there was not a clear-cut consensus.

"I don't think it's *simple* at all. It's an impulse, a temptation, and a deeply entrenched pattern of thoughts and behavior. It grows out of bad parenting, emotional and physical trauma, or sexual abuse when we're very young. The enemy is able to build a stronghold that's difficult to overcome on our own. There's also evidence that this tendency can be passed down from previous generations: the sins of the fathers and grandfathers."

Evidence?

"So we must align with what the Word has to say, rather than calling ourselves by that which God condemns. In my way of thinking, and in our program, as long as I differentiate between the actions and the identity, I can deal with my feelings."

"Feelings?"

"I still struggle with the desires," he replied, matter-of-factly, sweeping one hand in a nonchalant way.

My mind was racing with questions, but reason dictated a casual approach. "Will they—the feelings—will they ever go away?"

It seemed a shrug would be his only response, then he answered, "I've learned it's much like alcoholism. I'm successful if I go through this day and not surrender to the desires. Yes, I cling to the promise that with God, nothing is impossible, and I live in the faith that the Holy Ghost inside me is strong enough to give daily victory."

I resisted the urge to offer him an apology. "Is the group…are there other programs that are part of your ministry?"

"The Circle is just one element we offer as part of our overall approach."

It was clear I would have to pull specifics from him, as I had when he first came to my office.

"We? Are there others on staff?"

"No, it's just me, and I'm not even paid. From time to time, we've had those who've been in the program for a while who become trustees to help me. And we're affiliated with Exodus International, an umbrella organization for ex-gay groups like ours."

"Affiliated in what way?"

"I go to their national conferences, and they know the great work we are doing. If someone from Birmingham contacts Exodus, they direct that person to me. To Whole-Hearted."

"Am I asking too many questions?"

"Not at all."

"Since you don't get a salary, I assume you have another job."

"Yes, I'm the manager of the Homewood Library. I've been there for six years. It affords me a flexible schedule and access to all those books."

"You said the Circle is *one* element. What else is there? How is the program structured?"

He sucked on the straw, forcing some of the thick shake from the cup. Answering my question seemed less a priority than more milkshake did. "The weekly Circle meetings are open to all. There's a voluntary sign-up sheet, but we just ask for first names, and no contact information. They can attend the group as long as they feel comfortable, and there's no pressure. We've had guys come once, and we never see them again. There are some who are sporadic, showing up when they do something that makes them feel guilty and want absolution. There's not much we can do for them until they are serious about change."

"Let's say I show up at the group, and I know being gay is a sin."

Keep it abstract.

"What do you tell him?"

With his picture-ready smile intact, Scot looked at me for longer than was comfortable.

Does he suspect my not-so-detached interest?

"On the sign-in table we have pamphlets about what we offer for those who seriously desire change. It outlines our 'Path to Wholeness' program where we lead them into their journey of healing. We provide them with materials to discover root causes for their attractions, worksheets to identify their triggers, Bible studies targeted at resisting their temptations, prayers to claim God's promises. We also have workshops and retreats, and I provide one-on-one sessions."

"How many guys enroll?"

"If someone's interested, he fills out an application, giving his background, his involvement in the lifestyle, and his understanding of why he has homosexual tendencies. I also conduct a personal interview with him, where I go over the program again and ask more questions. If he wants to take the next step, we enroll him in the first workshop. We have had hundreds complete the entire Wholeness program. We are thrilled at their diligence and dedication."

Now I regretted not looking at that table; I could have gotten a brochure and saved the time of extracting the information out of him. "Does this—was it Exodus?—do they provide you with materials to use for the workshops?"

He sat up straight, his head moving back and forth with enough force to make another milkshake. "Oh, no. I write the materials."

OK, that hit a nerve.

To avoid sounding like I was conducting an interrogation, I waited to see if he'd continue.

"I mean, I *have* attended workshops and seminars and consulted with different ministry leaders. I use the resources offered by other successful programs as inspiration and information. For example, we hope to get a Homosexuals Anonymous program started soon, but we use some of the truths of Twelve-Step programs in our Circle meetings already."

"I'd love to read the brochure. Can you mail one to me?"

"Do you deal with this much?" he asked.

The question stunned my motor functions and my breathing. It also felt like my heart stopped. I wasn't ready for personal disclosure. I managed to blink and force a confused look to my face.

"Do you get many men who come to you with this problem?"

Forcing my lungs to release, I responded. "No, most of my clients come from within the church."

He snickered. "So do mine."

"Never thought of that."

"I think *every* one of those guys this evening comes from a strong church background. The exception might be Eddie, who was living on the street. One is the son of a Baptist pastor..." He used his fingers like he was counting. "Barry—you heard him give his testimony—was a student studying to become a preacher; one is married to the daughter of a missionary; they hope to also go into the mission field. Darrel, who helps me with the training, taught at a private Christian school and was engaged. He got fired when the principal learned he was having an affair with a man. And I play the piano for the youth at my church."

"Do they...how do their churches...do they know?"

"Most do. These guys come here because their church, or pastor, referred us. This is a matter the church either does not know how to handle or chooses to ignore. The only time it's addressed in the pulpit is with condemnation, or when someone in the congregation is caught in the sin or admits to same-sex attractions. We had a guy with us tonight who decided to open up to his pastor. He shared about the wonderful things God was doing through Whole-Hearted. The pastor promised to pray for him. The next week, the deacons informed the young man he should leave the congregation for the good of the fellowship. They were concerned that he might 'relapse' and involve one of the youth or children."

It was emotional, knowing I wasn't alone; other Christians understood my struggle. But hearing these stories also brought fear of someone discovering my secret desires.

I can never tell anyone!

"They are so blessed to have this ministry...and you...to help them."

He patted my hand. "That is very kind, but I am just God's chosen vessel. To give as I have been given."

"I would love to visit the group again."

Scot finished his milkshake, noisily making sure he'd gotten every bit from the bottom of the cup. "I can tell you have a heart for these hurting men. I am thrilled you are interested in helping. Would you maybe consider speaking to the group? You would offer valuable expertise."

Six

Boxes labeled "kitchen" and "living room" were unpacked; I'd flattened and discarded most and put the rest in the storeroom. The apartment was empty, and I'd spent my first week in the new house. "Our" bed was in the downstairs guest bedroom, where I was sleeping until I found new furniture for the upstairs master bedroom. The next major project would be my study—putting all my books into the bookcases I had installed. Susan and my mom thought the study should be downstairs, with the guest bedroom upstairs; I preferred the separation and privacy of having guests downstairs. And since I often studied late at night, and did my devotions early in the morning, having the study on the same floor as my bedroom made more sense to me.

I broke away from the stress of unpacking to get in a workout. I'd finished and was leaving the gym when Trey walked in. We almost collided, so avoiding him was not an option. In less time than a heart flutter, every emotion I'd felt the past weeks converged: sadness, annoyance, resentment.

I manufactured my best casual, chipper tone to ask, "How's it going?"

"Not too bad." He didn't look at me.

What a jerk!

With nothing else to say, I turned to exit. He touched my arm, then pulled back. "Do you have time to talk?" he asked, almost pleading.

He stood me up…for weeks…without explanation. I pushed

down the irritation and resisted my initial impulse to tell him how I felt. Against my better judgment, I agreed, and we walked to the snack area. After getting two bottles of water, we sat down.

"You're looking good," he started. "I can tell you've been staying on your program."

A warmth covered my face, undoubtedly accompanied by a crimson blush. "That's kind." I could at least be civil. "I confess I've skipped a few lately; my life is crazy busy these days. Then I reminded myself it's a great way to release stress and got back to it, by myself. It's good therapy."

"You're the expert in good therapy," he joked. "And don't take this the wrong way, but your efforts are paying off." This time, he blushed.

Compliments about my physical appearance had never been easy for me. Coming from Trey, who had that perfect body, they were both implausible and exhilarating. "Well, if that's true, you get the credit. After all, you're...you were...my trainer, until you vanished without so much as a phone call."

Civility lost out to anger.

"You're absolutely right. I've been a real ass since the last time we saw each other, and you have every right to be pissed at me. I apologize and hope you can find it in your heart to forgive me."

Crap. Now I can't be angry with him.

"Can you at least tell me why?"

"I didn't know what to say to you after...after that conversation."

"Well, the 'dead wife thing' can stifle any conversation," I answered, hoping to lighten up the mood. "I wish we hadn't left it like that, but I'm glad we're talking now."

"I've been avoiding you. I've seen you several times but left instead of risking running in to you. I felt guilty, embarrassed, and well...afraid."

"Afraid, of me?"

His gaze was on his water bottle as he ran his index finger around the rim. "No one likes admitting their feelings and being rejected."

My response upset him, but my feelings for him terrified me!

"Please know: it wasn't rejection. I wasn't expecting it; that's all."

"I'm attracted to you and just assumed...well, you know. I think you guys call it 'projection.' Staying away from you was easier than facing the humiliation. And the hurt. I ended a rather intense relationship last year, so I was protecting myself."

"If I were your counselor, and not your friend, I'd tell you that's a normal response."

"Friend?"

I nodded. "I hope so. Can we get past this?"

He looked up and smiled.

What a smile!

"So you wanna go back to our usual workout schedule?" he asked.

Not a good idea, Conscience warned.

It's just a workout, came the rebuttal from some other realm of my mind.

"Yes, please. I have an almost-big birthday coming up soon, and I *will* eat cake and ice cream."

"Birthday? When?"

"Not 'til May. I'll be twenty-nine on the twenty-ninth."

"Hey, I survived the Big Three-Oh, and several more since then. You'll be fine. Is your mother gonna get you a tie again this year?"

He remembered.

"Actually, she helped me buy a house."

"Wow. That sure beats a car."

"She's a real estate agent. Even though she lives in Memphis, her expertise was useful. It took weeks of looking, which had a Goldilocks quality: Some were too small, some were too far away, some were too expensive, and one was too ratty. I saw all kinds of dismal wallpaper and dreadful decorating. But then I found it: a townhouse just outside Homewood, toward Southside."

"How grown-up of you. I'm impressed."

"It needs work, but my realtor recommended a contractor, and that's being done. I'm moved in and living in the chaos of the noise, mess, and cardboard boxes."

"That has to drive your neatness obsession insane."

He wasn't wrong.

"If you need any help, I'm available."

"Thanks." Having him in my house...alone...was *not* going to happen, but it was still a kind offer. I noticed the time; I was meeting Susan at seven. "Gotta get going. My friend Susan is helping me hang curtains."

"I'm glad we talked," he said. I got the feeling he wanted to hug me but must have had second thoughts. We did a hearty handshake.

"And you're still my personal trainer? We'll resume our workouts on Friday?"

"It's a da—uh...yes, see you on Friday."

THE NEXT FEW SESSIONS, MY MUSCLES WEREN'T THE ONLY THING strained. Trey and I worked hard on the machines, but we were also working to appear casual, acting like things were the same.

They weren't.

"Are you settled into the new place?" he asked when we were having juice.

"*Settled* is such a subjective term at this point," I answered, followed by an exaggerated huff. "The place still looks more like a storage facility than a home. I'm sleeping in the guest room, on our... uhm...my old bed. I plan to buy some new furniture, just haven't had the time. Susan is helping me. Work is crazy right now. In the midst of the madness of buying a house, I've resumed working on my doctorate."

"*Doctor* Truett. Impressive!"

"It's way too early for that. It'll take three or four years, combining time in class with clinical work and correspondence classes."

Trey picked at the label on his drink.

"You seem pensive. Everything OK?"

"I was going to ask you something," he replied, "but didn't want... well, you might misinterpret."

"Ask me, and if I'm offended, the worst that could happen is I douse you with my Gatorade and storm out."

Apparently my levity helped. I always enjoyed seeing that smile. "I'd like to invite you to dinner. For your birthday. I mean, you probably have plans on the *actual* day, so we could do it on any day. Or, if you think it'd be too weird, we—"

"I do have plans on the twenty-ninth, but I'd love to get together. How about the Friday before that? Unless you have a date."

"Nope, no date. Would you be open to me cooking dinner? It might be less awkward than being seen together in public."

I agreed, and then he stood. "Now, how 'bout a game of racquetball? Let's see if you've improved enough to beat me."

I hadn't, and I didn't!

"WHAT'S YOUR PLEASURE, REVEREND?"

His question caught me off guard. After I arrived, we did an awkward handshake, and he posed his question. A very stupid sounding "huh?" was my response.

"We're not in public now. Would you like something to drink?" He whispered: "I won't tell anyone."

Alcohol could help my nerves.

"Just give me whatever you're having. And don't call me 'reverend.'"

"As you wish, *Reverend* Nathaniel."

Offering to help would be useless since I'd never mixed drinks, so I perused the room, which was sizable for an apartment, and nicely decorated. The couch and two over-sized chairs were brown leather and looked comfortable. Accent throw pillows brought color, perhaps the influence of Gennie. The painting on the wall over the sofa appeared to be hand-painted, loosely depicting a mountain lake and woods. A sliding glass patio door took up most of one side of the room and had beige sheers that allowed light into the room but offered privacy. A gigantic entertainment center filled one wall, with a TV, a turntable, two huge speakers, and a variety of unfamiliar equipment. Separating the living room from the large kitchen was a single bookcase with an eclectic library, including classics such as *Moby Dick*, *Robinson Crusoe*, and *Treasure Island*, all favorites of mine growing up. One shelf was romance novels, with provocative titles. There were law books, biographies, an assortment of Reader's Digest Condensed Books, fad-diet paperbacks, and even various Bibles.

Bibles and diet books for Trey seem ironic.

Of course I saw a large section of science fiction and fantasy; I recognized many of the authors: Asimov, Bradbury, and Heinlein. I pulled a copy of *Stranger in a Strange Land* from a shelf.

"That's one of my all-time favorites." The voice came from behind me. I turned, and he was handing a glass in my direction. "I've read it several times."

"I read it in college." It wouldn't have been on the school's approved book list, but several guys in the dorm were discussing it in the common area. One of the guys was cute, and I liked hanging out with him, so I participated. Of course, everyone in our small "book club" condemned the book's harsh treatment of religion, focusing instead on the themes of community and the "Christological allegories" in the main character.

I tried a small sip of the drink. It tasted sweet, followed by a slight burning in my throat, and then it made my face warm. In combination, it was rather pleasant. "What is this?"

"Bourbon and Coke. Not very exotic, but quick. Maybe we should share water instead."

I looked down at the copy of Heinlein's most famous book. In the story, the main character came from a planet where water was scarce, and he considered the act of sharing water the highest form of intimacy and friendship. A warmth moved over me.

It has to be the alcohol.

He lifted his glass toward mine. "Here's to our friendship."

His salute seemed sincere, so I raised my glass in response. "I grok that," using a term coined in the book.

"Have a seat." He motioned toward the sofa. "Dinner's almost done."

My nerves returned, so I took another sip of the drink. The polite thing to do would be to get him talking. Asking about his day or his job would be simple. I could learn more about his family. We could chat about movies or books. Instead, when I opened my mouth, the words I heard were "So, do you date much?"

His surprise was clear. "You're a therapist *and* a yenta?"

After he explained the reference from *Fiddler on the Roof*, I sought to cover the inappropriate question. "We've never talked about your…I mean, we talked about my deceased wife, but not about your…uhm…social life. I assume you're involved with…not sure how to pronounce his name. *Jayden*?"

"It's Jahlee. He's my best friend. We met in college. He works for my dad's law firm. Yes, we do hang out a lot, but we're not dating. His wife likes me, but she wouldn't allow that." He laughed and then returned to cooking. "To answer your question, though, I do date. Nothing serious right now. I did have a guy ask me out the other day. I met him at Quest, a gay bar in Southside."

The conversation—which I had started—was no longer enjoyable.

Why am I bothered about him dating?

"Sorry, I shouldn't…that was too personal."

"You can ask me anything." He peeked around the corner again. "I'm an open book, remember?"

"I didn't even know there *were* gay bars in Birmingham."

"They come and go."

"You'll laugh, but this is the first mixed drink I've ever had."

His chortle echoed into the living room. "I'm a corrupting influence."

A Bible verse stung in my mind: *Bad company corrupts good morals.*

"I'm also curious." I couldn't see him from where I sat, but he was loud enough to hear. "Why does a church sponsor a counseling agency?"

"It may be hard for you to believe, but the church cares about people."

"Hey, I'm not *that* cynical. I just have my reasons for not trusting religion."

"Yes, and at some point, I intend to discuss *that* with you, Mr. Open Book."

He again stepped into the room, gave me the fakest smile possible, and shook his head like that would never happen. "What kind of cases do you deal with?"

"All kinds. I have the mandatory premarital sessions with couples who want to get married at our church. Also marriage counseling. I do lots of conflict resolution: husband and wife not getting along, parents and kids not getting along, siblings not getting along. I work with teens having basic behavioral problems. Some of my clients are depressed, and others are going through major life transitions, such as job loss or retirement. I see myself as a general practitioner when it comes to counseling, so I have a large network of referrals I can use when the problems are more than I'm able to treat: psychiatrists, child psychologists, drug and alcohol rehab centers. But folks who can't afford counseling—the ones who often need it the most—come to us. The church takes up the overhead, thereby cutting the expenses to the client."

"What if they cannot afford anything?"

"I contract with them to work it off. It's important that they contribute to the process, or it tends to be meaningless to them."

"Indentured servitude?"

I knew he was joking. "See, you *are* that cynical. No, we have them help in the church nursery or around the office with mass mailings or folding newsletters."

He came into the room and announced that dinner would be a while but that the salads were ready. We were having grilled steaks, sautéed with mushrooms and mixed vegetables. He took the chair across from me and waited, perhaps to determine whether I needed to say grace. I picked up my fork and took a bite.

During the salads, he was uncharacteristically silent. When I asked, he gave his customary shrug and took another bite. I heard a sigh—the nasal kind, taken in and let out. My training kicked in, and I asked, "Is the fact that you're gay bothering you?"

"Not at all. Yeah, it bothered me that I didn't tell you. Then I did. Well, that was a disaster."

"How long have you known? I mean how...when did you first suspect?" I was unsure if my question was to draw him into conversation or help with my own questions.

"All through high school, I did the typical dating thing. Even had a few sexual experiences with girls. But I knew I was attracted to guys. When I was a senior, I actually made out with the nerdy kid who was tutoring me in math. It was amazing. In college, I had several actual sexual experiences and decided it was time to deal with the feelings. When I did, there was this sense of self-awareness that swept over me."

"And people...your friends...know?"

"As a junior in college, I fell head-over-heels in love with a guy and had to tell someone. My kid sister, Alena, came home for Thanksgiving holidays, and she noticed, in her words, "something different" about me. So I told her everything, and she was so cool about it, which gave me courage. Later, I came out to my parents. It took a while, but now they're great. Mom keeps trying to set me up with random guys she meets. I think everyone in my life, except maybe my paper boy, knows."

"How do you think your paper boy will react when he finds out?" I joked, seeking to relieve some his tension. And mine.

People knowing I even have these desires terrifies me.

"Do you think...what made you gay?"

He looked up at me but didn't speak. The scrutiny of his gaze made my heart rate increase while decreasing my ability to get air into my lungs. "I don't claim to have all the explanations, and I avoid detailed discussions about the origins of my orientation. However, I do believe it's who I am."

My mind was racing, besieged with conflicting information. The characterizations of the homosexual lifestyle from the materials I was reading and the stories I was hearing didn't line up with Trey and what he was saying.

Maybe he's the exception. An anomaly.

"It does, doesn't it?"

Trey had said something, and he was frowning. I'd gotten lost in my thoughts. "I'm sorry," I stuttered. "What did you say?"

"I can see that my sexuality is a problem for you. Maybe this was a bad idea." He stood and picked up his plate.

"Your sexual preference does *not* bother me, not in the way that you think. I apologize for my reaction. So much of what you're saying goes against…well, it's new, that's all. I'm trying to comprehend, and I wandered off mentally. I *would* like for us to continue our meal. I'll try not to ask so many questions."

He didn't respond but also didn't take his eyes off me. I wasn't sure if he was thinking about my invitation to continue with dinner or if he was peering beneath my facade, into the confusion that was driving my questions.

He sat back down. "I prefer *orientation*."

"Excuse me?"

"You called it 'sexual preference.' That sounds so trite. I *prefer* chocolate ice cream to vanilla. My attraction to other men is not a preference, it's an orientation. And it's unchangeable."

Unchangeable?

"And I don't mind your questions."

"'Cause you're an open book."

I liked that I made him smile, but knew I should change the subject to something less personal for him and uncomfortable for me. "You had sex with women, but you're attracted to men. How is that *gay*?"

Maybe I should shove a roll into my mouth.

"I messed around with girls in high school because it was expected. I was a horny teenage boy, and it got my rocks off. It was

OK, until I had sex with a guy. There was a connection I'd never had with girls. It satisfied something inside me that I wasn't even aware was there."

None of that makes sense.

"So once you were sure, even though you'd had sex with women, you accepted your sexual preference...uhm...sexual orientation?"

"Oh, it wasn't all that simple. I accepted that my sexual orientation was part of me but also had fears and reservations. I knew that not everyone would agree, so I kept it to myself. I did some research at the library to learn all I could about current thinking on the subject. Formed my opinions and settled it, once and for all."

Move on to a different topic.

"You were in a relationship." It was both a statement and a question.

"For almost three years."

I don't need to know about this. Such couplings are immoral.

"How did you two meet?"

"He was a lawyer at my dad's firm, and we met at a party my parents held for the firm. A bit older, but that never bothered me."

"What happened?"

"He moved. Jake—that's his name—took a position in Chicago. I wanted to go with him, but he never asked. The breakup was amicable."

"How long ago?"

Stop!

His forehead wrinkled as he thought. "Last summer. I've been out with guys since then, just nothing that lasted more than a few dates. I'm not big on the gay scene and not interested in one-night stands."

I took a sip of water. "Why don't you enjoy the 'gay scene,' as you call it?"

"It has nothing to do with being uncomfortable about being gay, if that's what you're getting at."

It wasn't. I didn't press since he sounded defensive. Still, he chose to continue. "Casual sex is fine for some people, and I've done my fair share of that. Maybe I'm just a romantic, but I'm not a giant hormone, waiting to be satisfied. I'm thirty-four years old and want something more permanent."

The books and materials I was reading focused on sex…lots of sex…as the primary element in homosexual activity. *Permanence* and *romance* were not words used to describe such relationships.

"Now, can I ask *you* a personal question?"

I didn't have an Open Book Policy, but a buzzer on the oven signaled and rescued me. "Never mind." He rose and spent several minutes puttering out of sight at the final preparations.

I used the break to think, stunned at our discussion. It was interesting, with a titillating, forbidden element. It stirred up old feelings and tantalized my imagination. And also made me afraid.

I wish he'd come back and talk to me.

As the old saying goes, be careful what you wish for!

"Everything OK? Anything I can do to help?"

"It's fine," he replied. "Dinner will be ready shortly."

I had been married long enough to know that "fine," when spoken in *that* tone of voice, meant things were *not* fine.

I walked in and stood by the narrow kitchen island across from where he was putting the final touches on our dinner plates. "I'm sorry if my questions got too personal."

"Don't worry about it."

"Nothing you've told me changes our friendship. Please believe that."

He didn't turn around.

"Trey?"

No answer.

"What is it? Is it something I said?"

"Just go sit down, please. I'll bring the food in a sec."

His tone was sharp, so I did as requested.

"What did I miss?" I asked when he joined me again. "You act like you're angry with me."

"I'm not angry. Sorry about being terse. It's just that I want to ask you something but am worried about—"

"If you're wondering about how I'm dealing with your sexuality, please relax—"

"To be honest, I'm more interested in *your* sexuality." He spoke his words with such calmness that it took a few moments to sink in. Without speaking, I pushed back from the table and went to the den. He followed, taking a seat in the chair facing me.

"What is *that* supposed to mean?" I sputtered from fear-pursed lips.

"It's something I've wanted to ask for a while."

Would it be rude to flee his apartment?

"Ask what, dammit? We covered this already, in my apartment, when you told me…you know…that you're gay and that you were attracted to me and all that. I believe you even apologized."

"We kinda did, but our discussion got derailed when you brought up your wife."

This cannot be happening.

"So why bring it up again?"

His shoulders shrugged. "Just evaluating the facts."

"Facts?" I questioned back. "So now you're Joe Friday?"

"I'm not trying to put you on the spot. Or force you to admit anything."

"Then why are you doing this to me?" My voice shook as I asked the question, and I couldn't muster much above a whisper.

"If you tell me to drop this, I will."

Yes, let's do that!

"You think I'm gay?"

"After our first conversation, I thought I might have been mistaken. That maybe you're just a sensitive and compassionate guy, essential qualities for your profession. But now I'm not so sure I *was* wrong."

I glared, demanding a further explanation.

"Something in the way you look at me, especially that first time, in the hot tub. There's the night we discussed my sexuality, and your reaction. I sensed your discomfort stemmed from something more. Tonight, the questions you ask. It's lots of stuff taken together."

"Sounds pretty circumstantial, Perry Mason."

"This is not an interrogation, and you are not on trial."

"It feels like it," I said petulantly. "Couldn't I just be a friend who's interested in your life? A therapist who wants to help?"

"Of course. But it's like pieces of a puzzle: as they come together, a picture forms."

"Racquetball *and* a jigsaw puzzle obsession. You have very diverse interests, Mr. Stavros, the third."

After a moment of silence, he apologized. "This is upsetting you. Why don't we go back and finish our dinner?"

Deal!

"I was married." The quick reminder kept him from standing up. "That should prove..." I was too drained to finish that last-ditch sentence with anything more than a slow exhale.

"You *are* an enigma. An intriguing mystery."

"So you've gone from Joe Friday, to Perry Mason, and now to Columbo. You are very versatile."

He laughed. "That's a different conversation altogether."

What's so funny?

"Look, I'm not trying to spoil our evening."

But you are!

"Just tell me you're not gay, and this conversation will be over. I'll never bring it up again." He stared at me for what seemed like an hour while I fumbled with a button on the pillow I held on my lap.

Freud would love this. I'm covering the very part I am most afraid of revealing.

"Well," he pressed, displaying his casual smile. "I'm waiting for an answer to my question."

"Yes."

"Yes, you'll answer, or yes, you're gay?"

"The question deserves some thought."

"The question *deserves* an answer."

"What is it that you want me to say?" My annoyance increased the decibels in my voice. "That I'm gay?" My hands were flailing around in exaggerated gestures, and I was screeching.

He didn't give an answer, but his eyebrow arched as his head cocked to one side. Waiting.

My throat felt scratchy after the outburst. I flopped backward into the sofa and made the effort to slow my breathing, which sounded like a dog in hot weather. "I don't want…I don't believe I *am* gay." I tried in vain to gage his reaction. "Am I attracted to men? Definitely." I was shaking, also evidenced in my quivering voice. "Are you satisfied?"

He took a seat beside me and touched my hand. "Relax, Nathaniel." He put an arm around my shoulder. Feeling him close brought a symphony of feelings, but the tune was very dissonant. His muscular arms brought an immediate sense of security. It also scared me how much I enjoyed the embrace. "Do you think telling me this would change anything between us?"

I jumped to my feet and shouted: "Of course it changes things. How can I be expected to help you deal with your sexuality when I can't even come to grips with my own?"

"I never asked you to help me deal with my sexuality. I just answered *your* questions about my sexuality."

He was so composed. Then his disarming smile appeared.

I tried not to laugh, but the situation was too ludicrous. "I must sound like a raving lunatic," I said, sitting back down. "The situation took me by surprise. I overreacted—"

"Please stop explaining. It's OK."

"You were able to accept your sexual desires—" He must have heard the quiver in my voice. "But all I've ever wanted was to get rid of mine."

"What scares you so much? Is it the idea of being gay? Or being here…with me?"

"I don't think of myself as gay; it's…"

"A sin?" He completed the thought, adding a hint of disdain.

I felt compelled to defend my beliefs and challenge his tone. I did neither. "I've spent years trying to ignore the feelings. Sublimating them. Trying to make them go away."

"Are you angry that I've forced you to deal with them again?"

"More like, surprised. Maybe because I was married, or a minister, no one has ever assumed I had this secret attraction. So I've never been able to talk out loud to anyone about the feelings. Not even my therapist. Just confessions in my journals. I'm pretty good at hiding them. Or thought I was, until you came along." I looked at him. His charming manner made it difficult to stay annoyed. "How did you know? About me?"

"I've suspected for some time. From the beginning, I'd say. It's like a sixth sense among gay men."

In an instant, fear asserted. "Then this—" With a gesture of my arm, I swept the room. "This invitation was designed to manipulate me into a confession?"

He stiffened. "Hell, no! Please believe that. I invited you here for your birthday. The rest just happened."

"It feels like more than that. This all seems *calculated*. You admitted you found me…that you were—"

He moved close to the over-stuffed arm of the couch. "If that's how you see me, maybe this was a mistake."

That's my cue to exit.

I could go back to my life and drive these desires back underground.

He was looking up at the ceiling. "You might be right," he finally said to the tiles above him. Then he faced me. "Not about me manipulating you here, I want you to believe that. But maybe I was orchestrating the situation. Not intentionally, but there is a definite attraction. I like being around you, so that might have clouded my motives."

This was a side of Trey I'd not seen: self-reflective and insecure.

"I can be direct, going after what I want without always considering the consequences. I've been told I have control issues.

Pushy. For some, that's…off-putting. So I apologize. I rushed you into something you were not expecting and are not ready for. I'll understand if this is too uncomfortable and you want to leave."

There it was again: my way of escape. Without warning, tears formed. Then I was sobbing. He moved in to hug me close, holding me until I stopped crying.

"I'm sorry," I managed through a runny nose. "I've fought these feelings for as long as I can remember."

"But you've never…?"

I shook my head before he completed the obvious question.

"Then all this must make you nervous." It was both a question and conclusion.

I bobbed my head side to side. "Yes and no. You intimidate me with your confidence. And the fact you admit that you find me… you know."

"The word you're looking for is *attractive*. And yes, I do, though I didn't intend it to cause you such anxiety."

You do that just by being this close to me.

"I meant what I said. I didn't invite you here with ulterior motives. I'm not planning to try and seduce you. Does that help?"

"Honestly," I said, looking him in the eyes, "I'm kinda *disappointed*."

Seven

For a moment, my words hung in the air like the smell of our uneaten supper. He cocked his head to the left and looked at me like a curious puppy. The questions he must have now, along with those that had just been answered, were practically written on his face.

Our eyes locked, and neither of us blinked. The world around us froze, but in a wave of warmth rather than cold. I sensed no movement, heard no noise. Cicadas were muted, and the wind wasn't whistling past the patio door. Even nature paused with us.

It was different...*noisier*...inside me. I was certain he could hear my heart beating; it banged loudly in my ears, and my throbbing temples were probably visible from space. My throat also pounded in syncopation. The cardiac increase spread directly to my face, which grew hotter with every beat. My lungs stopped functioning. I couldn't breathe.

It was frightening.

It was wonderful.

They say at death your entire life flashes before your eyes. I wasn't dying, so in this situation, I think my brain cataloged every sermon I'd ever heard and replayed them in fast-forward. Words—condemning words—clobbered my mind. Abomination. Sodomite. Sin. Judgment. Shameful.

None of them mattered in that moment.

I fixated on Trey, a motionless mannequin beside me. This man who'd long occupied my dreams *and* my daydreams was here. He was fantasy and lust, combined. He belied all I'd been told about homosexuals. He didn't fit any of the dire descriptions or warnings.

More memorized Bible verses sought to assert.

They were ignored.

Maybe just this once.

Necessity broke the silence—an audible intake of essential air into my deprived lungs. And I blinked.

As if by magic, the noise of taking in air, and the instinctual act of blinking, set everything in motion again. He inched toward me, and I knew what was about to happen. Conscience screamed in one more attempt at rebuke. To no avail.

The kiss was gentle; his lips were soft and tender. Not that I'd had much experience for comparison's sake, beyond a few girls in high school, but I guess I'd assumed kissing a man would somehow be *different*.

Internal warnings faded as the kiss intensified. His tongue separated my lips and probed inward. My head dizzied at the taste of him. Our tongues enjoined in an ecstatic wrestling of exploration.

I became aware that the blood, which seconds earlier had made my ears pulsate and my face hot, was now following a new downward path. It embarrassed me to think that if he moved much closer, he'd feel the erection through my jeans.

When he pulled away from the kiss, I gasped. My brain grappled to form words. My mouth tingled, still reveling in that kiss, and refused to cooperate, beyond addled mumbles.

"I didn't…I wasn't…" He moved backward on the couch.

The thought of his wanting to stop, especially out of a sense of chivalry, brought an outburst of a single word. "No!" Taking his hand, I kissed his fingers. "That was *incredible*."

"Are you sure?" Concern burdened his words.

Sure?

Not even close.

"You may not know this, but before we met in that hot tub, I'd been watching you. In the weight room."

He laughed. "You weren't that subtle. It was both entertaining and adorable, watching you trying desperately to operate the equipment."

"Always glad to be a source of amusement."

"Oh, you are so much more than that."

"Since that day, I could not stop thinking about you. I fought it of course. Like I've done all my life. Even after you talked to me and we were spending time together, I never imagined someone like you...as beautiful as you could ever...well, that's not exactly true. I *did* imagine. Sometimes you were in my dreams."

He looked surprised, which surprised me.

This can't be the first time someone's pointed out how gorgeous he is.

"You had dreams? About us?"

With my complexion full flushed, I nodded. "More you than me."

"I'm flattered. And just so you know, that first time we met, I was disappointed when you left. I looked for you every time I went to the gym. Then I saw you working out and *had* to talk to you. You were shy and funny and real. That's why I kept showing up and asking you to play racquetball. That's why I offered to be your workout buddy. I liked being around you. At one point, I worried you'd think I was a creepy stalker."

Am I being real now?

"Nathaniel." His voice was soft and hesitant. "It's important to me that you know I did *not* invite you up here to seduce you. I've had my fantasies as well, but that night, in your apartment, you were clear, and I respected your boundaries. When I learned about the death of your wife, I could feel your pain and wanted to be there for you. To get to know you. Thought we could be friends. Yes, I sensed you had *secrets* and might need someone to talk to, but this evening was *never* intended to expose those secrets. More than anything, this night was my birthday gift to you. Am I making any sense?"

"And now?"

"Now?"

"You said you wanted to get to know me. Thought we could be friends. Does this change that?"

"Playing racquetball together is different than...well, sex always changes things. We don't have to do anything you'll regret later."

He's making sense. We should stop right now.

"I want this," I asserted, ignoring my thoughts to the contrary.

SILENCE IS OFTEN AN EERIE ABSENCE OF NOISE. OR IT CAN BE an unnerving void in a conversation. But sometimes, it's the welcome interlude when there's nothing more to say.

Without looking away, he began unbuttoning my shirt. Upon reaching the last button, he slipped it over my shoulders, letting it drape across the back of the couch. I remembered the time he lifted my T-shirt at the gym, and now I had the same apprehension about him seeing my body. I stiffened.

Did he notice?

"Want me to stop?"

"I'm...I've always been...self-conscious about my body. Having *you* see me is somewhat intimidating. Terrifying is more like it."

He had that confused puppy look again. "I think you're gorgeous. You *and* your body."

I snickered, which he must have interpreted as permission to continue. His hands, strong yet gentle, stroked my bare chest, moving downward to my navel. Swirling. Barely touching. The lighter the touch, the more my nerve endings energized to experience the sensation. I arched back and shut my eyes.

The creak of the leather cushion let me know he'd left the sofa. Resisting the urge to look, I felt the warmth of his breath on my stomach. Then his tongue found my navel, circling it, probing it. He licked upward and found my left nipple. He ran his wet lips around the brown spot, stopping to suck it.

How did I not know they were so sensitive?

I heard loud moans, then realized: it was me. I wasn't sure I could make them stop. Or if I even wanted to. My arms were perpetual motion, moving from behind my head to gripping the sofa cushion to holding his shoulders. Everything—my anxiety, my fears, all the nervous energy pent up in my squirming body—converged into an uncontrollable sound reminiscent of a scream. Rather than bother him, or even slow him down, it seemed to drive him to more determined action.

"Relax," he said.

He's kidding, right?

"How can I, when you're doing *that*? If I don't move, I might explode."

Trey chuckled. It was throaty, almost wicked. "Well, we can't have that, can we?" His palm rested on the front of my jeans. "Not yet, anyway."

The tremor that raced through me was almost painful.

"I think these might be too restrictive. Don't you agree?"

He's going to see me naked.

Before I could answer—I absolutely *would* have agreed—he was unbuckling my belt and popping open the single button at the top. He took the metal tab of the zipper and pulled it down at a pace that would have made a turtle impatient.

Click.

Click.

Click.

As he guided the zipper down, each notch sounded loud, building anticipation. Wanting him to be done, but not wanting it to end.

Will I ever be able to hear the sound of a zipper without getting an erection?

Nothing else happened, so I squinted my left eye. I was draped half naked, off the edge of the sofa. Trey was on the floor, between my legs, looking up at me. It was the most riveting sight I'd ever seen. "You'd tell me if we're moving too fast, right?"

"I don't know the posted speed limit, but I'm enjoying the ride so far."

I raised my hips, and he slid my pants and underwear down around my ankles. The coolness of the leather on my bare skin was jarring but forgotten the instant he took me into his mouth. When I tried to sit up to get a better view, he held me in place, massaging my nipples in the process. Leigh would touch me down there, but we never discussed doing this. I worried that telling her I wanted such an intimate act would somehow expose too much about my hidden desires to her.

"Wait," I implored, pushing him away, too embarrassed to tell him what would happen if he continued. His sly grin revealed he understood.

He sat down in front of me. "Take as much time as you need." When I bent down to pull up my pants, he put his arm out. "I'm just gonna drop 'em again. Might as well take them off and save us both some time."

"If that's the way it's going to be, then you have *too* many clothes on."

"I'll make a deal with you. You can pull your pants back up long enough for us to go to my bedroom." He didn't wait for my answer. I kicked off my shoes and, holding my unzipped jeans in place, hopped after him.

"LIGHTS ON OR OFF?"

Choices…now?

With the lights off, I wondered if I'd fumble in the dark, searching for his lips or his *whatever*. Having the lights on would provide me the best means to look at his body.

He'll also be able to see mine.

My indecision lasted too long, and he moved into the room, leaving the light on. He took a few steps, then turned to where I stood in the doorway, clutching my jeans. "I hate to sound like a broken record," he said. "But we don't have to do this. Or *anything*. In fact, we can go back to dinner—which is cold by now—and talk. Pretend none of this happened and never speak of it again."

He was right, of course. More than that, I should have left earlier. Done what was right and *righteous*. But pretend it never happened? I was not that good an actor.

"Just *talk*?" Holding on to my belt loops to keep my pants from falling down, I leaned on the door jam, and crossed my legs, in a casual pose. "Sure, we could do that. Maybe discuss the weather. Our favorite TV show. I like *CHIPs*. Hey, does Auburn have a chance at a national championship this year?"

"You have a hidden Krystle Carrington side I've never noticed before. And *CHIPs*? Really? We'll have to come back to that one."

I saw he was going to remove his shirt. "Let me," I said, walking to where he stood beside the bed.

The fingers on one hand clutched my jeans to keep them up, while the other fumbled with the buttons on his shirt. When that proved too difficult, I decided getting the shirt off was more important, so I let my jeans fall. He used that as an invitation and occupied himself fondling between my legs. It was such a distraction that I somehow lost the ability to operate buttons. I pushed his hand away when he tried to help. "I *want* to do this." The confidence in my voice proved I was a better actor than I gave myself credit for.

Once I tossed his shirt to the nearby chair, I watched as he slowly...willfully slowly...removed his slacks. His erection pushed his jockey shorts tight against it. It was flattering to notice a sizable wet spot in the front and fascinating that I could have that effect on this good-looking man who'd been with more experienced guys.

I stepped out of my jeans as he slid backward on to the bed. I climbed up and straddled him. Having no idea what I was doing, I followed his example from earlier: kissing up from his stomach and licking around his nipples and along his neck.

It was unclear how long to linger on any one area or at what point he'd expect me to move on to something else.

What if I'm doing all this wrong?

His aroma filled my nose. I detected several scents as I moved over his body: the soap he used to shower and perhaps a hint of his deodorant. Maybe an aftershave or a musky cologne. Even the steaks he'd cooked for dinner. He smelled, and tasted, great.

I moved up beside him and ran my fingers over his chest and stomach, each time moving closer and closer to the elastic band of his underwear, once even slipping a finger under and skirting along the edge. I circled the dark hair on his chest, then followed the path back to his shorts. From the look on his face, the noises he was making, and the way his muscles tightened at my touch, he seemed to enjoy what I was doing. He arched his back, thrust his hips upward, then placed both of his hands on mine and guided me over the front of his shorts. His firmness twitched as I closed around it.

"Oh, God, that feels great."

"Trey." The apprehension was evident in my voice. "I'm…uhm…I want you to enjoy…to satisfy you, but I'm not sure how…I don't know what to do."

With his left arm, he cradled my head into his chest. I could hear his heart and feel his breathing. And his smell was more intense now. "Baby, you are incredible. What you were just doing is great. So hot."

Baby.

It had a foreign quality to it, coming from a man, directed at me. But it also touched something in me and felt safe.

"If there's something that you like done to you—that gives you pleasure—chances are it'll feel good to me."

"I liked it when you…you know…"

He sat up in bed. The sudden action startled me. "I keep forgetting that this is all new to you. Not just the sex but even talking about it. Right?"

The reddening of my face was my answer.

"There's no need to be embarrassed."

Too late!

It was true though. Growing up, we didn't discuss sex. I remember once—I was seven or eight—my mother came in during my bath and warned me about touching myself. I wasn't, but her horrified tone made the implications clear. Around thirteen, my father left a biology book in my room with chapters about changes in my body marked for me to read. He'd also included a sheet of Bible verses about sexual purity. In Southern Christian culture, sex was outside the realm of polite conversation. I'd counseled several married couples who had difficulties talking about it. In my own marriage, we had a healthy sexual relationship, but what we liked or what we'd like to do wasn't discussed.

"You can be yourself with me."

Be myself?

I wasn't even sure who that was right now.

"Use whatever words are comfortable for you. Now me, I can get a bit dirty. I admit I'm not familiar with the religious terms for body parts."

"Something like, 'I wish to sucketh thy male member?'"

"Now we're talking." He shed his shorts and threw them on the floor. "Bless you, my child."

Moving down to his erect penis, I touched it. First with one finger, circling the slippery liquid leaking from the head. I wrapped my hand around him. "I always wondered about...you know." I was stroking his erection, so I hoped the implications would be obvious.

He propped up on both elbows to see me. "What it'd be like to see another man's dick?"

"No, I've *seen* plenty. I played tennis in high school and college, so I've been in the showers with naked guys." Just to be clear I explained, "Guys were naked, but it's not like I was gawking at their..."

"Their dicks. Well, you certainly looked at mine that first day we met."

"You noticed that, did you?" I was blushing. "I thought I was subtle."

"Why do you think I stood halfway in the water for so long?"

"If I remember your explanation, it was to massage your injured leg."

He snickered. "Yes, the jets were nice, but I was giving you an unobstructed view."

"Yours is bigger than mine." I coupled my statement with a long, slow stroke.

His hand joined mine. "Actually, it's in the average range."

"You measured it?"

"I assumed every man has, at one time or another. Gay men for sure."

"I haven't."

And I'm not a gay man!

"Maybe my dick is a little longer, but yours is thicker. It stands hard and sturdy, like a good soldier."

He tugged at my arms, returning me to the pillow next to him. He reached over and grabbed my *soldier*. "Standing at attention and ready for action, sir."

"I feel like I should salute," he said as he crawled down the bed, "but instead I'll…" His mouth engulfed me.

That night, he took me through the experience of sex between two men. He told me when he enjoyed something I was doing, and his instructions about things I could do to him were explicit. He was gentle and patient, erotic and sensual. At times, funny. "Did your Bible college teach you to do that with your tongue?"

At first, his penchant for "dirty talk" intimidated me. I'd spent my entire life in the church, so the words sounded coarse to my ears. But something in me seized them as fuel, which inflamed me with increased desire. When at last I reached a climax—he had insisted on my finishing first—it was powerful.

"Jesus Christ," he exclaimed at the sight of my release.

"Please," I panted. "No shop talk."

Later, we lay naked—his front to my back—just holding one another. "This is nice." He snuggled close.

It is nice.

I was so content, feeling the closeness that comes in just a touch, a sense of security that awed me. When I heard his rhythmic breathing, I rolled over and settled in for a night of glorious sleep. Given the events of the evening, I expected Trey to fill my dreams with continued joys of now-fulfilled fantasies.

I would make a terrible prophet!

Dark nightmares replaced the erotic dreams I'd experienced in the past. Years of moral training, biblical teaching, and doctrinal constraints reasserted with a vengeance. The inner voice of Morality pointed an accusing finger and condemned my actions, manifesting in a variety of scenes. Everything from having my senior pastor walk in on Trey and me having sex to being tried in court for the crime of homosexuality, with my father as the judge and a jury of former professors, Sunday school teachers, and Grace staff members. It made for a fitful night with little rest.

For me, our night of heated passion dawned to a morning of chilling reason. And regret. With the light of day came the glare of remorse and the renewed conviction of Conscience's strong voice.

Eight

"So?" Trey asked at breakfast.

I'd managed to find my shirt and jeans before he got up. He was seated across from me at the small kitchen table, dressed in a pair of lightweight gym shorts and no shirt. I stopped my spoon mid-bite. The milk from the cereal dribbled into the bowl. "What?" I responded in honest innocence.

He gave me a you-know-what-I'm-talking-about look.

"Are you asking the 'How was I?' question?"

He laughed. "That'd be wasted on you since you have no criteria to judge me by. I'm asking about what's going on inside you. How are you dealing with all this?"

"I'm not," was my frank answer. I put down the spoon and picked up my coffee cup.

"You're…*not*? As in, you're fine?"

"As in: I'll deal with it later."

"Is that the Scarlett O'Hara method of deflection?"

I was tired, my nerves were raw, and my emotions were being held together by repeating the promise that I'd deal with everything later, once I was alone. Affecting an exaggerated Southern accent, I batted my eyelashes at him. "Yes, Ashley, I'll think about this tomorrow, when I get to Tara."

Maybe a little levity would prevent the inevitable confrontation I saw coming.

He didn't like my solution; that was obvious. He pushed away his bowl. For a while, he paced the room and then went out on the patio, standing by the rail with his arms crossed, staring out at the wooded area behind his complex. I poured myself another cup of coffee and joined him, taking the chair closest to him, though not sure what I should say. While the afternoon May temperatures had been in the eighties, it was chilly outside this morning.

He has to be cold without a shirt.

"You're gonna walk out of my life, aren't you?" Emotion rippled through his question.

I wasn't ready to admit that he might be right. With both hands, I massaged my temples where a headache was forming. "I think we both knew that…we knew the impact…that what we did…" I also rubbed under my tired eyes. "This is hard for me, Trey."

He returned to the kitchen chair, and I followed.

"Oh, it's hard for you now?" He spit his contempt out like bitter coffee, prefaced by a mocking snort. "Last night, when your dick was *hard*, it overpowered your precious religious restrictions, and you were fine. More than fine; you fucking enjoyed it."

I liked it better when he silently brooded. I'd never heard him raise his voice or seen his face red with emotion.

"Now, when your dick is soft again, you're the nice Christian with the hard…morality, imposed by that damned church that forces you to deny who you are and what you want. You're Dr. Jekyll and Reverend Hyde."

Every harsh thing he said was true. Emotions and tears were being held back by a tissue-paper dam. "Can we please not have this conversation right now?"

"You would think I'd know better." He was pacing again. "I should have…I knew you weren't ready for this. God, I hate playing games, and I detest bullshit even more."

"I resent the suggestion…the presumption…that I could have predicted how I'd feel today and your accusation that I'm playing games." My voice and volume caught him off guard. "Though I should have listened when you told me how pushy you are." I expelled my own exaggerated huff. "You underestimated yourself.

You're a bulldozer, rolling over anyone who doesn't comply with your high and lofty standards. But I will not be bullied to abide by your timeline or your expectations."

He drew in a loud breath, which he released through his mouth like blowing out birthday candles. "You're right. I'm pushing again. I'm sorry. But you do *need* to have this conversation. You're a counselor. You know it's not healthy to keep it bottled up inside you."

How dare he tell me how to do my job!

But expressing such a reaction would escalate, not resolve, our conflict. "You're correct: I *do* need to talk about it. And I promise I will. But *not* with you!"

"Why? Because I'm not part of the church-going elite or because I seduced you?"

The words stung. "That's not fair. I do not think you seduced me, and I made that clear last night. I take responsibility for my own actions."

"Then please let me help. Don't you get it? I care about you."

"If this...*when* all this comes crashing in on me, there'll be so much to deal with. In my own way, in my own time."

"All what?" He threw up his arms.

"You know...this...uhm...our night together and what we did."

"You still can't even say the word, can you?" It sounded weak, like he and his voice had run out of energy. He collapsed into the chair. "I thought what happened last night meant something to you. It did to me. We had sex. I sucked your dick, and you sucked mine. We had sex—gay sex—and you *liked* it. Why can't you say it, Nathaniel? Quit avoiding the truth."

"Oh, and I suppose you know the truth?" I wanted to ask if he could recite *any* of the many Bible verses that condemned what we had done last night.

I certainly can.

"At least I accept who I am."

"But you can't tolerate others who aren't as secure, can you? Believe differently than you? Who still have questions, and fears?"

I was sure the entire building could hear my screaming. "I'm not you, so stop being so damned critical."

"I think the person most critical of you is *you*." He put his hand on mine. "I didn't intend to come across that way. I'm just concerned."

So am I.

"I'm concerned because I've seen what that religion you hold so dear does to people like us."

People like us?

"If I'm being pushy, it's because I see the wonderful, caring, passionate man who's trapped inside. I spent last night with someone finally able to express and experience the desires he's denied for so long. I like spending time with *that* man."

That man is not real!

I headed for the den. When he came into the room, I was putting on my shoes.

"What are you doing?"

"I have an appointment."

He sat down and put his arms around me. He felt so good holding me, tempting me to stay.

Not today.

"Look, I'm sorry. Just…don't do this."

"I have to." He released me and watched through tears as I tied my shoelaces. "I need some time. Alone. To think. To…" I wasn't about to say 'pray.' "I really *do* have an appointment."

"Will you call me later?"

With a put-on smile, I agreed.

Fake promises don't merit a genuine smile.

"Sorry I'm late."

By the time I arrived, the sky was overcast. We'd had several days of rain in the past weeks, with afternoon storms. Even as that possibility loomed in the dark clouds overhead, I couldn't *not* come, today of all days. My umbrella was in the car in case I needed it. Placing the Styrofoam cup of coffee on the bench, I sat in silence.

What was there to say?

Thunder rumbled in the distance. Those who put stock into coincidental natural phenomena might interpret it as a sign from heaven.

"I'm so ashamed."

I knew our dead loved ones couldn't hear us. That went against my Christian beliefs. Nonetheless, every Saturday I came and talked to her. Everyone needs somebody who will listen, and Leigh was my somebody. The week I returned to work, I admitted my anxiety. Before I cleaned out her things from the apartment, I expressed the sadness and loneliness I felt. When I found my house, I told her first. I even bragged about how well I was doing at my workouts and weight loss. I didn't provide details about the person who had helped me with that.

Forest Hill Cemetery was located on the east side of Birmingham, about fifteen minutes from Homewood. Though not my choice for her burial, I gave in to her parents' wishes. It was near where they lived and where she'd grown up. They had the cemetery install a nice two-person concrete bench next to her headstone, which I had purchased, but with an epitaph written by her mother, who took the death of her youngest child extremely hard.

Leigh Anne Truett
Wife. Daughter. Sister.
Child of God.
No more suffering in the arms of Jesus
Earthly Birth February 21, 1955
Heavenly Birth October 28, 1981

I stood and put my hand on the large granite marker. "You must be so disappointed in me right now. I sure am."

My faith taught that Leigh was in a perfect place where such petty human emotions don't exist. Where God wiped away all her tears. And she now lives where there is no sorrow. Being a counselor, I understood that saying it aloud had more to do with me than her.

I walked back and forth along the boundaries of her grave. "I can't explain it, 'cause I don't understand it myself." I sat back down. "When you were here, I could resist these desires. That's not an excuse. Please believe me. It's just that your love surrounded me and protected me. I would have never thought of doing anything like this."

A large raindrop hit the seat beside me, followed by more hitting me on the head. The air filled with the smell that comes before a storm. Logic would dictate getting the umbrella. "Having sense enough to get out of the rain," as Mom would say. I didn't move. The more it rain, the more I cried.

"I'm sorry, sweetie. Please forgive me." I was wailing like a paid mourner. "I need you to forgive me."

A crack of thunder almost masked hearing my name. "Nate."

That's Leigh's voice.

"Nate," it spoke again. "What's got you so upset?"

When a hand touched my shoulder, I jumped, screamed, and spun around. My arms, swinging like rag doll limbs on my body, knocked the cup of coffee into a nearby headstone.

"Regina." I almost poked out an eye on her oversized umbrella. "I didn't hear you drive up."

Until that moment, I'd never noticed how much Leigh's mother sounded like Leigh.

"I know this is your time with her. But yesterday I saw a bit of overgrowth and thought I'd trim it up." There were caretakers to do that, but Regina was not one to give up control, not when it concerned her daughter.

"Why were you asking Leigh Anne to forgive you?"

She held out her umbrella, inviting me out of the downpour. I carefully brushed the water off my face and hair to not splash her. It also allowed me to think of an answer that didn't involve anything close to the actual truth.

“What’s going on, son?”

Taking in extra air through my nose, I launched into my *reasonable* explanation. “Things have just been difficult. My birthday is next week—the first without her. Moving out of the apartment… *our* home…hit me hard. I guess it came crashing down on me this morning.”

“You know she loved you. She’ll always be in our heart, and we will all be together one day in paradise.”

“I’m gonna get out of this storm.” Reacting to her not-helpful platitudes would prolong the conversation. “There’s lightning, so you should consider that as well. It was good to see you, Regina.”

Nine

"Do you have any special plans for your birthday tomorrow?"

I was looking over the next week's schedule. More accurately, I was staring at the page and thinking about Trey. For days, I replayed our angry exchange. He had been so nasty. So had I. Miss Gert's question interrupted my thoughts.

"Susan's coming over to help me put up some curtains in the guest bedroom before the open house and then taking me to dinner. She's being all mysterious."

Please don't let it be a surprise party.

"You still have two weeks before the open house."

Don't remind me.

"All of the workmen are gone except for the painter who's finishing the kitchen. Most everything is done, except the master bedroom furniture."

According to the dealer, it would be delivered Tuesday.

"I have some extra invitations," Miss Gert said. "In case you think of anyone else to invite."

The open house-slash-housewarming had been Miss Gert's suggestion, but before she asked me about it—whether I even wanted it—she'd talked to Dr. Shannon, who thought it was an excellent idea. My townhouse wasn't big enough to invite the entire church. In fact, the thought of everyone in the church knowing where I lived, and showing up at my house, made me queasy, so the event wouldn't be included in the bulletin or newsletter. We decided on having personalized invitations printed and mailed. Even with that, the list was more extensive than I'd preferred, but Miss Gert convinced me some were necessary: elders, Grace staff, leaders of partner agencies, donors, and board members. Though it felt odd, I included Leigh's friends and coworkers. I'd also invited Scot, but requested he not mention it to the Circle. In total, we had mailed and given out about two hundred invitations.

What if they all show up at the same time?

Or worse, what if no one shows up?

The after-church hours would be between two and five, and the invitation emphasized "come and go" in large, bold letters. Miss Gert explained it was to discourage "a bunch of chatty folks hanging out at your house the entire time, taking up all your attention."

She and Susan were coordinating the food: snacks and finger foods. Of course there would be chips, nuts, and a variety of sodas. Our minister of music's wife owned a bakery where they'd be getting cupcakes and pastries. I also requested some healthier choices such as veggies, fruit, and cheese.

"I think everything is taken care of."

If only.

I FINISHED A PRODUCTIVE SESSION WITH A MOTHER, HER TEENage son, and the man she'd just married after a divorce from the boy's biological father. They came to me because the boy wasn't responding well to his new stepfather; I was helping them develop communication skills to bring harmony to the transition.

As the trio and I were walking to the reception area, Miss Gert said, "Brother Truett, this young man has a delivery for you." I turned, and on the counter of the receptionist's desk sat a huge fruit basket. Standing beside it was Trey. I almost dropped my notepad, and the lunch I'd eaten threatened a return appearance. Turning to the family, I forced a steadiness to my voice. "See you in two weeks."

My impulse was to follow them out, get in my car, and drive away. I resisted every urge to scream: *What the hell are you doing here?*

He stepped toward me, and I stiffened. "Sorry to interrupt your day. I was dropping this off," he said, indicating the basket with a nod of his head. "You know, for your birthday."

"It's beautiful," Miss Gert observed.

I looked at her, then back at him, and repeated the motion.

He reached across the counter. "I'm Alex, but my friends call me Trey."

She took his hand and did a modest nod. "So you must be Alex, the third."

"I am." He gave his most amiable smile. "Not everyone understands the meaning of my nickname."

"Not everyone is as old as I am."

My brain decided to kick in. "Sorry. Trey, this is Miss Gert. She's the receptionist and my administrative assistant."

"Nate...Brother Truett...has told me all about you," he lied. "He couldn't do what he does without you."

I think she blushed.

Always the charmer.

"I'm Brother Truett's personal trainer. And we play racquetball. He's quite the competitor."

"Oh, you're his standing afternoon appointment."

"I am." He glanced over at me with that roguish grin. "Though he's missed his workouts lately."

Did he think I'd show up after how we left things?

"He's having a busy month, what with his birthday, the board meeting, and the open house coming up in two weeks."

I couldn't think of a way to stop what I knew would happen next.

"Will we see you there?" she inquired.

And there it is.

"I appreciate that, Miss Gert, but I'm not part of the church. I wouldn't know anyone there."

I could say aloud that I agreed, plus having him there would be awkward. He would be, as always, a distraction.

"You should come," I declared, surprising myself. I snatched an invitation and thrust it at him. "You know, if you want to."

He looked confused.

"I'd like you there. To...you know...see my new house."

He put it in an inside pocket of his tailored, form-fitting suit. "I'll check my schedule."

"Thank you." I pointed to the basket. "It looks scrumptious."

He picked it up. "Let's take it into your office. You can show me where you work."

I couldn't think fast enough to offer a valid objection. Besides, a few weeks earlier, I'd met him at Birmingham Center for Legal Services where he worked. He'd given me a tour of the facilities, introduced me to coworkers, and shown me his office before we went to a movie. I should return the favor.

"You can put it there." I indicated the credenza under the window by my desk.

Then, awkward silence.

"I'm sorry about just showing up here unannounced." He spoke in a whisper. "This way, I make sure you got it and that no one reads the card." When my face showed curiosity, and possible shock, he explained, "It's nothing scandalous, but not something I'd want anyone else to read."

I closed the door and then wondered if he'd misinterpret that action. He gazed around the room, walking to the bookcase where he looked at my library. I sat in my chair in the counseling area and pointed to the sofa.

"More than anything," he said once seated, "I'm sorry about the things I said the other night. I was impatient and harsh, letting my own feelings eclipse what you must have been going through. I'm an insensitive ass. I hope you can forgive me."

"You *did* hurt me, but you are not insensitive. Blunt and impatient, but not an ass. I also said some things I wish I could take back."

"So let's talk about what happened."

His directness is so annoying.

"I do forgive you, but I'm still sorting all this out."

"And I get shut out while you do? Isn't that unfair since I'm part of what you're sorting out?"

"This is more about me and my ministry."

"Are you telling me I have to compete with God?"

"That's not what I'm saying."

What am I saying?

"I need time. Can you be patient?"

"I think you've seen that patience is not my strongest trait, but I'll try." He stood to leave. "Please read my card."

A hug of support and gratitude will be fine.

As soon as we embraced, all my resolve vanished. I touched his face and moved my finger across his lips.

"Have a wonderful birthday, Nathaniel." He kissed the inside of my hand. "Give me a call when...*if* you'd like to talk."

WITH TWO BACK-TO-BACK APPOINTMENTS, READING HIS CARD needed to wait. Knowing him, I was concerned the contents would hinder my ability to concentrate on my client. As it turned out, *not* reading it caused me to wonder about the content throughout both my sessions.

At four-fifteen, I told Miss Gert to call it a day since there were no more appointments, and I wanted to leave early and pick up extra drapery hardware, just in case.

"Happy birthday, Brother Truett," she called out. "Be sure to take the cake home with you." Of course she'd baked me a birthday cake, which was delicious.

Trey's card was buried inside the cellophane that covered the basket. I held the envelope in my hand but didn't open it. He'd written my full first name on the outside.

He has nice handwriting.

My sense of dread was stronger than the anticipation, keeping me from tearing into the envelope. There was even the fleeting thought that I should throw it in the trash. Not read it at all.

How can I overcome this sin if I keep toying with the person who's my biggest temptation?

That would be the prudent thing to do, but curiosity won out over prudence, and I sat down to read.

Dear Nathaniel,

I can't tell you what knowing you means to me. Our time together last weekend was amazing and special. It's clear you have lots to work through, and I get that there are things in your life that make this more difficult.

Hopefully, it's not impossible.

You've endured pain and grief I could never comprehend. I find it beyond admirable that you've come through everything with your desire to help others remaining intact. My heart hurts for all you went through. I can't believe my selfish actions last week added to that pain. Please forgive me.

I think we might be something worth exploring. I hope you'll give this...you'll give us...a chance. I'm ready and willing to try...if you are.

Happy birthday!

P.S. Just so you know, there's no hidden pun in sending fruit except that it's healthy. I wish you all the best, and please know that you're on my mind. And in my heart.

I reread the card several times before shoving it into my briefcase and heading home.

When the phone rang just before seven, I was still asleep. I'd worked until after midnight on a presentation I was doing at the Circle next month. But Mom always called me on my birthday—she liked to be the first person to wish me a "Happy birthday" and sing to me—so I wasn't surprised. We talked about the open house, and she again expressed her regrets that she couldn't attend. She taught a

Sunday school class at her church—the "widow women," she called them—and also didn't like to travel on the Lord's Day.

Awake, I made coffee and did my quiet time. In my journal, I recorded anxiety about the upcoming open house and the possibility of Trey attending.

Don't think about him.

I went for a morning run around the complex to clear my head and sweat off some stress. The phone was ringing as I returned.

"You sound winded. Did I interrupt something? Or someone?"

"Susan, get your mind out of the gutter. I was jogging."

She giggled, unruffled by my reprimand. "If it's OK with you, I'll bring my clothes over to your place. That way we can hang the curtains, then clean up and go celebrate your birthday."

"Or—" I stretched it out for effect. "We could hang the curtains, stay in, order pizza, and watch a movie."

"I'm taking you out for your birthday, and it's not up for discussion. But when you find out where we're going, you'll thank me. I was able to get us a reserved table at..." The pause was for dramatic effect, which was typical Susan. "Gionelli's."

That did make it more interesting. The place was a hole-in-the-wall diner near EPCS, the college where she and I had met. A favorite haunt of college students, the restaurant boasted Italian food that was renowned throughout the city. "I haven't been there in years."

"I booked us at six, so I'll come by around three, which will give us plenty of time to get the curtains done. If not, there'll be time after dinner."

"You are the best friend ever."

"Don't you forget it either."

I moved Trey's gift basket into my bedroom closet to avoid answering her questions about who had sent it. I was rummaging through my clothes for something to wear to dinner when the phone rang.

That's Susan telling me she'll be late.

"Is it redundant to wish you a happy birthday again?"

"Trey."

"Did you read my card?"

Pushy, as usual.

"Yes, it was kind and moving."

"But was it convincing?"

"It's possible you might have missed your calling. You could write greeting cards."

"Can we talk? I could come over—"

"I have dinner plans with Susan."

"Are you two *dating*?"

That made me laugh. "Heavens, no. I'll tell you all about her later."

"So there will be a later?"

Bad idea!

"I'm thinking we could put all your muscles to work. I have furniture being delivered on Tuesday. Once that's done, I could use some help moving boxes upstairs before the open house. I'll spring for pizza."

"Tell me the time, and I'll do some extra push-ups to be ready."

I gave him the new address, and we agreed he'd come over on Friday after work.

It'll be fine.

I ARRIVED AT THE RESTAURANT BEFORE SUSAN. NO SURPRISE. She had a habit of being late, but got offended if others were.

Could I get away with ordering a glass of wine?

Susan wouldn't care, but it could have repercussions if someone from church were to see me.

She arrived carrying a brightly colored package. The bow was as big as the box, and a giant Mylar balloon bounced over her as she walked. They stood out against her usual wardrobe of black with gray accents. She must have kept the gift in her car while we were working at my house.

Once she put the gift down, the attached balloon hovered above, like a lighthouse, telegraphing to all in the restaurant that we were celebrating my birthday. It almost guaranteed the waiters would sing to me.

She gave me a peck on the cheek and whispered, "You hate the balloon, don't you?" She didn't allow me to respond. "I knew you would. Which is why I *had* to bring it along. Anything to help you loosen up."

She did like to torment me.

Susan insisted I have a glass of wine. "It's your birthday, darling. Besides, it's not like you're Baptist." She still didn't comprehend that our church made many Baptist churches look progressive. She grunted in disdain when I poured the wine into a tea glass to disguise what it was just in case someone might see me.

Once we'd ordered, we exchanged "war stories" as Susan called them, talking about our work and the rigors of ministry. We laughed at some of the people we had to deal with. Susan had an active but unsuccessful dating life, so our conversations often involved her latest boyfriend or another breakup. Today, she went on and on about an accountant she'd met in her yoga class.

"So what's going on with you these days?"

I dodged the issue and made a nebulous comment about trying to discern God's will in several areas.

She frowned. "I'm not that certain God gets too involved with the mundane affairs of our life. After all, he gave us a brain and common sense. What purpose does it serve to spend hours trying to discover God's will about whether to wash my hair or not?"

"Well maybe this is more important than washing my hair!" My annoyance was evident.

"I'm sorry," she said. "It wasn't directed at your particular struggle. I was just…I'm sorry."

"No, I overreacted."

The meal, as usual, was incredible. During dessert—a mildly sweet panna cotta topped with tangy fruit compote—she insisted

I open my gift. As feared, this signaled a band of troubadour servers to converge on our table and sing an Italian birthday song. I tightened my lips to mimic a smile and nodded, glad the dim light hid my embarrassment. When they finished, the entire room applauded. Nothing like being on display while opening a present: a beautiful shirt with a coordinating tie. The shirt was labeled *fitted*, and Susan must have seen me reading the tag. "It'll look great on you. It's obvious you've been working out, and this will show off your hard work and your hard body."

More gratitude for the dark room that hid my embarrassment.

"I'm glad we're here. This place brings back such memories." She pointed to a table in the back near the kitchen door. "That's where we sat when you introduced me to Leigh Anne."

"Oh, I remember. She thought you and I despised one another because all we did was argue."

She took another sip of wine—her second glass. "Then I moved away and was so terrible at keeping in touch."

"Hey, I was just as bad. But I'm glad we reconnected."

"So tell me. This new dedication to getting in shape. Does it have anything to do with someone special?"

If I'd been eating, I might have choked on my food.

"Sorry if that was intrusive. Is it still too soon?"

"Yeah, Mom's concerned that I'll be…in her words…tempted by the lusts of the flesh and start dating too soon."

"That sounds like Charlotte. But you didn't answer my question."

"Right before Leigh died, she told me she didn't expect me to stay single."

Susan was nodding. "I didn't know if she'd had that conversation with you. She and I talked about it in her final months."

"You did?"

"She loved you, Nathaniel. And she would never want you to stop living your life."

"It's not easy, my life without her. And…well, it is something I've been thinking about."

"So there *is* someone?"

My mind raced. "Not sure. Maybe. More like an attraction. But it's complicated."

"These things usually are."

"This...uhm...this person and I are very different. We have a great time together, but it's—"

"Yeah, *complicated.* Is this related to what you talked about earlier? Looking for God's will?"

"Sorta. I mean, not really. It couldn't be God's will. Even though it's..." I almost said "complicated" again. "It's confusing."

She reached across the table and placed her hand on mine. "Be happy, kiddo. That's what I want for you *and* what Leigh Anne wanted for you."

"Allow me to wish you a happy birthday," our friendly waiter said, bringing our check. He didn't move his hand until I glanced up. The accompanying look conjured up new birthday wishes to go with blowing out my candles. "If you need *anything* else, let me know. And please come back anytime. Ask for Julien, and it'd be my pleasure to serve you again."

As we stood in line at the cashier's counter, Susan laughed. "Well, *that* wasn't subtle."

When I pretended ignorance, she motioned back into the restaurant. "That waiter was hitting on you."

I waved her off. "He's just being nice. Gets him a bigger tip."

She changed the subject and asked me about the open house.

"Everything's pretty much done. Once the furniture arrives, then it's down to the wire getting both bedrooms presentable."

"Do you need me to help?"

"A friend's coming over."

That got a raised eyebrow, so I prepared for an explanation.

"Good. Knowing how anal-retentive you are, I worried that you might be trying to do it all yourself."

Ten

"Brother Truett, you never cease to amaze me."

The sheets had twisted around our legs, with enough to cover myself.

This was not how I'd envisioned the evening. In my plan, he would come over, and I'd tell him how it had to be from now on: we could be friends, but we could *not* have sex.

Then he arrived, and I saw him, framed in the doorway with the light of the late afternoon sun illuminating behind him like a saint in a stained-glass window. I couldn't help but marvel at how majestic he was.

Definitely not a saint, but an example God's finest handiwork.

The planned speech faded to a vague echo.

"Don't think this will get you out of helping me move boxes."

He propped up on his elbow and looked at me. "So you wanted me for my body…to move boxes?"

My fingers scraped across the hair on his stomach. "Guess I get both." Then I slapped him in the same place. "Now get your cute butt up and let's get the work done."

He helped me move boxes from the downstairs guest bedroom to the upstairs master bedroom. I put clothes in drawers and closets as he watched, making occasional comments about an item of my clothing. We ate pizza, drank beer, talked, laughed, kissed, and playfully touched one another.

It was after ten-thirty when we finished. Tired and sweaty, I suggested we shower. And I didn't spend the first night in my new bedroom alone.

After all, it would've been rude to send him home at such a late hour.

"I didn't hear you get out of bed." Trey was in the doorway, "nekkid as a jaybird" to use my mom's phrase. His hair, usually so styled to perfection, looked like he'd grabbed a live electrical wire in his sleep.

And yet, he's still adorable.

"Couldn't sleep and didn't wanna disturb you." The clock revealed it was six-eighteen. "Why are you up so early?"

"Had to pee and noticed you were missing." His brow was scrunched; he nodded to the open book on my desk. "What's that?"

"This—" I answered, closing the book, "is where I record what's on my mind: feelings, observations, questions. Helps me think through stuff."

"Am I in there?" He pressed his fingers against his chest and then slid them down his stomach at a slow, deliberate pace, stopping just below his navel.

Such a tease.

"There are no bounds to your arrogance."

"That's a *Yes*. So, how long have you kept a diary, Ms. Frank?"

"Since high school. And it's a *journal*, thank you very much."

"Maybe you could call it a 'Captain's Log,' like in *Star Trek*. That sounds sexy."

"You're standing in my doorway, naked, talking about a way to make my journal sexy?"

He walked over and kissed me on the top of my head. "You hungry? I can fix us some breakfast."

"That'd be great." As he left the room, I hollered to him: "Oh, and lots of coffee, please."

"Let me get dressed."

"Where's the fun in that?"

When I came downstairs, he'd donned an apron with nothing

underneath. I gave him a kiss on his shoulder and patted his bare butt.

"The coffee's ready, and I cut up some fruit."

The smell was pleasing, but the caffeine it promised was what I most wanted.

"Everything all right?"

"Yeah, just a bit tired."

"You were jerky during the night."

"I let you sleep in my new bedroom, and you call me a jerk?"

"Be serious. Did you get any sleep?"

"I…well, no, not much. Lots of stress right now. Writing helps." While he cooked—his bare butt facing me at the table—I told him about the high school youth retreat where I'd learned to journal. "I can go months without writing anything, and then there are weeks when I write every day."

He wanted to know more about my past.

"Listening to my life story is not recommended while operating heavy machinery; it could cause drowsiness."

"I'm making an omelet. I think I'll survive. You already mentioned you grew up in a strict, religious home. I wanna know about your childhood. Tell me about your family. Do you have brothers, sisters?"

"I'm an only child. I always thought my childhood was normal, until I got to college. That's when I discovered just how sheltered I had been. It's a wonder I didn't go wild."

"Were you a good student?"

"Honor roll, in high school and college. I guess you could say… well, Susan says I'm an over-achiever. I completed my bachelor's degree in just over three years by going year-round."

"That's impressive. And you majored in marriage and family counseling at Evangelical Presbyterian College of the South."

My head snapped up from staring at my coffee. "How did you know that?"

"The diploma's in your study." He snickered. "Now tell me one thing about you that most people don't know."

"Well, I'm not just an only child. I'm adopted. And other than Leigh and my parents, no one knows it was a kinship adoption."

"That's unusual and way cool."

"My parents had always wanted kids but could never conceive, and as they got older, they'd pretty much given up. Then a distant cousin on my mother's side, fifteen years old, had a baby out of wedlock. This cousin and her folks lived in a mobile home on a remote lake about twenty miles from civilization. They were destitute and not able to manage the responsibility of a baby. They contacted my mother, and she offered to take me. A lawyer in Dad's church helped them through the process. So I was born on May twenty-ninth, but my mother also liked to celebrate August tenth, the day I came to live with them, and then October third, the day the adoption became final."

"Have you ever met your birth mother?"

"No, after she gave birth, she cut out. No one knew where. My mom...my *adoptive* mom...later learned that her cousin—my biological grandmother—had died when I was about seven, and we have no idea what happened to my biological grandfather." I chuckled. "I know it sounds like a bad episode of *Dukes of Hazzard*."

"That assumes there's such a thing as a good episode of *Dukes of Hazzard*," he quipped. "But you don't want to find her? Your birth mother?"

"It awful of me to admit, but no. I wonder about her from time to time, but she made the best choice for her and for me. Mom always said that..." The story was so familiar, I'd started it without considering whom I was telling.

"What?"

"I know you don't like stuff like this, but Mom always explained it as God bringing me to them for a reason. She used to read to me about Moses and Esther, who were raised by someone other than the birth parents. Both became great leaders."

"I find that beautiful and inspiring." He dropped two pieces of turkey bacon on my plate.

"In fact, she named me Nathaniel because it means—"

"Gift from God."

I was stunned.

He laughed. "I looked it up after we met. And I, for one, am very thankful that God brought you to them."

It was difficult to imagine Trey and my mother agreeing on something.

"Are you comfortable talking about...uhm, your wife?"

"Leigh Anne. I don't mind if you say her name. Most of her friends called her Leigh. Well, except for Susan, who has this quirk of calling people by their full given name, like Nathaniel instead of Nate. I'm sure *you* understand."

"I'm in good company then. When, and where, did you and Leigh Anne meet?"

"My junior year...her sophomore year...in college. She was born and raised in Birmingham and would show me around the city. We married the week after my graduation."

"Sweet," he injected. "Did you know then?"

I didn't like the thrust of the question though I understood his intent. "I think so. More subconscious, I'd say. It wasn't something I would have *ever* acted on."

"How long were you married?"

"Just over five years."

"How did she...Is this too much?"

I pointed to the bacon on my plate. "It's just two pieces." I knew what he meant but needed to lighten the mood. Instead, I got a sympathetic look and then silence, which was my cue to tell him the entire cancer ordeal.

"It's so tragic," he replied. "It must have devastated you. I can't imagine. It only makes me care about you more."

I'd worried that the conversation would upset me; instead it was Trey who teared up. I sensed the awkwardness that comes in discussing a dead person. "I appreciate your interest. It's not easy for me to talk about her and our marriage. My therapist says I need to do it more. It's kinda strange talking with you."

"I totally get it. She was your wife, and I'm just your...your personal trainer. But Leigh Anne inhabits a major place in your past and in your heart. I want to know every part of your life, so that includes her."

Every part?

That was a scary premise.

He scooped up the omelets, placed them on our plates, and sat down at the table. "I wish I could help."

I waved him off, shaking my head. "You were very helpful with the boxes—"

"I wasn't talking about the open house. I'm talking about *you*. When I came to your study, you had this look of sadness. I've seen it before. I don't know if you're thinking about her or if you're sad about choices you're making right now."

Why...how...is he able to know me so well?

"You're right; Leigh has been on my mind more for the past few weeks. The new house. And...other things." I didn't elaborate that I meant him. "She seems to have this way of just showing up, unexpectedly, in my mind for no apparent reason at all. All of the sudden, I just *remember* her. It's like she decides to materialize to prevent me from forgetting. Whatever, it's a kick in the heart. "

"It hasn't even been a year, Oraios, I'm not an expert, but that sounds kinda normal."

"Thank you, and...wait, did you call me *Oreo*?"

"You *are* sweet," he said with a laugh, "and oh so creamy on the inside, but no. *Oraios* is a Greek word that means 'handsome.'"

Did my heart just flutter?

"Look, I recognize that you and I...*us*...come with limitations. There are parts of your world that are exclusively *yours*. That's why I was so apprehensive showing up at your office with the gift basket. You have so much to lose and a lot at stake. This is all new, and you need time. I'll be patient because I think you're worth it. I think *we're* worth it."

Time? For what?

It's not like I could *ever* tell anyone about us. Or introduce him as anything other than a friend.

"And you're OK with that? With our *arrangement*?"

After his usual shrug, and a solitary puff-of-air snort, he said, "Not thrilled with referring to us as an 'arrangement.' It sounds like something set up by our parents or the way we placed the furniture in the bedroom yesterday. But for now, I think we shouldn't worry about what we call us. We're still in the early stages. It's fun and exciting. Let's not get bogged down in trying to figure it all out."

What a relief.

"What would you think about maybe getting in a workout?"

He grinned. "At the gym or upstairs?"

"Silly boy. Why does it have to be either-or?"

"You're getting stronger." After our workout, we played a racquetball match.

"Is that your way of acknowledging that I beat you?"

"You won *one* game, not the match. Don't get cocky."

Decorum, and the fear of being overheard, prevented me from making an off-color pun.

"It's my first victory against you. Don't deprive me of my celebration."

"Any plans for dinner?" he asked. "We could stop and pick up something." His question was so loud that I panicked and looked around, thinking others in the snack bar might have heard.

"Relax, we're alone."

"I'm more interested in lunch. You hungry?"

"Should we shower here or go back to your place?"

We both knew the answer to that question.

After lunch, we walked around the Riverchase Galleria, and he insisted I try on shirts at an upscale men's shop. A few of the shirts cost as much as my car payment or were colors I wouldn't wear. Regardless, he was complimentary—everything from how the color made my eyes look bluer to how the shirt accented my body. One knit pullover was skintight, and I refused to come out of the changing room, so he stuck his head in.

"Pardon my language, Reverend, but you look fucking hot."

"I can't even breathe in this one."

"It sure takes *my* breath away."

"I think if we go back to my place, I can find other ways to do that, without spending ninety dollars on a shirt I'll never wear."

His exaggerated pseudo-pout was then replaced with his naughty smile. "I have no doubts. Now hurry!"

Eleven

The open house was the next day, and I was near frantic. Susan tried to convince me that the house was ready and looked great. Around five, while I was still finding things to do, Trey surprised me by showing up with salads, some fresh fruit, and a bottle of wine. "I was worried you'd forget to eat," he explained.

How did he know?

After we ate, he helped me with final touches in the living room and guest bedroom. Around ten, I stated it was time for bed and motioned upstairs.

I mean, it would be rude to send him home after all he'd done.

"Can I ask…I have a question." I was undressed, sitting on the edge of the bed in my underwear. "It's kinda embarrassing."

"Those are the best kind." He finished taking off all his clothes and propped himself against the headboard, the sheet up to his waist.

"Is our…uh…what we do together…satisfying to you?"

He grinned. "I'm not sure what you mean."

We both knew he did.

"I know there are other aspects of sex that, well…if you'd like to—"

"Oh, and where did you learn about these 'other aspects?'" He used air quotes with the last two words.

I wasn't going to tell him that I'd overheard a conversation at Scot's group.

"It was mentioned—" I answered with my obligatory blush, "—at a seminar I attended recently."

"What are you Presbyterians teaching these days?"

In spite of his teasing—*Is he avoiding my question?*—I pressed on. "Well, if you, I mean, if those other intimate…uhm…activities are important—"

"Fuck."

I'd offended him. "I'm sorry."

"No, the word you're looking for is *fuck*. You're asking me about *fucking*." He flashed his boyish grin.

He's enjoying this.

My embarrassment radiated to my face. I'd never used that word in my entire life. It sounded so obscene. I guess I expected him to continue. Hoped he would so I wouldn't have to bumble through this conversation. When it became apparent that he wasn't going to make this easy, I huffed. "Well, are you going to answer?"

"I don't recall a question. But I assume you're asking if I like to fuck. Or be fucked."

More silence.

"We both know you aren't shy, so you must enjoy tormenting me."

"Yeah, that part is amusing."

"Well?"

"You might be moving too fast."

"For you or for me?"

"Not to be crude—"

"Yeah, 'cause that would be so unlike you."

"Be that as it may, you're just now getting comfortable giving a blowjob without gagging."

"I understand, but if it's something that you want."

He twisted around in the bed to face me. "If I'm being honest, I wasn't sure if you had any idea what it was, or what was involved, so I never brought it up. Many gay men consider fu…uhm…doing *that*…well, it's kinda expected. Two guys meet, jump in bed, and go at it like horny little bunnies. I've done my share of *bunnying*, but not so much in the past few years. Being that intimate with someone shouldn't be indiscriminate."

"Is that like *top* and *bottom*?"

"I really must rethink going back to church if these are the current topics."

"It wasn't at church, you knucklehead. I was at a...uhm...support group, and a homosexual guy used those terms."

"Damn. And I thought I was the only gay man you knew."

"Hardly. But if it makes you feel any better, you are the only naked gay man I've ever been in bed with."

"Good answer. As to your earlier question—and I'll try not to be pornographic—you've no doubt guessed it has to do with anal intercourse. A 'top' is someone who prefers to penetrate—inserting the penis into the anus, and a 'bottom' likes to be penetrated."

The idea that two men could have intercourse shocked me and brought up questions about hygiene and cleanliness. At the same time, it was intriguing.

"Which did you...I mean, were you...do you—"

He mercifully rescued me. "That aspect of a relationship is like nothing else. I've enjoyed both, depending on the person I was with. I haven't done either for a while now. In general, I prefer being a top."

He moved in close and brushed my hair with his index finger. "It's a big step. You've never been with another man, and the fact that I'm the first man in your life is flattering, but it also brings out a protective quality in me. So to address your original concern: I *am* satisfied with our—what was your word?—our sexual relationship. We don't need to rush anything. I think we'll know when we're ready for more. At that time, it will be right, and we'll both enjoy it."

His soft words of explanation comforted me and sparked a small amount of arousal.

"I could ask you the same question: are *you* satisfied? I know all this is new, but you've never talked much about what we do together?"

"All the stuff we've done—that you've done to me—has been incredible."

When Trey and I had sex, I let him take the lead. After all, he had the experience. He took his time, and I never felt pressured to do anything. He had a way of skimming his fingers over my skin—touching, but almost not touching—that tickled and excited. It apparently didn't bother him that I was *reserved*, though he encouraged me to let him know what I liked. Sometimes what felt good—what provided pleasure—also created "control issues." That didn't seem to bother him either. "If you let me know, we can slow it down or take a rest. But if you come, that's great. I like seeing you shoot your load. And we both like it when you come while I'm sucking you off."

He was right, but the first time it happened—I couldn't stop myself—I was horrified, thinking he'd be grossed out that I hadn't warned him in time. But he assured me that he intended it to happen. I had not yet learned to reciprocate.

He threw off the sheet. "I want you to explore my body. You can use your hand, but also use other parts as well. Your fingers, your lips, your tongue. Try rubbing your face or your chin across my skin; the stubble of your face can be highly erotic. Run your foot, your toes, up my leg. No part of me is off limits. If I like it, I'll let you know. If I want you to stay in one particular area, I'll tell you. And at any time, feel free to ask me and verbalize what you are feeling."

"Oh, it's a dirty treasure hunt."

"And you are the pirate."

As I slipped off my underwear, he held up his hand. "Just one more thing. When you're done, we switch, and I get to do the same with you. And—" he added, precluding any inclination I might have later "—with the lights on!"

"But—"

"You have a great body, Oraios. It's obvious you've worked with a skilled trainer."

Whose bright idea was it to have this open house on a Sunday afternoon?

Trey didn't leave my place until around seven, and having him in my bed was not conducive to sleep. I still didn't know if he would attend. I also still wasn't sure if I wanted him to attend.

Although some see Sundays as a "day of rest," for the staff at Grace, they were demanding. There was the mandatory morning staff meeting at eight-thirty in the conference room of the pastoral suite for a quick debrief of the upcoming service, the announcements that would be made, and an overview of the Order of Worship. We were given a printout of the liturgy and those who would participate: acolytes, Scripture readers, and the elders who would lead the various prayers. Once adjourned, we would greet people and help direct them to their respective Sunday school classes so the teachers could start on time. At ten-thirty, we had a short, also mandatory, staff prayer prior to worship.

Today, I skipped the usual time of after-church chatting and rushed home to finish up last-minute details. Around one, Miss Gert arrived. Susan did so about ten minutes later. People began to show up before two o'clock, the scheduled starting time.

Not long afterward, Miss Gert advised me that standing at the entrance, greeting everyone, was hindering "the flow of traffic" into the room. "Go and talk to your guests," she instructed. "Have some fun."

The steady stream of people was impressive, but the room never felt overly crowded. Susan directed traffic, providing directions to the food and various parts of the house.

I moved through the rooms and talked to...*mingled* with...folks. Dr. Carl Randall, a local psychiatrist who served on our advisory board was there with his wife. He sometimes recommended clients to us if he felt they needed—in his words—a more "religious approach" to therapy, or if they couldn't afford his rates. When a Grace Center client needed more than we could provide, he was one of our referral doctors, and his practice supported us financially.

Several of the Grace staff came, and we chatted. Joe Sawyer, our minister of music, was there with his wife. She owned the bakery that supplied, at a huge discount, the cakes, cookies, and mini cheesecakes for the open house.

"Your home is lovely," Rebecca said when I walked up.

"And your food is amazing. As usual." I gave her a hug.

"Brother Nate," Joe inserted, putting his arm around the waist of a petite woman next to him, "This is Cheryl, Becca's sister. She and her son, Charlie, are staying with us right now."

I extended my hand. "Welcome."

"Sorry to crash your party. I'm just tagging along with them."

The resemblance was unmistakable. Cheryl was about an inch shorter than Rebecca and thinner.

"Not at all. I'm honored you came. Is Charlie here as well?" Since she didn't mention her husband, it was best not to ask.

"Oh, no," Cheryl answered with a laugh. "If he had any of Becca's sweets, he'd be bouncing off the walls all night long." She bumped shoulders with her sister, and they shared a loving sibling glance.

"I have the same problem with too much sugar late in the day," Joe offered.

"Well, they are so delicious," I reaffirmed, "it's hard to stop eating them."

Dr. Shannon arrived, so I excused myself.

"Claire and I are thrilled to be here for this milestone with you."

Mrs. Shannon moved in for a motherly hug. Unlike her husband, Claire was overtly affectionate. "Nate, you've done an amazing job. It feels so homey."

"Thank you. My real estate agent put me in touch with a talented decorator, and she helped me maneuver through everything from picking out paint colors to area rugs. I would have never guessed there are so many shades of beige."

To my surprise, Leigh's parents showed up. They gushed about being proud of me and how much Leigh would've loved the house. It was no surprise when Regina choked up.

As they walked away, I turned, and Trey was standing there.

"Oh, hey." It wasn't as casual as it might have sounded; I was glad to see him and resisted the impulse to hug him. The crowds and the chit-chatting were stressing me out, and seeing him provided an unexpected comfort. "You're here."

"I am. I brought you a housewarming gift. It's on the dining room table."

"You know you didn't have to do that. I wasn't sure if you'd show up."

"Well, Miss Gert did invite me."

"Indeed I did," came the voice from behind me. "Now, come with me and let's get you something to eat. You boys are too skinny."

As the afternoon wore on, I'd scan the room to find him. Once he was talking to Scot, which made me cringe. Then I noticed him and Susan in an animated conversation. She caught me watching and took him by the arm and walked him upstairs. My stomach knotted up. Around four, I saw him with Regina and Cecil, Leigh's parents. Regina was crying again, and Trey was hugging her. As I got closer, it was evident he was emotional as well.

"Is something…what's going on?"

"It was so nice to meet you both," he said to the Madisons. "My condolences on your loss." Wiping a tear, he looked at me. "Good to see you, Natha…uh, Nate."

He'd never used my short name, and I didn't like how it sounded coming from him.

"He's such a kind man." Regina was dabbing her eyes.

"Said you guys play racquetball." That was Cecil.

"Uhm…" I couldn't stop looking at the front door, wondering if I should go after him. "Yeah, we met at the gym. He's a…he works for a nonprofit law firm."

"Well, we have to leave, sweetie." We hugged again, and Regina shed more tears. "Thank you for including us."

After the last of the guests had left, Susan and I convinced Miss Gert to go home.

"I ain't gonna argue. These old bones just don't have the endurance they once had."

I fought the urge to laugh. Miss Gert was active with the Prime of Life group at church, was a member of a knitting circle, participated in a book club at the local library, and volunteered with the Congregational Care ministry, visiting nursing homes. I could imagine her leaving my house and going home to sew clothes for everyone at a homeless shelter.

"So I met Trey." Susan was washing the dishes, and I was drying.

Be cool.

"Yeah," I replied. "I saw him, but we didn't have much time to talk."

Don't look at her.

For further explanation, I included, "He's my personal trainer."

"OK."

The single word was ripe with innuendo, so I replied with my own one-word question: "What?"

She held up both hands in a gesture of surrender. "I met him, and he's very nice."

"He's the friend I told you about. Remember? He and I went to a science fiction movie and dinner."

Oh, and we've had lots of intense sex.

"He seems to think highly of you."

"I'm very likable."

Why was he so upset talking to Leigh's parents?

"Did you happen to hear anything Regina and Cecil...did you hear their conversation with Trey?"

"No, did he...was it a heated exchange?"

"They were talking, and when I went over there, Regina was crying. I think Trey was, too. She must have said something to upset him. He left abruptly."

Susan groaned. "Regina could put a damper on a funeral."

With the last of the dishes done, I dried my hands. "I can finish this tomorrow. I think I should...I'm gonna check on him. Make sure he's—"

"I understand."

I hoped she didn't, but that was a conversation for later.

TREY OPENED THE DOOR WEARING A PAIR OF GYM SHORTS AND no shirt. For a moment—an *extended* moment—I was fixed on his sweaty upper body.

Had he been working out?

The thought also crossed my mind: it could have been something more intimate. I'd always assumed he dated—*why wouldn't he?*—but we'd never discussed it.

Now is not the time.

"What are you doing here?" The question, which sounded more like bewilderment than reprimand, forced me to glance up. "Shouldn't you be at your party?"

"Yes, but I...you left before I could thank you for the beautiful gift."

While Susan gathered some of the food, I snuck upstairs and opened it—a beautiful replica of the lion that sits at the entrance of the New York City Library. The small card inside read, *Knowing your love of lions, this one would look great guarding your new bookcases.* The fact he remembered my affinity for lions was impressive. It came up once in a conversation about favorite books, and I talked about *The Chronicles of Narnia* and the character of Aslan, the lion.

"I'm glad you liked it."

"You left so suddenly."

Inviting me in, he motioned to the den and disappeared into his bedroom. When he returned and sat across from me, he had put on a T-shirt.

"Talk to me, please."

"I think this—" He didn't look at me but waved his arm back and forth, in my direction and then toward himself. "I think you and me...*us*...is a bad idea." His face relaxed, and his eyes filled with tears. "You've been through so much, Nathaniel. I cannot imagine. You're undoubtedly confused, and I'm some kind of experimental *rebound*. You'll realize at some point that we are a mistake. Let's not wait until then."

"What did Regina say to you?" My annoyance at her came through in the question.

"She's a sweet woman. Still grieving her loss. *Your* loss."

"She's histrionic, and I wish she hadn't inflicted that on you."

"She reminisced about her...about Leigh Anne's childhood. She remembered the day you two met. She talked about your wedding. How beautiful Leigh Anne looked. Your work in the church *together*. You were trying to have a baby." The tears were streaming down now. "We should never...I'm sorry."

I walked to the chair and knelt in front of him. "I'm a willing party to what's happened between us. This was not all you."

"It scares the hell out of me how much I care about you in such a short time. But you're...you were married. We are very different. You're deeply religious. All of your friends are, too. I'm the opposite. You're a minister for God's sake." He was rubbing his face with his hands.

He's right. About everything.

"I never considered all our differences. I just liked being with you. I like...*you*. But talking with Leigh Anne's parents, it all came crashing in." He looked at me. "To borrow your line: I need some time to process."

Twelve

It was ten-twenty when I got in. I'd driven across town, on a Thursday night, to a small theater and watched *Making Love* by myself. The movie's gay content had generated national publicity and outrage. It also piqued my curiosity. The lead actress, Kate Jackson, was from Birmingham, so it was well-covered in local media. Being recognized was terrifying, so I'd worn a baseball cap, sunglasses, and an oversized jacket. In the stifling summer heat, the outfit alone probably garnered scrutiny.

The story intrigued me and made me sad. Driving home, I wondered: *If Leigh had lived, would that have happened to us?*

At home, there was a message on my machine. "I'm having Nathaniel withdrawals. I know I'm the one who asked for space, but I miss seeing you. And talking to you."

For the past three weeks, I'd honored Trey's request, giving him time to think. I'd changed my workout schedule to afternoons and resisted the urge to call and tell him about something that'd happened during my day. To keep from thinking about him, I occupied my mind with reading, TV, and movies.

Diverting my lusts was not as easy. I had had a brief encounter with a guy I met in a department store. We chatted, then he followed me into the restroom where we masturbated one another. While driving to a meeting on the other side of town, I purchased several provocative magazines from a truck stop and used them in the evenings while I pleasured myself. I met a young man at a convenience store who was upset, and we talked for hours in between customers. When his shift ended, I went to his apartment, and we gave each other blowjobs.

Hearing Trey's voice made me realize how much I missed him, but it also brought up all the guilt. It reminded me of my actions in the weeks we'd been apart.

My life is out of control.

It sounded similar to the first confession in a twelve-step program, which was appropriate since I was learning that giving into these urges is like an addiction. Perhaps illicit sex should come with warning labels or require a prescription: only available after attending extensive certification training.

No wonder Scripture speaks so strongly about keeping our passions in check and provides explicit examples of what happens when we ignore the Truth.

Maybe the Bible is the warning label!

And I should have heeded that warning because now I was seeing the consequences of my choices. My bad choices. Once I had made the decision to have sex with Trey, I had opened Pandora's Box. Afterward, each time I was confronted with a choice, the urge seemed stronger and my will weaker. Steadfastness vanished, and it was impossible for me to refuse. Worse, the compulsion grew, and I wanted...*needed*...more and more.

Trey told me once that gay men have some kind of sixth sense about other gay men. But I'm not gay, so I have to wonder if sin is an aroma, oozing out of me, that calls out to the sin in others? All of the sudden, men were noticing me. Flirting with me. Flattering me. Somehow, having sex with Trey activated some kind of secret signal, like the carnal version of a dog whistle, which alerted every horny gay man in a thirty-foot radius that I'd had sex. Gay sex. I'd suddenly become some kind of penis-to-penis magnet.

I listened to Trey's message again.

He misses me.

I had no idea how to close Pandora's Box.

What would happen if I didn't call him back?

Sure, it was passive-aggressive, but in the long run, it would uncomplicate his life. And mine.

Jesus' words gave me hope: "If you have faith the size of a mustard seed, you will say to this mountain, 'Move from here to there,' and it will move; and nothing will be impossible to you."

I had the faith. Trey was the mountain.

Then the phone rang.

"You sound tired."

What good is my mustard seed if You keep throwing the mountain in my way?

"Hey," I said, forcing cheerfulness. "Just got in and heard your message."

"You're getting in late."

"I had an evening appointment, then needed to catch up on paperwork."

It was true enough for this conversation.

"How was your evening?"

"So exciting. Gennie and her boyfriend left for Gulf Shores yesterday. I've done my laundry, and now I'm in bed, reading."

"You wanna put some of those clean clothes in a bag and spend the weekend here?"

This is not the conversation I'd planned.

"I was hoping you'd say that."

"You already have clothes packed, don't you?"

"Maybe."

For now, the example of Scarlett O'Hara would prevail, and Pandora could wait until tomorrow.

TREY WAS STILL ASLEEP AS I SHOWERED ON SUNDAY. MY SKIN was crusty with the residue of last night's activity. There was an ache in my rectum area; it wasn't unpleasant, more like an unusual throbbing sensation. When I touched my anal entrance, it brought back last night's experience with vivid details and accompanying pleasure.

As I'd watched him seductively take off his clothes, I summoned my courage and announced, "Uhm…I think I'm ready to…you know."

"Wanna be a bit more specific?" The mischievous glint made it obvious he knew what I was asking.

"You're going to make me say it?"

"If you don't, I might think you're ready to try mountain climbing, raise alpacas, or become a philatelist."

"Philatelist? Did you find that one on your Word of the Day calendar?" I crossed my arms over my chest and fabricated a pout. "You're mean."

He slid into bed next to me and ran his palm across my stomach, sending a shudder through me. "What brought this on?"

He didn't need to know about my late-night visit to an adult bookstore across town where I'd seen pictures in a magazine of guys doing it. The images were intriguing and alarming. And an incredible turn-on.

It was difficult to concentrate during church; my mind would wander back to Trey inside me. A light movement in the pew, and I could feel a tinge of pain, reminding me of the experience. I forced myself to listen to Dr. Shannon's message about prayer, both as petition and thanksgiving.

So I prayed: *Dear God, please don't let me get an erection during church.*

At home, Trey had gotten us salads from a neighborhood deli. When he greeted me in the kitchen, he wrapped his hands around my hips and squeezed. My butt cheeks tightened, my body trembled, and I sucked in a gasp of air.

"Still sore?" His question came with a concerned tone.

"A little." My face warmed as I added: "It might need some internal massage."

Susan had been out of town for a few days, and it had been weeks since we'd had time together, so we agreed to dinner after work to catch up.

"You've been so elusive lately," she said as we stood in line at one of our favorite barbecue places near the college we'd attended. The heat and humidity of August were brutal, and I wished I'd stopped by the house to change. Inside, the overactive air conditioning blended with the aroma of slow-cooking meat in the ovens to welcome those willing to wait the usual thirty to forty minutes to be seated.

"Me? Elusive? Every time I look in a mirror, there I am."

"Do I need to guess where you're spending your time or who's been taking up so much of your time?"

Does she suspect something about me and Trey?

"Is my *private life* what you wanted to talk about?"

"It's on the list, but fine. A woman in my church needs some legal advice. Isn't Trey a lawyer?"

"Not an attorney, but he manages a nonprofit law firm. He could help or find someone who could."

"Are you OK? You're white as a ghost."

"Stomach's a little upset." I walked outside to get some air that wasn't thick with the smell of cooking meat.

"You were sick the other night too," she reminded, following me to the small park next to the restaurant. "What's going on with you?"

I shed my sports jacket and took a seat on a concrete bench. Hoping to sound casual, I responded, "Nothing major. I'll figure it out."

"Maybe I can help."

I considered tactfully ending the evening. After all, I *wasn't* feeling well. But at the moment, standing up carried a high chance of losing what might be left of lunch.

"I'm worried about you."

I blame you, Leigh, for telling her to look after me!

"That makes two of us."

"Then spill it." She placed her hand on mine and caringly squeezed. As usual, she was going to be persistent. "Is this about Trey?"

She does suspect.

"You're the one who brought him up."

"Yeah, then you got sick. Is there more to this story?"

"I'm not pregnant if that's what you're asking."

"Do you love him?"

Deflect!

"What's that supposed to mean?"

"If you're not comfortable talking to me, I understand. But I can see it's bothering you, and I'm willing to listen."

"It's wrong," I managed in a whisper. "Me and Trey. We're morally and biblically wrong."

Her hand didn't move from mine. I did a quick glance at her face. She was waiting for a more complete explanation.

"It started with us working out, and we became friends. He's such a great guy, and I love...uhm, *like* hanging out with him. I didn't even know he was...you know. When he told me, I stopped seeing him. Then I did again. And something happened, so I stopped again. Now, we're, you know, *involved*."

There was no reply

She's disgusted.

"Please don't hate me."

"Nathaniel, I could never hate you."

"I wish I didn't hate myself. When we're *together,* it's kinda great. I've never felt..." I didn't know how to end that sentence. "Then there's this guilt and shame. I can't sleep, can't concentrate, and can't keep food down. I never intended for it to happen. Surprised and horrified that it *did* happen.

"It's obvious he cares about you."

That was not what I was expecting. "What do you mean?"

"At your open house. From the moment he arrived, he would look around until he found you. I watched him. I mean, he's drop-dead gorgeous, so it's difficult *not* to look at him. But as he talked to guests, every so often he'd scan the room until he found you. Then this sweet smile would light up his entire face."

It is an amazing smile.

"He's hooked."

But I'm the one who feels trapped.

There was relief telling Susan even though I remembered those agonizing stories at the Circle of men who'd revealed their secret or had been exposed. Those did not end well. "I can't be—" I whispered, hoping to prevent anyone around us from hearing. "I don't want to be *gay*."

"I don't wanna be a redhead either."

Her response startled me. "But you changed your hair color." To further make my point, I motioned at her head.

"Miss Clairol helps me alter the outward appearance, but DNA encoded my *real* color. I'm a redhead because it's part of my basic design."

As I shook my head in disagreement, my hands were in front, waving back and forth with similar fervor. "There's no evidence that a person's sexual preference is predetermined." Even as the words came out of my mouth, I heard Trey's voice correcting my terminology. Sexual *orientation*, not preference. "Being homosexual is a choice. One that God condemned as unnatural."

"Oh, absolutely." Her sarcasm was undeniable. "I mean if God had wanted men to have sex with each other, she would have given them a hole in their butt."

"Susan, that's *gross*!"

I was not going to talk to her about *that*.

It did feel incredible when Trey...Stop!

"Sorry, I forget your provincial upbringing. Then tell me this: when did you decide that you liked guys? Did you wake up one morning and say, 'Hey, from now on, I'm gonna lust after men?'"

The genesis of homosexuality—how a person *becomes* gay—was a topic I was researching. I'd read numerous books, with more on my reading list. There was little agreement about origin, which resulted in no definitive methodology for cure. The materials theologians and Christian counselors had written presented it as a choice but suggested additional factors as well, depending on the author—everything from demonic possession to damaged emotions to parental influences. But one shining truth was common to all these Christian writers.

"The Bible clearly teaches homosexual activity is a sin, and to engage in these behaviors is a violation of my Christian principles. Of my ministerial ethics."

"Our history has shown we'll disagree on Scripture, but as far as the principles of ministerial ethics, you *are* correct. The church—my denomination at least—has not adequately confronted this matter; I'm not sure *your* church ever will. So technically, being sexually active while unmarried is a violation of our vows. I wrestle with that one too. You and your conscience will have to come to a workable *compromise*."

I felt like my entire life was compromised right now. Not just because of my ongoing sexual involvement with Trey, but also because of the encounters I'd had with the other guys while I was giving Trey his "process time."

There was also the hypocrisy of my continued involvement with the Circle.

"It's tearing me up inside. Making me physically sick."

"No surprise, knowing your commitment to the church and your sincere nature."

"So you do think I should end this with him?"

"I can't tell you what you should do, kiddo. I hope, in time, the church will rethink this untenable position. I mean, it was able to change on matters such as slavery and child labor. It's changing on divorce. The role of women in ministry is evolving. I guess my position comes down to this: does God intend you to live your life unfulfilled simply because the church refuses to acknowledge your sexual inclinations? I cannot imagine such a callous Creator."

"But God *did* provide a way to satisfy these desires: a man and a woman joined in holy matrimony. That's natural and normal. To give into these urges—to lie with a man as with a woman—is an aberration. Giving in to these feelings makes a mockery of my marriage to Leigh. That she was not enough."

Susan got quiet again, giving me hope that the conversation was over.

"I spent time with her in those last weeks. The Leigh Anne I knew—the one who was so accepting of everyone—I think she would give you her blessing. In fact, she might even have known, or suspected, that you had these attractions."

Anger flared. "That's just cruel, Suz. I'm stunned you'd resort to throwing my dead wife at me just to win an argument."

People walking by were looking at us.

"Take it easy. It's your life, and I won't tell you how to live it. I was just giving my perspective, not trying to upset you."

Why did it upset me?

In an instant, my mind replayed one of my final conversations with Leigh.

"I NEED TO KNOW YOU'LL BE OK." SHE WAS SO THIN AND FRAIL, I thought if I held her hand too tight, it could break.

"Please don't…" I turned aside. She didn't need to see me cry.

"Being married to you has been my great joy. God's providence and timing brought us together *for a season*."

"You can't give up, Leigh." My plea was unfair.

"Neither can you, my love. You have your whole life ahead of you."

"I can't even think about that." I was ashamed at the harshness of my tone.

"I'm not telling you to forget me or what we had together. Our love will endure after I'm gone. You just need to know I don't expect you to be alone. That doesn't honor me, and it's not God's intention."

I nodded, hoping to end the conversation.

She managed a smile that seemed to hurt her face. "You have such a tender heart, with so much to give. It's why you're so good at helping others. Promise me that you'll be open to God's providence again. Promise that you won't limit who He wants to bring to you." Her tone made it clear she wasn't being rhetorical.

"I promise."

We'd missed our place in line, so I walked across the street and got us tacos and sodas.

"I always thought she was good for you," Susan said when I sat back down. "She balanced you."

"In what way?"

"Let's face it, Nathaniel: your background, your education, your church are very restrictive. You've been *incubated*. Leigh Anne was creative and curious. She liked all kinds of people. I watched the folks who visited her; it looked like a United Nations parade. I can't believe she didn't ruffle feathers with the folks at Grace."

Susan was right. Leigh and I were so different. Her philosophy was "God didn't give us interests, and talent, and imagination to spend all our time coming up with reasons, and rules, not to use them." She loved movies, theater, books, music, and art. I'd never owned a TV until we moved into our apartment, but she wanted one. She enjoyed comedies, like *Happy Days*, but also the steamier shows like *Dynasty* and *Dallas*. She got me interested in detective shows like *Magnum, P.I.*, *Simon & Simon*, and *Hill Street Blues*. And we always watched *Little House on the Prairie* together. Before we married, I'd never tasted alcohol, but she liked wine, so we kept bottles hidden in the pantry. The first movie I ever saw at a theater was with her. She didn't care about PG or R ratings; she enjoyed the stories. Everything from *Nine to Five* to *E.T. the Extra-Terrestrial* to *Star Wars* and *The Muppet Movie*.

"Susan, I apologize."

"About?" Her left eyebrow raised in anticipation.

"I overreacted. When you suggested Leigh might have known." I related the troubling conversation I'd remembered. "How did *you* know? About me and Trey, I mean?"

She paused, as if deciding how to answer. Or whether to answer. "I've suspected for years. Trey just confirmed it. I mean, we've been friends for a long time, and I guess I know you better than anyone, other than your mom. I'm not Heather Locklear, but at least when I'm with straight guys, they look at other women. You tried to hide it, but you would linger on other men."

"I wasn't aware…I'm…that's kinda embarrassing."

"Don't be. You look at guys because it's part of who you are." She followed with a casual sweep of her hand. "Plus, you never showed any interest in girls in college. You never dated. Then you met Leigh Anne, and you two were getting married. If you ever wondered why I wasn't overly enthusiastic about your marriage, that's the reason. I assumed you were gay and afraid she'd get hurt."

"Well, I'm not certain I am."

"Am what?"

"Gay. I mean, I do have certain desires, but that's not definitive. Or defining. Those can be ignored. I did it for years."

"You think you can just stop being attracted to men? To Trey?"

"Yes, I think so. I wasn't gay when I was married to Leigh. If she'd lived, none of this would be an issue. I've been visiting a support group that helps eliminate these unwanted desires. To be *normal.* There are many who've successfully done that."

"Does he know?"

"Know what?"

"Any of this. That you don't want to be gay? Or that you're going to a group to make you *not gay*? Have you told him that you believe what you guys are doing is sinful, that you don't see the two of you as *normal*?"

I couldn't argue. I should tell him and walk away.

"Look, I cannot begin to imagine what all of this does to that conservative theology of yours; just know that I love you, and I'm here to help if I can."

"Maybe there's a simple solution. I mean, if I'd moved on enough after Leigh's death to get involved with Trey, doesn't that mean I'm ready to start dating? I should go out and meet some good Christian girls. Get my life back on the straight and narrow."

Straight and narrow.

Freud would revel in that slip.

Thirteen

"What do you need from me?"

The past week, it was all I could do to go to work, and I was too depressed to eat. I lashed out at Trey's gentle reminders of my need to keep up my strength. He had endured the multi-spectrum of my moods. Several times, my temper boiled over into an outburst of unkind words. Last night, when I broke down and cried before bed, he held me until I fell asleep and was there when I woke from a nightmare. He had been patient, understanding, and supportive.

But answering his question carried implications difficult to admit. It would confirm the recurring awareness of how much a part of my life he'd become. Not just that I enjoyed being with him but how much I depended on him.

What do I need from him?

Every time I planned to tell him that we could not continue our involvement, something happened. Mom fell and broke her wrist. One of the teens in my Sunday school class was killed in a car accident. A man I'd been counseling died of cancer. Through it all, Trey was there for me.

I shouldn't need him at all, because he shouldn't even be in my life. That unresolved quandary was why I continued my involvement with the Circle. In a twisted way, being part of Whole-Hearted kept me connected to the possibility of change—a way to convince myself that I could…that I *would* at some point… conquer these desires.

Now is not the time to deal with all that again.

"We'll be back in about an hour" was my response to him.

Today is about her.

For weeks, I'd tried to prepare myself to face this "anniversary." I hoped people wouldn't remember. I wasn't prepared for more tearful condolences, well-meaning platitudes, or emotional remembrances. I had intentionally been reminding myself of our life together. Before cancer, and doctors, and treatments.

She's been gone a year.

Remembering her led to the inevitable personal introspection... and journaling...of my life since her death. My heart was healing from the pain of losing her, and I was fulfilling her exhortation to go on with my life. I reflected on the choices I'd made, the weaknesses I'd allowed to take control. And Trey.

This can't be what she meant.

Now the day had arrived. I felt numb, detached, and ashamed that I felt numb and detached.

I wasn't surprised at the dreary weather. My Calvinism blended with my cynicism to conclude the intermittent storm had been predestined before the foundations of the earth to make this day as miserable as possible. Once I parked the car, I looked up through the windshield. Nothing like divine set decoration to reinforce my sullen disposition.

Could this day get any worse?

"I would've thought Trey'd be here with you," Susan said when she got to my open car door. She'd taken the rest of the day off to spend with me.

"He knew this is a personal time."

Even though I'd talked to Leigh about Trey on several of my visits, having him with me would heighten my guilt about our activities.

Not today.

"At least the rain stopped," she noted, interrupting a rehash of my conflicted thoughts. A foreboding rumble of thunder emanated from heaven, serving to punctuate my internal warfare. I pulled the hood of my sweatshirt over my head and grabbed the umbrella.

I envisioned a serene observance. Susan agreed to pray, and I wouldn't say anything, afraid my emotions would overwhelm me. To compensate, I brought flowers to put on her grave. Just as we sat down on the bench, Leigh's parents arrived.

"Oh shit," Susan whispered.

I guess it can get worse.

Regina was sobbing before they reached Leigh's marker. Susan and I spent nearly an hour listening as she cried and recounted again tedious details of Leigh's life.

When we got back, Trey had made a big pot of vegetable soup and corn bread muffins.

"You have a thoughtful boyfriend," she stated. He laughed and nudged me. I didn't have the energy to correct her designation.

The three of us ate in the den and, at Susan's insistence, watched *It's the Great Pumpkin, Charlie Brown.*

On the liturgical church calendar, Christmas is part of Advent, when we spend the four Sundays before December twenty-fifth in meditation and anticipation of the birth in Bethlehem. At Grace Presbyterian, Advent was full of required activities for the staff: decorating the building, coordinating a live Nativity scene in the church's parking lot, hosting concerts by the youth and children's choirs, holding a toy and food drive as part of our stepped-up benevolence and outreach to needy families in the community, and offering multiple worship services to accommodate the "Eastmas" crowd—those who only attended church at Easter and Christmas.

The holidays presented another challenge for me: the client load at Grace Center increased with people overwhelmed by the demands of parties, family, or financial responsibilities. Often, expectations were unrealistic, which led to disappointment and depression. For many, Christmas was not the *hap-happiest season of all.*

Trey and I navigated the flurry of holiday activities, finding time to spend together at Thanksgiving and Christmas while also fulfilling our separate responsibilities to families, friends, and our jobs. I left on Wednesday to visit Mom in Memphis for Thanksgiving, so he and I fixed our own traditional dinner on Saturday when I returned.

I attended numerous Christmas events at church—senior adults, ministerial staff, singles, youth—all involving food and decadent sweets. Over and over, people asked, "How are you holding up?" I answered that Advent was my favorite time of the year, when we remembered that Jesus was born. "That gives me joy and peace." It sounded pious enough to satisfy their concern.

Trey had his own holiday parties as well. He tried to convince me to accompany him to one. "It's just friends I've known for years," he explained. I interpreted that to mean *gay* friends and declined, citing a nonexistent obligation at church.

I'd planned a small gathering for the Grace Center board and supporters, so he helped me decorate my house, including picking out and trimming the tree. We put on music, ate homemade sugar cookies, and drank colorful cocktails. At one point, when I returned from the bathroom, he was naked beside the tree, with a bow strategically placed below his navel.

"Don't think for a second this will substitute for buying me a gift," I said before we had sex by the twinkling lights of the tree.

Early in our relationship, Leigh and I agreed not to exchange extravagant gifts at Christmas but to set a spending limit and give that same amount to the church's benevolence fund. Trey loved the idea, minus donating to the church, so we chose a local homeless shelter. I made him promise to stick with the budget, but it turned out that it was I who went over our agreed-upon limit. I was at a bookstore downtown and saw a vintage lithograph reproduction of the movie poster for *The Day the Earth Stood Still.* With the cost of having it professionally framed, it was ten times our agreed-upon limit. The stunned look on his face when I gave it to him was worth the expense.

Grace had a Watch Night service on New Year's Eve. It was casual, consisting of hymns, reflections on the past year, communion, and a short devotion. Rather than make resolutions for the coming year, we were encouraged to dedicate our hearts and lives to finding a new way of doing God's work here on earth. The service was over by nine, and then Trey, Susan, and I went to a midnight showing of *The Poseidon Adventure*, which I'd never seen but that he insisted was *the* definitive New Year's Eve movie.

The holidays had been amazing and exhausting. I'd anticipated the memories of Leigh emotionally swallowing me, but Trey and Susan kept me upbeat. He and I spent most of January relaxing and working out to reverse the excessive eating. The flurry of activities at Grace dissipated, and Lent wouldn't begin until February.

In contrast to the joyous celebration of Advent, Lent was a somber season on the church's calendar—a forty-day period beginning with Ash Wednesday in which we were encouraged to fast and repent of our sins. It all led up to the observation of Jesus' death and burial.

My attitude must have also been in sharp contrast from what it had been during Christmas. After one of the Circle meetings, Scot pulled me aside while others were milling around. "You have such a sad look on your face. Is everything OK?" I gave a vague answer about being overwhelmed and exhausted from the holidays.

In modern religious life, the fasting observed during Lent wasn't on a par with Jesus in the wilderness, with no food at all. Typically, people would choose something important to them and abstain from it. It could be drinking alcohol, watching TV, or eating candy. The goal was to contemplate the essentials of our faith and refocus on Jesus' sacrifice for us.

The entire emphasis served as a bitter reminder of the choices I was making in my life.

I'm such a hypocrite.

My fast—giving up an indulgence in my life—was obvious.

"Can you get some time off the second week of February?" Trey asked as we drank water to rehydrate from our racquetball match. "And are you able to take a Sunday off?"

"It can be done, given enough lead time," I said through my panting. "Whatcha got in mind?"

"I have a weekend conference in Atlanta and wanted you to go with me. I'd have seminars on most days, but we could fit in some sights and have breakfast and dinner together. Lots of hotel sex."

I shushed him, looking around to make sure we were still alone in the snack bar.

"Give it some thought," he said. "If you think about it, it's also our anniversary—the first time I saw you, trying to work out on the machines."

I had mixed feelings at that memory.

"Since I'm a presenter, the hotel is covered. But if you go with me—" He lowered his voice to a whisper. "—I'll upgrade to something more...*romantic*."

Out of the question!

The invitation required no thought. As a professional, I owed it to my clients to make them a priority. I had responsibilities at church, including the youth Sunday school class. There's no way I could ask Dr. Shannon's permission to skip a Sunday for a weekend of debauchery. Plus I was fasting from our sexual activities.

"I think I can arrange that."

Why would he say that to me?

It had been a wonderful weekend. The suite he'd booked was beautiful and included a small sitting area, a spacious bedroom with sliding screens for privacy, and a luxurious bathroom with a huge walk-in shower. We arrived early enough to do some sightseeing, including driving by the home of Margaret Mitchell, who wrote *Gone with the Wind*. It was disappointing since the house had been damaged by fire and was in serious disrepair. Trey wanted to see where one of his heroes, Dr. Martin Luther King, Jr., had been born, along with the Ebenezer Baptist Church, where the great civil rights leader had served until his death.

Atlanta brought a bunch of firsts for me. Trey and I held hands in public walking around Midtown, which was once the center of gay life in the city but now seemed kind of seedy. At a local restaurant on Friday night, he kissed me, and no one screamed in disgust. I went to my first gay bar, which was also my first bar. I saw my first drag show, which I found disturbing *and* hysterical. We went to a huge gay dance club, and it was the first time I danced with a man. Several, in fact.

On Saturday, while he was attending workshops and, in his words, *schmoozing*, I visited a gay and lesbian bookstore in Midtown. It took me several walks around the blocks to garner the courage to go inside. My first impression was from the *Chronicles of Narnia*: it was bigger on the inside that it appeared on the outside. Greeting me when I entered were shelves of various sized bottles labeled "personal lubricant" and an array of flesh-toned products whose purpose I chose not to ponder. There were cases and carousels with every imaginable kind of rainbow-emblazoned product: T-shirts, underwear, dog collars, coffee mugs, bracelets, picture frames, kites, stuffed teddy bears, and umbrellas. In an alcove that had probably once been the adjoining building was a small coffee shop, complete with six round tables and chairs and a glass case of pastries and muffins.

I walked up and down the rows of books, which included sections I could find in most bookstores: history, bestsellers, and biographies, but there were also shelves with gay fiction, lesbian fiction, biographies of gay and lesbian leaders, and gay erotica. I perused books on "gay theology" and set one aside to purchase later.

In the back, I saw a black door labeled in oversize letters: *Adults Only*.

Wonder what's in there?

A cute young guy—*a mind reader?*—walked up behind me. "That's where they keep the hardcore stuff. And they have booths that show gay flicks. I was heading back to get a magazine...or two. You know, to get me through those *hard*, lonely times. Wanna *come* with me? We could *browse* together."

He was brazen, with the unique ability to make ordinary words sound nasty. The invitation was absurd but exhilarating. I followed him into the dark, dank back room where he invited me into one of the booths. Inside a small screen and coin slot were built into the plywood wall. Permeating the area was the acrid scent of sweat, merged with the unmistakable odor of discharged bodily fluids. He inserted several quarters, and we watched part of a pornographic movie while he gave me a blowjob and jacked off, adding our smells to the cubicle.

He left without saying a word.

I bought a steamy novel about two firemen, along with a couple of books to use in my research—one by a psychologist and the other an autobiography of a minister who came out as gay, left his denomination, and formed his own church for gay and lesbian believers. And I got Trey a souvenir of our trip: a magnet with a peach—a symbol for the city—on a rainbow background, which he promised to display in his office.

Overall, it had been an exhilarating adventure.

Now we were driving back to Birmingham and barely speaking to one another.

I blame Trey!

Love is sacred, central to the Christian faith. It should be treasured, not trivialized like "I love chocolate," or "I love Scott Baio."

I stared down at my journal. Writing had occupied significant attention today, grabbing five or ten minutes here and there and in between appointments. Now I was staying late, scribbling my scrambled thoughts. I'd been back from Atlanta for two days, and there was so much to figure out. Decisions I needed to make!

Perhaps it was the somber message of Lent, reminding me that rather than self-denial or repentance, I'd spent the past ten months in the worst kind of wanton promiscuity.

I've been too easy on myself. I ignored everything I believe and all I've committed my life to be. It was satisfying of course. Forbidden things usually are. That's how the world was cast into sin in the first place!

It was our last night in Atlanta and another of my firsts. At Trey's request, I was inside him; he'd coached me in what to do. Being "top" was interesting, but I preferred our usual position. Just before he climaxed, he exclaimed, "I love you, Nathaniel." I went rigid. The room didn't have sufficient air; I couldn't breathe. He had to have known; I was buried inside him, and my intense reaction drove me deeper, causing him to shoot all over his stomach and chest.

Having someone say, "I love you" should be a good thing. Or so I thought.

A look of horror crossed his face, replacing what had been pleasure seconds earlier. "Please don't freak on me. It just slipped out."

I assumed he wasn't talking about my now-limp dick. "Then you didn't mean it?" I asked as I moved off him.

"No, I meant it but hadn't planned to say it. Yet."

The expected response was obvious, which was *not* going to happen!

He sat up, crossed his legs, and looked at me. "In the year we've known each other, I've always been honest with you. Should I not have told you how I feel?"

Not about that! I wanted to scream.

Three simple words jarred me back to reality. He says he loves me, and I know in my heart that's not true. Such deception can only come from Satan, the Father of Lies.

His declaration was like a wind pushing away the clouds, allowing the light to come through. For months, I'd made a conscious effort to ignore nagging concerns. Now there was clarity.

How have we stayed friends?

He was unapologetic about his sexual orientation, believing it was inherent and unchangeable. I didn't see myself as gay and was convinced I could defeat my desires. Most of all, there was our fundamental disparity, an obstacle I could *not* continue to overlook: I was a Christian, and he didn't believe in God. The Bible labeled us "unequally yoked." I should be sharing the Gospel with him, not sharing a bed with him. Praying for him instead of having sex with him.

It was after seven o'clock, and I hadn't eaten since my small salad at the senior adults' potluck luncheon Miss Gert had insisted I attend with her. I put today's client notes in the file drawer and locked it and then did a quick security walk-through of the Center before turning on the alarm and locking the front doors. I stopped by Arby's for a roast beef sandwich. Back home, I nibbled at the meat, contemplating the dilemma that was now too blatant to ignore.

I pushed aside the remainder of my sandwich, sensing the early churns of nausea, and went back to journaling my jumbled anxiety.

Sex is <u>not</u> love. It's lust, expressed. I will not elevate lust by relabeling it. Worse, by dignifying it. Lust cannot be equated with something as precious and unique as Love. I refuse to adopt his delusion.

I reread the pages written throughout the day. Once again, putting it all down on paper had helped alleviate anxiety. Some observations about myself were blunt and harsh. There were blistering denunciations about my behavior for the past months. A few of my "revelations" were unsettling. According to the rule I'd followed for years, I wouldn't go back and edit.

I was left with one recurring question still banging inside: *Now what?*

Fourteen

Alone in my car, driving home, afforded me too much time to think. Turning the radio on loud didn't work, so I tried silence. I replayed the positive testimonies of change from the Circle meeting I'd just attended. I wanted to be one of those success stories.

My name is Nate, and I'm a new creation in Christ.

But it would require some hard choices.

Mostly, just one.

Trey!

The sounds of my car tooling along the road and the noise of traffic around me faded. Verse after verse from the Bible barraged my mind, chastising me, warning me of the seriousness of my actions, calling me to renounce these feelings.

And Trey.

It had been weeks since Atlanta, and I was still rattled. And confused. And sad. For our trip back to Birmingham, I'd pretended to be sleeping, and Trey pretended he believed that I was asleep. When we got to my house, he reiterated his apology. "I'm sorry I fucked up our weekend, Nathaniel."

What about how you fucked with my mind?

"I'm not upset," I'd lied. "I was shocked, that's all. It will take me some time to absorb."

He'd graciously agreed to "give me space," which meant, at least for me, not seeing or talking to him. Ever!

My bad mood was noticeable to those around me; both Suz and Miss Gert had expressed concern.

I chose to lie to them also, telling them I was tired and overwhelmed with my doctoral studies.

During tonight's Circle meeting, Scot talked about sin leading to more sin and losing our ability to know right from wrong. He quoted Scripture about reprobate minds, being devoid of understanding and darkened by sin. He used the example of rolling a snowball down a mountain. It starts out small and slow, but as it grows bigger, it rolls faster and becomes impossible to stop.

My first thought was: *he's not talking about me*. Then Conscience reminded me of actual examples to prove Scot's point. Since meeting Trey, I'd done things I had *never* thought possible. I had ignored my convictions to fulfill my lusts and violated my ministerial standards. We'd had sex. Many times. He had been inside me, and I'd been inside him. *An abomination*. I'd also had sex with random guys, and a minister I had met at a conference. I deceived people I cared about, including my pastor, to get the time off for the trip to Atlanta. Through it all, I'd justified those actions.

What else was I capable of?

In an instant, everything I'd had for dinner—perhaps every meal I'd had in my entire lifetime—revolted in my stomach. There was barely enough time to pull over to the curb before it all erupted.

As if my body wasn't already excreting enough liquids, I began to cry.

"Do you need assistance, sir?"

Seeing the formidable cop who'd walked up to my car stopped my tears but not the rumbling of my insides. "Uhm, something I ate."

"Have you been drinking tonight?"

Not yet.

While I enjoyed wine or cocktails in the evenings, it was something I did only after my day had ended.

"No, officer." I sensed the need for a more detailed explanation. "I'm a therapist and was leading a support group. I'm on my way home and suddenly got very sick."

"Mind if I see some identification?"

Before fishing out my wallet from my back pocket, I raised my head and inhaled the night air.

"Here you go." I also included a business card to add validity.

He shined his flashlight on my driver's license, then on me, and then back to the card. "Will you be OK to drive home?"

"I think so. I don't live that far away."

"Hope you get to feeling better. Drive careful, sir." He returned to his squad car and drove away.

I could use a police escort!

At home, I undressed and showered, still able to smell the sickness that permeated my pores. Even after brushing my teeth and using copious amounts of mouthwash, the taste lingered. When I fell into bed, I noticed the light on my answering machine was blinking.

"'Evening, Oraios. Had you on my mind and thought I'd check on you. I know you want space, but I'm…I miss you. Have a good night. Sweet dreams."

Sweet dreams? Yeah, wouldn't that be nice?

His thoughtfulness was charming, but his impatience was aggravating. I resented his pushing me. Rushing me.

Calling him back will not make me feel better.

There was also a message from Susan. "Please call when you get a chance."

I didn't want to talk to her either.

Rip off the Band-Aid.

Step up to the plate.

Face the music.

Man up!

Clichés were not helping. My fingers were not dialing Trey's number.

It was just after two o'clock; I was exhausted, so I was leaving the office early.

OK, let's get this over with.

He answered on the second ring.

"Hey, sorry I didn't get back to you sooner. It's busy around here."

"Are you all right?"

"Why?"

"You sound *funny*."

"But you're not laughing."

"I'm serious. Tell me what's wrong."

His sixth sense about me is annoying.

"On the way home last night, I threw up on the side of the road. I took some Pepto Bismol, and it's better."

"How 'bout I come by after work and bring chicken soup?"

No way!

Even though it sounded like I was avoiding him—which I *totally* was—I told him I was having dinner with Susan. "We haven't done anything together in weeks, and she's coming over to the house."

"I have something to discuss with you. Nothing urgent, but I'd like to talk in person. Before I leave on Friday."

Alena, Trey's younger sister, was getting married, and his dad was insisting that the entire family be present. "The wedding is in Mykonos," he'd told me back in January.

"That's a long way for a wedding."

"It's where our family is from originally. Papa retired there. I wanted to say no. Taking two weeks off work puts the agency in a bind, but the entire family hasn't been together in several years. And he isn't getting any younger."

"Are you all packed?" I asked, deflecting the conversation.

Seeing him was never a good idea. Like ice under a heat lamp, my resolve tended to melt when in close proximity to him.

"When *can* we get together?" His impatience was coming through again.

"It's gonna be tough." Might as well get started weaving the web of lies. "I have several workshops at my alma mater this week, and I'm teaching a training seminar for church leadership on Wednesday night. Thursday night I'm having dinner with our minister of music and his wife." Most of that was true but inaccurately compressed into a single week.

"I understand," he said. Even on the phone, his disappointment came through. It might have been anger. "Perhaps more time apart will be a good thing right now. For both of us. I'll check in with you when I get back."

"Enjoy the time with your family. I want what's best for you."

"I want what's best for *us*, Nathaniel. And family is more than biology."

It was unfair. This kind, thoughtful man—who worried about me and called me sweet names in Greek—was forbidden. He had feelings for me that I could not...must not...reciprocate.

Mom always said that God won't put more on us than we can endure. Scot regularly reminded everyone that "we are more than conquerors through Christ."

Seriously?

"You seem distracted," Scot said as we packed away the supplies.

Trey had been gone for more than a week, and while I missed him, I knew it had to be this way. Had to stay this way.

"Things are crazy these days. I've been preparing for several workshops and seminars coming up. The client load at work is growing so fast that we're hiring a new therapist 'cause I can't keep up. I'm also busy with my doctoral studies."

"You have so much on your plate, which makes your service to this ministry even more special."

"This is important." It was the answer I'd given him on several occasions. "I like helping out."

"Not to pry, but is it more than that?"

I'd expected this conversation. I had thought about how to initiate it myself. Now that it was happening, I had uncertainty about what, and how much, to reveal. Or if I should even confide in Scot.

Standing there, holding a chalkboard and easel, I reminded myself: *I'm a new creation in Christ.*

"For now, let's just say that my interest is not *merely* academic or altruistic."

He picked up the box of Bibles and brochures.

Had he heard me?

"I will respect your boundaries," he said as we were locking up. "But as they say: inquiring minds *will* want to know more when you are ready."

I HAD ONE SHOE ON AND WAS TYING THE OTHER WHEN THE doorbell rang.

I hoped it wasn't a church member with a crisis. Those didn't happen often, but when they did, they could disrupt or derail all other plans.

How much time do I need to get ready to be on time for—

My internal conversation came to halt when I opened the door.

"Hello, Oraios."

My brain and my mouth froze in surprise, so he shrugged and walked past me into the den.

"You getting ready to head out to a function tonight?"

Why can't I speak?

An unusual look—almost a shadow—fell across his face. "Do you have a date?"

I reached out and touched his arm. "I have some time before I have to leave…for a planning meeting."

Scot, Barry, and Darrel were coming to Grace Center to work on some classes we were adding to the *Wholeness* curriculum.

"I'm sorry for just dropping by like this. I should have called first. In fact, I should have called two weeks ago, as soon as I got back. I just didn't know—"

"You don't owe me an…I'm glad you came by. I *do* want us to get together soon and talk."

His strong arms enclosed on me. “Name the time and the place.”

Damn, he smelled good. Sexy. Familiar.

“I brought you something from Mykonos. An early birthday gift. I’ll give it to you when we get together.”

“Well, you can’t tell me you got me a present and expect me to patiently wait.”

His expression revealed he’d anticipated my response. “It’s in the car. I’ll get it.”

I imagined it was something along the lines of the small magnet I’d gotten him in Atlanta. Instead, it was an exquisite stained glass window, encased in a beautiful wooden arch, and mounted on a stand. The entire piece of art was about two feet high. In the middle was a white dove surrounded by the most beautiful starburst of colors, radiating out on all sides.”

“It’s a replica of one of the windows in my family’s church in Mykonos, done by a local artist. It’s *Iremos*, which translates into English as ‘calm, tranquil.’”

“Trey, it’s beautiful. I’m overwhelmed.” I couldn’t imagine what this had cost; I was afraid to hold it for fear of breaking it.

“When I saw this in the marketplace, I thought of you. Maybe it could go in your study—” He pointed upstairs. “When you’re having your morning reflections and writing in your journal, this might be a source of peace.”

I hugged him and gave him a kiss. For gratitude. Which became more passionate. With every ounce of willpower in me, I stepped back. If this continued, I would not get to my meeting. We agreed that he’d come back the next night, which was Friday.

As I finished getting dressed, I wondered if I’d be strong enough to make my decision known to him once and for all. Being near him always muddled my brain and weakened my will.

Shit. Meeting at a restaurant would’ve been the better plan.

I FIRST MET RICH HOWARD WHEN I SPOKE AT A CITYWIDE YOUTH conference. He was a minister of youth—adorably cute—at a small Baptist church south of Birmingham and had stayed after my session to talk. Or flirt.

Since I'd returned from Atlanta, Rich had become a regular sexual partner. He was six years younger, and married, so there was the explicit understanding of "no strings attached." Sex with him satisfied those desires that had become accustomed to regular release with Trey, and I didn't worry about hearing "I love you." It was always intense, without emotion or affection, as though we were recreating one of the porn movies he enjoyed watching. One unique dimension was that Rich and I could talk about our ministries, our faith, and things going on at church. Such conversations became as easy as the raunchy talk he liked when we fucked. During one of our serious discussions about both of us wanting to overcome our desires, I talked about Whole-Hearted and the Circle.

When he called, I could tell something was wrong. He didn't want to discuss it on the phone, which wasn't unusual, so I invited him to come by the house after work. I figured we'd be finished before Trey arrived around seven. It *seemed* like a workable plan, except that I hadn't anticipated that Rich would be running late or that he would be so upset when he arrived, just after six.

"My wife knows," he informed when I opened the door. Then he burst into tears.

I let him cry while selfishly wondering if I was part of her discovery.

"She found my stash of porn magazines and decided to follow me. Saw me go into the park, pick up this guy, and take him back to my car. She's filing for divorce." The crying intensified. "Informed the pastor, and I was terminated."

"What will you do now?"

"I'm staying at a cheap motel in East Lake, but I have *got* to get outta this city. I mean, more and more people from church will find out, and I just can't endure their contempt."

"I'm sorry, Rich. You have to do what's best for you, and I support you. I will miss our time together."

"I have a gay cousin in Dallas who invited me to stay with him. Told me there are gay churches out there, so maybe I can find a way to…you know…combine my faith *and* my feelings. I deserve to be happy." He gazed at me through his wet eyes. "You deserve happiness too, Nate."

"Me? I'm doing great."

The look he gave was familiar. I'd seen it often in the days after Leigh's death when I said I was doing "fine." Sadness, concern, pity. And disbelief.

"Oookay," he said in that doubtful tone I also recognized.

"I'm serious. Things couldn't be better right now."

The doorbell interrupted any additional rebuttal.

Trey stepped in, and I backed away to prevent his kiss. "Trey," I motioned to the den. "This is Rich. He's a youth—" *No, he was fired.* "He's a friend who came by to tell me he's moving to Dallas."

They shook hands. "If you two need to continue, I can come back later."

Rich answered. "I was about to leave." He hugged me. Then, for some reason, probably driven by God's twisted sense of righteous indignation, Rich decided to tell more of the story. "My wife found out I'm gay and wants a divorce. She told my church, and I was fired."

"That's horrible."

I knew this would not help Trey's already negative opinion of the church, but couldn't think of anything to redirect the conversation.

Rich leered at Trey with explicit lust. "He's stunning. If I weren't leaving town, I'd be very jealous."

"I...uhm...thank you." Trey glanced at me in confusion.

"When you arrived, I saw you lean in to kiss Nate, so I kinda figured you weren't a church member."

"Hardly," Trey answered.

Any explanation would trigger questions I preferred to avoid, so I remained silent—praying this conversation would end.

"Not to worry," Rich said, clearly still under the direction of divine whimsy. "Nate and I were just casual sex from time to time, but it's good to know he won't be alone once I'm gone."

Shit!

I could feel the glare without looking up, but Rich thwarted my response. "I thought about joining that group of Nate's. If folks thought I was trying to change, maybe I could stay in town."

God, is all this necessary in one conversation?

"What group?"

It was like watching a car rushing toward a brick wall, with no clue how to stop the impending crash.

"The one that promises to cure our homosexuality."

My impulse was to run screaming out of the house, but since it was my house, that didn't seem practical. "It's a ministry our church supports," I offered, still hoping to divert the careening car.

Of course God obviously prompted Rich to impart more information. "This guy, who used to be gay, has a ministry that helps other gay guys who don't want to be gay to change."

"And *you* are involved with this group?" Trey asked me, but didn't wait for an answer. "What a waste of time and money. Sexual orientation can't be changed. I'm surprised you, a trained therapist, can't see that. But then, sound science, and your feelings, always take a back seat to your religious beliefs."

Rich looked uncomfortable. "Seems you two have stuff to talk about."

Trey shook hands with Rich. "I wish you the very best in your new location."

Once Rich was gone, I prepared for a grilling. Instead, Trey sat down. The extended silence made me anxious, hoping he would talk. Until he did, and I wished he hadn't.

"Were there others?"

If I lie, we can bring this conversation to a quick close.

"Yes."

No reaction or response.

"I can explain—"

Like trying to see a nightlight in thick fog, there was such sadness settled on his face, it was difficult to remember his infectious smile and caring eyes.

I did that to him.

"Here's the thing, Nathaniel: I'm not sure I want your explanation."

I would try anyway. "You said we needed time apart."

"Which you thought meant you could fuck around."

I should have lied.

"I get it. And I don't blame you." His voice remained steady and soft. It was annoying, and a bit scary. "This is my fault."

"How is this *your* fault?"

"I was your first." He waited for me to confirm. I'd lost his trust, which annoyed me more. I nodded to reassure him.

"You need to sow your wild oats; we all go through that stage. The night of your open house, I made up my mind that we should stop seeing one another, thinking I might be just a rebound or a confused experiment. I shouldn't have ignored that instinct."

"I'm sorry, Trey. I never meant to hurt you."

He gave me his cocked-head, puppy-dog look. "I believe that, Nathaniel. In fact, I believe that in everything you did, I never crossed your mind. At all." He took several deep breaths. "Trust me. I understand the allure of sexual encounters. It's all new and exciting. I wish you'd been honest instead of cheating on me."

I resented that term. People cheated on their taxes. On exams. On their spouses. "We're not married!"

"No, we're not, and to me, that's part of the problem. You and your narrow system of beliefs see only one kind of sanctioned relationship. Everything else is sinful. And I always felt like your dirty little secret."

"You *never* understood the turmoil I've felt being with you." Fighting tears and mounting anger gave my words a harsh edge.

"I did try to understand. And to be patient. You think I didn't notice that we never had sex on Sundays, after you got in from church? You would be so moody. So conflicted. I knew it was that damned church that kept you torn up inside."

Even I hadn't picked up on that pattern.

"Did it ever occur to you that I was conflicted, too? I could never compete with the power of your dogma. I held out hope that things would get better. That you'd get more comfortable with us. And your sexuality."

That will never happen.

"You...*us*...was unexpected. All my life, I'd been able to control those feelings and ignore anyone who enticed those desires. Then you came along. It never made sense."

"If I believed in the God you talk about, I might be tempted to see *that* as a sign that we were meant to be together." Before I could object and offer theological reasons that such a providence would never happen, he continued. "I believe you do have feelings for me, but admitting them would go against everything you've ever been taught by your family and your religion. Your tenacious adherence to that church never made sense to me, but it was important to you. Because you were important to me, I set aside my concerns. Now to learn that the whole time you and I were making lo...uhm... fucking, you're attending meetings to become straight and telling other men how not to be gay. It's demeaning to both of us. Worse, it's duplicitous, and I'm appalled at your involvement. You are innately a good person, and I'm awed by you, but all that is overshadowed by the darkness of what you've been taught."

The sadness in his face had changed to disappointment. I couldn't believe I'd done that to this kind, generous man. I wanted to fix it, to make it right.

How do I make something right, out of something's that wrong?

"Trey." My voice tremored. "Do you regret *us*?"

For reasons I couldn't have explained, his hesitation hurt.

"I'm very glad...you might say *thankful*...that you came into my life. I do wish that *us* meant as much to you as it did to me."

His use of past tense wasn't lost on me, and I thought my heart might explode through my eyes.

"It does. I like having you in my life."

"And that's where we're different. You *like* having me in your life, but I love you. You have to do what you think is right, and so do I." He stood and moved to the door. "I do love you, Nathaniel. I just love myself enough not to be party to your deception."

Fifteen

"What is all that?" I asked, following Susan into the kitchen.

"Comfort food: ice cream, chocolate chip cookie dough, Krispy Kreme donuts, potato chips, burgers from Hamburger Heaven, and wine." She lifted two bottles. "One white and one red."

"I invited you to watch a movie, so I was thinking popcorn and Diet Coke."

"These are for heartbreak, dear boy."

"More like a heart *attack*."

"I also brought flicks to help you get over your breakup."

"We weren't technically a couple, so it's not really a breakup."

"Whatever bullshit you need to tell yourself."

The problem was that nothing I told myself seemed to work. When Trey left after finding out about Rich, I cried for hours and moped around for days, all while reminding myself it was what I'd wanted. What God intended. Trey occupied large amounts of space in my journal and was conspicuous in my dreams. I almost called him on several evenings just to talk. Once, I drove by his office, hoping to see him and invite him to lunch.

Susan held up the cases. "We don't need any sentimental rom-coms, so I was thinking *Airplane*, to make you laugh, and *Bedknobs and Broomsticks* because...well, because I love this flick. Maybe we can learn a spell to turn him into a frog."

I didn't tell her that our not-a-breakup was my fault, not his. Knowing it was useless to argue about the evening plans...and all that food...I grabbed a burger and the bag of potato chips and poured us both a glass of wine.

Angela Lansbury was singing with a cast of animated sea creatures when the phone rang. Susan huffed as she stopped the tape and muted the TV.

"Nate?"

"Hey, Cheryl. How's it going?"

"Charlie and I were wondering if you'd like to come over some time. For dinner. I'm not as good a cook as my sister, but Joe and Becca are doing a choir retreat next weekend. If you're free."

"Dinner sounds great. What can I bring?"

"Something for dessert? We'll plan to eat around seven."

"*Cheryl*?" Susan questioned when I hung up the phone.

"She's a friend. That's all."

The intensity of her gaze—a combination of confusion and shock—demanded more information.

"She's the sister-in-law of our minister of music and the sister of the woman who provided the desserts for my open house. That's where we first met. She came with them. Then Jim and Rebecca invited me over to dinner, and Cheryl was there. She just went through a divorce and is living with them with her son, Charlie. I *was* kinda shocked when it dawned on me that it was a 'setup,' but we had a good time. We're friends. Nothing serious."

"Are you sure such a *friendship* is a good idea?"

"You mean because she's divorced? Or has a son?"

When I'd talked to my mom about Cheryl, both of those things were thrown in my face.

"I mean because she's a *she*."

"Maybe this is God's answer for me."

"Please be sure that it's not just the answer you most want to hear."

"Hey, Nathaniel. Sorry to bother you."

Trey's voice on my answering machine was unexpected. I stopped unbuttoning my shirt and sat on the side of the bed. We hadn't spoken since he had left my house five long, lonely weeks earlier.

"I was cleaning out my bedroom and came across some of your things. I've put them in a box. I can bring them by...on second thought, let's meet at a neutral location. Anyway, call me, and we'll set that up. If you could, please get back to me in the next few days. Thanks."

I dialed his number, and Gennie answered. "Oh, it's you."

That frosty acknowledgment screamed everything about her attitude toward me.

"Trey asked me to call. Is he there?"

"He's working late, finishing a few projects and packing up his desk."

"He's pac—"

She'd hung up.

Two days later, on a mild Thursday night at the end of May, Trey and I were parked side by side at McDonald's. I stayed in my car, with the air conditioner running, while he got out, salvaged a beat-up box from the backseat of his new truck, and put it in the trunk of my car. He propped himself on the passenger-side door of his truck. He was dressed casually, in shorts, sandals, and a T-shirt. I fought not to stare at his physique, so visible through the tight shirt.

"Thanks for meeting me," he said with professional politeness. "I know this is a big weekend for you, and I didn't want to intrude on your celebration."

Of course he remembered it was my thirtieth birthday.

"Susan and my friends are there for me."

That probably sounded like a jab, directed at him.

Was it?

"Gennie said you were cleaning out your desk."

"I've taken a job with the Southern Poverty Law Center. They work for justice and civil rights for the disenfranchised and to expose hate and extremism. I had the first interview right before I left for Alena's wedding and wanted to tell you then, but—" He shrugged. "I'll be part of the legal communications team, helping craft the messaging that goes out to the media and the public."

I'd heard of the organization because he'd attended events it had sponsored. "That sounds exciting. Right up your alley. Is it located near your apartment? We both know how much you hate to commute."

"Not close at all." In the stark parking lot, I saw the street lights reflected in his teary eyes. "Southern Poverty is in Montgomery, and I'm moving there. Next week, in fact. I've been going down the past five weekends to find a place to live. That's why I wanted to get this to you so quickly."

He's leaving?

Before my tears became evident, I reached into the backseat and wrangled a small trash bag from the floor of the passenger side. "After we talked, I realized I had some of your things as well." I didn't disclose to him that I'd kept one of his T-shirts. I liked the way it smelled.

"Thank you."

Why won't he look away?

"Trey, I just want you to know that I..."

I miss you!

"I think you're gonna do great in your new job. Let's just hope there's a theater down there that shows old science fiction movies."

I noticed a meager movement around his mouth. An almost smile. It brought me some comfort that he might be remembering better times.

"If you ever need me, Nathaniel, I'm here for you. I wish...well, I wish things had been different. You are one of the kindest, most compassionate people I've ever known. You don't want to hear this, but I love you. Please be good to yourself. You deserve that." After his signature shrug, he got in his car and drove away.

What now?

"HAPPY BIRTHDAY, SWEETIE."

We have differing views of "happy!"

"Thanks, Mom."

As on every birthday for as long as I could remember, Mom would recount the story of how I came to her and Dad after years of praying. She recited the details of my adoption to me like I'd never heard the story. I would hear once more what a gift from God I was and the meaning of my given name. It was our version of Oral History. She would close with her own version of the traditional birthday song that added non-rhyming lyrics about God's blessings and following Jesus. I'd learned long ago not to balk but to listen in silence. I used it as a time to catch up on opening the mail, organizing files, or reading Tolstoy.

"Do you have big plans for your big day? I do wish I could be there with you."

"I'm having dinner with one of our ministers and his family. Susan will be there, too."

I chose not to tell her that Cheryl and Charlie would be there to prevent another lecture from Susan on why Cheryl and I shouldn't be dating.

This year was one I would have preferred to forget. It wasn't about my milestone age but my overall mood.

"Couldn't I stay home, in my pjs, and watch TV?" I whined to Susan.

"First, I seriously doubt you wear pajamas, and second, your friends...and your *girlfriend*...want to do this for you."

I yielded but requested my party not be a gigantic gathering but include just close friends. Susan brought George, the social worker she was dating. Several staff members from Grace were also there. Between Susan, and Miss Gert and Rebecca, the food was amazing. I endured all the over-the-hill gag gifts, and jokes about getting old, making every effort to appear *happy*. Several times I looked at Susan. She saw my pretense.

When I got home from the party, I found a card from Trey among my assorted mail. For the most part, it was casual and innocuous. He wished me a happy birthday. It was signed: *Love, Trey.*

It brought up so many memories from last year and the first time Trey and I...

Dammit.

Part II

Blind Guides

Sixteen

"How can I love my neighbor as myself when everyone goes out of their way to tell me what a fuck-up I am?"

"Thanks for the question, Brandon. But might I suggest that you not take out your anger on Nate?"

I waved off Scot's attempt to protect my feelings. "He's fine. It's important for us to be honest here."

My topic was the biblical foundation for healthy self-esteem. Scot thought we could spend the summer talking about our identity in Christ and how it was different from what the world taught, especially within the gay lifestyle.

"I *am* being honest," Brandon screeched.

Brandon was intimidating in both stature and disposition. He was the kind of tall that made basketball or football coaches salivate—at least six-foot-five or taller. His bulk and muscles gave him an imposing presence, so most wouldn't challenge his antics. At times, his anger and short fuse would explode as he vehemently disagreed with others in the group. He did *not* respond well to being told what the Bible taught. It was impossible to know whether that was his general demeanor or if it was because his parents forced him to attend under the threat of military school after they had found out he had a boyfriend. Most evenings, he'd sit sullenly silent, refusing to participate in any part of the meeting.

"Modern thinking tells us we must have self-worth, which comes from how smart we are or how much money we have or the car we drive. It's based on physical factors, like if we're tall, well-built, attractive—"

"And got a big dick." I couldn't see who made this comment.

"Language!" Scot rebuked.

"But the Bible teaches there's nothing good in us apart from God. We must learn to value who we are, and who we are meant to be, based on the One who created us. God loves us, and He knows us best." I asked if anyone could share obstacles we face to self-esteem—things, events, circumstances, or people who might prevent us from loving ourselves.

A black guy, new to the Circle, stood. He was fit, like a body builder, which was evident through his tight jersey. If he continued to attend regularly, Scott or Barry would quietly take him aside and suggest he wear shirts that wouldn't trigger the others in the group. "When I was in the lifestyle, men would cruise me because of the way I look, and then they'd make fun of me because they weren't expecting a big, black nelly bottom."

"Tops love to tease bottoms," Alton offered with a snicker. "But what would they do without us?"

"OK, guys," Scot interjected. "Let's remember to keep our conversations in the righteous realm and references to sexual activities in the past tense."

"You tell us that God loves us and that in the sight of God we have value, but I still have to listen to those jerks at school call me faggot and queer." I didn't know this boy's name.

Scot stood. "We know that Satan is a liar, and he will convince us that who we are is based on these feelings inside us. He will use external voices to defeat us. He is the accuser. We take our name from God, not the devil."

"God says I'm an abomination and turned his back on me," said Dante, one of the regulars. "How am I supposed to feel good about myself?"

"Two men having sex—lying together as with women—that's the abomination." Scot's voice was patient, with no hint of retribution toward the questioner. "It's the act, not the person." He walked over and placed his hand on the boy's shoulder. "God does not turn his back on us; we turn our backs on God. As long as we are here—" A sweeping gesture encompassed the room. "—doing the work to change, the Holy Spirit is on our side. No one wants us to succeed more than God." I sensed that my portion of the evening was finished, so I closed my Bible and notebook. "We have lots to think about this week. I invite everyone to come back next week with any questions you might have."

We stood, recited the Lord's Prayer, and dispersed.

"We make a pretty good team," Scot said as I helped him put everything away. "You should have an official title."

"I'm just happy to help where I can."

I couldn't dissuade him.

"At our next meeting, I'd like to introduce you as our associate director. It will add credibility to your ever-increasing involvement. I've talked with Barry, and we're giving him the title of outreach leader, and Darrel will be our education coordinator."

"If this is what you think's best. But again, it's not necessary."

"It will be seen as evidence that the ministry is growing and expanding," he mused, with a self-satisfied smile. "It shows others that God is blessing what we are doing."

"He's being difficult."

"Want me to talk to him?"

Without a second of hesitation, Cheryl put Charlie on the phone.

"Hey, buddy. What seems to be the problem?"

I could almost hear his shoulders drop and his lips pout. "You said we were gonna get ice cream."

"We are, I promise. You and me and your Mom will have lunch, and for dessert, we'll stop at Baskin-Robbins. I plan to have *two* scoops."

"Can I have two?"

"For sure. *After* church."

There was silence, then a thump. "He dropped the phone and ran to his room," Cheryl informed. "You sure do have a way with him."

"I suspect it's more about the ice cream."

When Cheryl and I first began spending time together, it was always at Joe and Rebecca's house. I'd go over, and we'd order pizza, watch movies, or play board games. Then she and I ventured out to restaurants, but always with Charlie. After a couple of months, I asked if she'd like to have dinner.

"Just the two of us," I clarified.

Initially, we made a choice to be discreet. She had concerns about Charlie getting attached to me, and I was aware that some in the church might not look favorably on us as a couple. It had only been six months since the divorce was final, and while Grace Presbyterian didn't forbid divorce, being part of the ministerial staff came with higher expectations.

On Sundays, Cheryl and Charlie attended church. Because she was the sister-in-law of our minister of music, there weren't many awkward questions in the beginning. But for the past three Sundays, they'd sat with me, and we would go out to lunch afterward. People caught on quickly. Not much pleases church busybodies more than watching "God bring two people together," as one of our venerable widows put it. Because they'd known Leigh, there was some kind of personal ownership, a divine response to their prayers that God "heal my heart."

I was thirty years old, but dating slipped me back into my teenage years. I heard the sermons my father had preached about God's righteous standards of moral purity and keeping the "marriage bed" undefiled. I remembered all those "talks" with my mom where she warned me about the sinful nature in boys, which must be daily surrendered to God lest it threaten to explode in unholy behavior. Our youth minister taught workshops on godly dating and the pitfalls of premarital sex, using vivid warnings about sexually transmitted diseases, pregnancies, grieving the Holy Spirit, and becoming trapped in a life of rampant lasciviousness, unable to control our sexual impulses.

I half expected to wake up one morning with pimples.

With Cheryl, I was the perfect Christian gentleman shaped by my strict upbringing. We didn't kiss until our third date. I avoided any PDA—public displays of affection—which included holding hands when we were out together. There was no sexual intimacy.

I got the impression she wanted…that she *expected*…more but congratulated myself for this high moral stance, ignoring the keen sense of hypocrisy raging inside me.

"How is it that you're engaged and chose *not* to tell your best friend?"

Susan swept into my office with the force of a winter storm. And the chill was just as evident.

"So nice to see you, too." I took the chair next to her, determined to avoid a flat-out denial.

The glare let me know this cold front was not in the mood for levity.

"Who told you that?"

"You know how I feel about people answering a question with a question."

One more attempt to agitate her seemed in order. "Soooo, you don't want me to ask you a question?" After all, it was Susan, someone who loved busting my balls whenever she had the chance. And I suspect with this news, I'd need a steel-reinforced athletic cup.

"You should know that the Birmingham church grapevine is efficient, and I have my spies everywhere.

"We are *not* engaged."

Technically, that was true. I had *not* proposed, and there wasn't a ring on her finger. I didn't need to disclose more specific details right now.

I remembered the night the idea was first dropped into a conversation. It was in mid-July. Joe and Rebecca were going to a Bill Gaither concert, and Cheryl and I were staying home with Charlie and Rebecca and Bill's nine-year-old son, Benjie. Before the concert, we were all having dinner. "I think I found an apartment," Cheryl announced as we ate.

"That's great," Rebecca responded, exchanging an eyebrows-raised glance with Joe.

"It has two bedrooms and a small playground for Charlie. It's affordable, now that the house has sold, and since Todd agreed to pay child support."

"We just assumed," Joe said, "that you would stay here until you two—" He gestured to us. "—decided to make it permanent."

Permanent? I thought. *We haven't even been dating that long.*

Reminding myself of that time line didn't bring me comfort. I'd proposed to Leigh after less than two months and was having sex with Trey within weeks of meeting him.

Rebecca agreed. "Why get locked into a lease until you know what's ahead?"

She and Joe grinned affectionately, their expectations evident.

My stomach got queasy as my mind went into manic mode, spontaneously spooling out a stream of questions: How would we all fit in my townhouse, could I afford a family, would I be a good stepfather to Charlie, where would he sleep, did I need new furniture? The questions pummeled my imagination.

"Why does she *think* you're engaged?" Susan asked, bringing me out of the recollection.

"It just kinda evolved, over time. I think people *assumed* it was the next logical step."

"Is this what *you* want?"

"Cheryl's great, and we get along so well. Charlie is an amazing kid. And face it: being married is always a plus in the ministry."

Susan was silent. Thoughtful.

"I can't argue with any of those facts, Nathaniel, though none of what you said answered my question. And this kind of decision is not about facts. Or what others want. I know you, kiddo. You don't like conflict or confrontation. I worry you'll get swept along in the expectations of others. I'm not going to push you on this one, and whatever you decide, you know I'll support you. But you do need to decide. For yourself. Do you love her? Why do you *want* to marry her? Are you even attracted to her? Without those answers, you run the risk of making the wrong decision, at the wrong time, and with the *wrong* person." She stood. "Now, I'm starving, and we don't want to keep your *fiancée* waiting."

I no longer had an appetite.

Seventeen

"Hey, Leo," I stopped at his door as I walked to my office, next to his.

"'Morning, Patrón."

Since hiring Leo three months earlier, he used the Spanish word he explained was a respectful term for the person in charge. I appreciated the deference, but I suggested he call me Nate. Miss Gert thought it should be Brother Nate or Brother Truett. He ignored both of us.

"You're here early."

"I can get some paperwork done before everyone arrives." He pointed to the breakroom. "I made coffee."

Leonardo "Leo" Palma had been raised in Costa Rica by missionary parents. Both were born in America; his father was first-generation Cuban, and his mother was of Mexican descent. Leo was fluent in Spanish, and because we'd had clients who struggled with English, I thought he'd be an asset. There had been a little resistance to hiring him from one elder who wouldn't come out and say it but seemed to have an issue with Leo's skin color.

"I just hope our church members don't mistake him for the janitor," he'd quipped.

"That won't be a problem," I replied with all the politeness I could simulate. "He'll be in an office, with his name on the door, wearing a shirt and tie instead of the green maintenance uniform; these facts should alleviate any confusion as to his position."

I hoped Dr. Shannon wouldn't think I was being insubordinate to an elder and was relieved when he offered, "I think our church members are fairly astute."

Leo finished his master's degree in marriage and family counseling ten months ago and was now completing the requirements for his license—two years of supervised clinical experience. His position at Grace Center would count, but he also volunteered at Hill Crest, a psychiatric hospital where I'd worked after college. Our clients liked him. For now, he was content to work part time, but if we couldn't make him full time soon, I knew he'd move on, which would be our ministry's loss.

I heard Miss Gert come in and drop her purse and Bible on her desk. "Good morning, Brother Nate. Good morning, Mr. Palma."

"Buenos días, Miss Gert." He stood, walked to her, and gave her a hug. "I took the rest of your delicious German chocolate cake home with me on Friday. Allison and I had it for dessert, and she wants that recipe."

He had no trouble showing affection, and Miss Gert loved the compliments to her food. He was also teaching her words and phrases in Spanish, which he liked inserting into conversation. His love of food, especially desserts, was evident in the extra thirty or forty pounds he carried. He referred to himself as "hefty" and didn't seem at all self-conscious.

Once I invited him to go with me to the gym. "The body is a temple," I explained, trying to be tactful.

"Yes," he replied, patting his belly. "And some have larger vestibules."

I envied his positive body image. When I noticed a few weeks ago that I'd put on a few pounds, I renewed my trips to the gym and even considered hiring another trainer.

A *female* trainer!

"Do we need a staff meeting this morning?"

"*Tú eres el jefe.*"

"That means 'you're the boss,'" Miss Gert interpreted, making me smile.

"Are there any prayer requests?" Scot always asked this before the meeting adjourned.

I raised my hand. "My friend, Elliot—a guy who used to be a member of my church—was severely beaten the other night after leaving a restaurant. He's in bad shape, physically and spiritually."

After Elliot graduated from high school, he stopped attending Grace. I didn't know the reason. About a year later, he dropped by my office to tell me he had "come out" as gay and that his parents refused to allow him into their home. I attempted to arrange a family session, but Elliot's father refused.

"His mother asked me to visit him in the hospital. He's living an unrepentant homosexual lifestyle. I saw him yesterday, but he was so resistant to the message of transformation. Demanded that I leave and not come back. It broke my heart."

"You reap what you sow," Barry offered, quoting from the book of Galatians.

"I'm sorry, what?"

"Was he coming out of a gay bar?" he asked.

"No, he'd just left a restaurant. It happened behind a church in Southside."

"That's a notorious gay section of town."

I looked to Scot, hoping he would have something to add. He gave a slight head-tilt in Barry's direction and offered: "Romans one does tell us that when men reject God's natural design to be with women, there's 'due penalty of their error.'"

"Isn't that harsh, given that this might not have even been about his sexual orientation?"

"Homosexuality is a behavior, not an orientation," Barry corrected with a sternness that could have been accompanied with a wagging finger.

"So you're saying he deserved to have the shit beaten out of him?" That was Brandon, and this time, I agreed with his angry question.

"Language!" Scot warned.

I was close enough to Brandon to hear him whisper: "Fucking hypocrite."

"Regardless of the circumstances," I pushed, "I'm asking us to pray for him. Christians, lifting up other Christians."

"I do not accept your designation that he is a Christian," Scot snapped back. "That is contrary to God's Word."

Giving in to my anger would be counterproductive, so I switched approaches. I steadied my voice. "Maybe I confused the issue here by bringing up his sexual…his homosexual behavior. That wasn't my point. My friend is in serious condition, with a long road of recovery ahead of him. Shouldn't that be enough for us to pray?"

Scot shook his head with defiance. "When we pray, we must join our petitions with God's promises. We must not find ourselves praying against what God intends in this situation. Perhaps He will use this tragedy to bring your friend to repentance."

The anger dialed up to livid level. "Help me out here, Scot. How is this attitude…this approach…anything close to compassionate? I'm not trying to get into a battle of Bible verses here, but we're commanded to pray for one another and to pray for the sick. There are no conditions placed on those commands. I'm not asking that we condone his lifestyle, but shouldn't we show love and mercy? As Jesus did?"

Several in the circle were staring down at the floor; the rest were looking back and forth between me and Scot.

"We will add Nate's friend to our prayer list tonight," he said tersely, turning away from me. "Now are there other concerns before we close?"

I hung around until all the members were gone. "I didn't expect that kind of response to my prayer request," I told Scot as we gathered up the supplies. "Please know I wasn't trying to make it an issue, but—"

He put down the box of Bibles with a thud that cut off my statement.

"It is *imperative* that as the leaders here we present a united front. We do not want our members and guests to think we are not in agreement on the seriousness of this sin."

"You think I gave that impression?"

"You challenged me in front of the group."

"First, it had nothing to do with his sin, and second, I don't see it as a challenge. I was seeking *clarification*."

"You should have come to me privately."

"How could I come to you *privately* when the discussion was happening right then, *in public*?"

"I appreciate your help, Nate, but I will not be diminished as founder and director of this ministry. *My* ministry. We must maintain our individual roles and responsibilities. Abiding by God's chain of command brings harmony and blessing."

I still didn't understand his reaction to my prayer request, but the fact that it was *his* ministry came through loud and clear. I was too tired to argue.

I need a cocktail.

"SCOT NELSON IS HERE AND WOULD LIKE TO SEE YOU," MISS GERT said when I answered the intercom. I was updating the file from my last session. "You're next appointment is in thirty minutes." Her emphasis on the last statement was intended for him, not me.

I walked out to the reception area where he sat, erect and smiling. "Hey, Scot. Nice to see you."

I opted against the more accurate "What the hell do you want?"

"Can we talk?" He cut his eyes to Miss Gert. "It won't take long."

As we walked by Leo's door, Leo looked up. Courtesy demanded I introduce them. "Scot is the director of a ministry our church supports. I do some work with them as well."

"What ministry?"

It wasn't clear whom Leo was asking, but Scot had made it clear it was *his* ministry, so he could answer!

"Whole-Hearted."

Leo waited through one of Scot's long pauses; I was tempted to jump in with an answer, but Scot continued. "We are a transformative support group for guys wanting to turn their backs on the homosexual lifestyle."

Leo was too well-trained to exhibit a reaction.

"Reverend Truett is an excellent asset. We're grateful for the time he devotes to helping with what we do."

Except when I challenge your domain.

They chatted as Leo asked questions about the ministry and got Scot's short, reticent answers.

"It was nice to meet you, Scot."

I saw that as Leo's professional way of wrapping up our intrusion.

As usual, Scot took a seat in the counseling area. "We should talk more about the incident at the meeting. Just so there's no misunderstanding in the future."

"It was never my intention to cause problems or conflict, for the group or for you."

"It did feel...*confrontational*, but I accept your apology. We should put it behind us."

Apology?

"I've spent much time in prayer about what happened."

"Scot, if you want me to take a more backseat position, or even to stop attending the group, I will understand."

"No, I do see where you were coming from. My heart does go out to those trapped in the lifestyle. They can't give up the drugs or the sex or the enticements of the world. In fact, last week we lost a young man who attended off and on. His name was Eddie; you may have met him. An addict who made his money by selling his body."

I did remember that kid. He looked so young, and his story of abuse was dreadful.

"They found him behind a liquor store in Norwood, dead from an overdose. I am just devastated with grief."

I shifted from remembering Eddie's tragic life story to listening to Scot's narrative. He was using words that described emotions without actual evidence of those feeling.

Is this his way to manage the loss of so many folks who come and go through the ministry?

I WAS NIBBLING ON APPLE SLICES AND READING THE LATEST issue of *Christianity Today* when Leo knocked on my door.

"What's your role with *that* organization?" he asked as he took a seat.

I didn't know Leo all that well yet, so I downplayed my involvement. And omitted my personal motivation.

"How well do you know Scot?"

"I met him early last year."

"And you trust him?"

Was he trying to tell me something?

"He's never given me a reason not to. Granted, he's a bit uptight, somewhat ostentatious, but he's doing good work. There are some desperate stories along with some moving examples of God's power to change lives."

"What kind of success do they have?"

"Success?"

"Your friend said y'all help people—what were his words?—turn their back on the homosexual lifestyle. Are they successful in that goal?"

The Whole-Hearted promotional literature boasted an eighty percent success rate, but I'd never asked how that figure had been determined. "This is an ingrained sin pattern. As you know, it's difficult to quantify behavioral changes."

His professional demeanor, which would be perfect for poker, was intact. "So you think being gay is merely behavioral?"

"Don't you? The Bible is pretty clear."

"I know what people *tell me* the Bible says, which I try to balance with psychological research that seems to indicate that homosexuality is innate."

He and Susan would get along great.

"Since it's sin, then it can be overcome like any other sin."

"Sure, we can modify the behavior, but is that the same as changing the orientation?"

I was rethinking my decision of hiring Leo.

"My sister's gay, so I'm not totally objective. She's kind and compassionate. I see her personal faith in action—working for a food bank in Nashville, active in a Methodist church, teaching a Sunday school class." He paused, but when I didn't respond or react, he continued. "I've heard the theological arguments and have listened to the sermons about gay people. But at the end of the day, I love my sister."

Eighteen

The meeting opened with prayer, and Scot reminding everyone of the guidelines for the group. He handed out a printed schedule of upcoming *Wholeness* workshops, then everyone stood, joined hands, and prayed. During the share time, I noticed that Brandon was back; he looked miserable, slumped in his chair with his arms tightly wrapped across his chest. In spite of the intense heat outside, he wore a heavy jacket.

"Hi, my name is Jerry, and I'm a new creation in Christ."

Brandon was murmuring something, and when Barry called him out, that led him to become red-faced angry, screaming back, "Leave me the hell alone!"

Once everyone was done, it was my turn. Scot had recently read a book about cognitive therapy and wanted me to guide the group in a discussion of how "godly self-talk" can bring about transformation. I showed examples from the Bible of people who talked to themselves during times of great emotion. "King David, in the book of Psalms, asks himself, 'Why are you cast down, O my soul? And why are you disquieted within me?'" My eyes moved around the circle to gauge their reaction. I lingered on Brandon, who was staring at the floor, saying something I couldn't hear.

"Have any of you ever felt cast down, which is like being disappointed, or discouraged?"

"Every week, listening to this bullshit," Brandon said loudly enough for all to hear.

"Let's keep our language appropriate," Scot warned.

"How is any of this helping?" At first, he fixed his gaze on me. Then frantically he looked around the encircled chairs. "Our souls have been turned over for destruction. We are abominations. We're all going to hell."

It was obvious that most of the guys were uncertain how or if they should respond.

"You bring up an excellent point," I exclaimed, hoping to engage him. "What we tell ourselves can often make us feel desperate. But when we turn our hearts to hear God—"

"God is not listening. We are controlled by demons, and they tell me there's nothing I can do to be free."

Scot stiffened more than his usual upright posture.

"Are these voices telling you other things, Brandon?" I moved closer to him.

"You won't believe me." His head was nervously shaking side to side. He extended both hands in front like he wanted to stop me from interrupting. "They told me…"

Scot inched forward in his chair, so I spoke to prevent him from entering the conversation. "When did you first hear them? These voices."

"I'm not supposed to—" Tears rolled down his face.

"I'm here to listen to you, Brandon. To help you."

"You can't help me!" he screamed. "No one can help me."

Then he cackled—something that sounded like it came from a horror movie. Several of the guys were now standing by the chalkboard.

I got on my knees, facing him. "Breathe with me, Brandon. Deep, slow breaths. In and out."

"I'm so afraid," he whimpered. "I can't make them stop." He put the palms of his hands over both sides of his head and let out an earsplitting screech, followed by wailing, uncontrollable crying, and sporadic laughing. I got in close to speak softly to him, but it was doubtful he heard over his shrieking. Then the sounds stopped, and he went limp in my arms. He was too heavy to hold, and we both fell on the ground. I could hear him heaving for air, and his entire body shook.

I looked to the cluster standing by the wall. "Someone find a phone and call nine-one-one. Ask them to send an ambulance."

Scot sat down next to me, laid both hands on Brandon's chest, and prayed aloud. I was too busy with Brandon to pay much attention to the garbled language. Barry stood at Brandon's feet, shouting. "In Jesus' name, I command the demons to come out. In Jesus' name, loose him and let him go."

"I can't." Brandon and the commotion grew louder. "It hurts." He was sweating profusely, and his body was quaking. "It hurts."

"Demons of hell, release him, in Jesus' name." Barry, the resident demon slayer was trying to out-bellow Brandon, repeating a version of this command several times, each time with more intensity, accompanied by foot-stomping and hand-clapping. Several guys were weeping. I couldn't concentrate, and the pandemonium was making Brandon even more agitated.

"Please stop," I said to Barry. To the crying guys: "I need you all to settle down. The best way to help him is to pray *silently*. If you need to go to another room, do that."

Barry wanted to debate. "We've been given authority over all the powers of darkness, and—"

"Authority is not synonymous with volume. Please go to the parking lot and watch for the ambulance."

As the noise hushed, Brandon became calmer.

"Can you stay with him?" I asked Scot. "I'm going to call and get everything set up to have him admitted."

I called Brookwood Hospital, gave my name, and referenced Dr. Carl Randall, a psychiatrist on my advisory board. He'd told me that if I ever needed it, he would have my name listed for emergency admission. The nurse would contact the doctor, and they'd be ready when Brandon arrived.

I should call Cheryl and let her know I won't be coming over.

Then I heard the ambulance arrive, so I returned to the fellowship hall. By the time the paramedics got him loaded, it was after nine o'clock.

"Are you riding with me?" Brandon asked.

"I can't, brother. But I'll follow in my car and see you as soon as you're admitted."

"Can you manage them?" I cocked my head in the direction of the church.

"Yes...go," Scot answered. "We will talk later."

"You are very composed under the worst of situations," Scot said to me at lunch. It had been almost a week since Brandon's episode. "It was commendable."

"Thank you."

I drove to the hospital behind the ambulance and had to wait more than two hours before they got him in a room. I talked with him briefly, then he was given a sedative. I didn't tell Scot that after I had left the hospital, I went home and drank until I passed out on my bed.

"But we have to address how you spoke with the other guys trying to help."

"What do you mean?"

"You were rather harsh with Barry, and you upset guys who were already upset."

Count to ten.

"Barry was hurt and embarrassed. He felt like you disrespected his beliefs."

Or maybe to a hundred.

"I have nothing against his beliefs, just the way it was manifesting at that moment."

"You punished him because he was dealing with the situation in a different way from you."

Deep breaths.

"That is *not* what happened. We were in an emergency situation. My training told me that Brandon was having a dangerous, emotional crisis."

"You sent Barry outside, like a child being punished."

"I stand by my decisions but will talk to Barry."

"Do you believe the Bible is the Word of God?"

I wasn't prepared for the question, and the context confused me. "Yes, I do."

"Do you believe in the devil and that he can influence our lives?"

"My first answer informs that one." It was blunt, but I didn't appreciate this grilling.

"But do you believe demons can possess a person?"

"Truthfully, I don't know. I can't deny it's there in the stories of the New Testament, but it's not part of my faith tradition or training. I don't *not* believe it could happen, but my *years* —" I paused to let that word sink it. "—of professional mental health education and experience convinced me that was not the case the other night."

"But you do not know that *for certain*. Yet you rejected the efforts of another Christian who *does* believe that's what was happening."

"What's this about, Scot?"

"This ministry grew out of *my* experience and *my* understanding of the Bible. We believe that the Holy Ghost speaks to us. We believe in casting out demons that have set up a stronghold in people's lives. We believe in speaking the Word, in faith, before we see it come to pass. That is how we do this work of transformation and why we see such wonderful results."

Should I ask him about those results?

"But we both know *your* approach is not the only way to overcome homosexuality."

He looked at me, surprised.

"Oh, yes. I've done my research. There are other ministries working with men *and women* struggling with same-sex attractions, but they do it in different ways. There is no defined methodology for success."

"The Word says, 'a good tree bears good fruit.' I cannot speak for those groups but point to our results brought about by the grace of God and the Holy Ghost."

Yeah, about those results.

"The issue here is whether you can operate under the founding beliefs of this ministry and submit to the principles that have made it successful."

I think it's more about whether I can submit to you.

"I'm a firm believer in submission, but you made me your associate director. In fact, you insisted on that title. So I think my skills, my training, and my experience should count for something."

"Not when they ignore our core values, or disregard the teachings of the Word."

"That's a total misrepresentation—"

Do I even care about this argument?

"Scot, I support the work you're doing…that *we're* doing…and I'm grateful to be part of Whole-Hearted. I just don't understand your reactions to me sometimes. Do I intimidate you?"

His always precise posture went rigid in the booth, his face flushed red with outrage. "I am not intimidated by *you*."

That hit a nerve.

"Got it!" I punctuated my statement by standing. "I'll give what you've said some serious thought and let you know what I decide. Until then, I think it's best if I take some time away from the group."

"Brother Nate, there's a young man on the phone. Says his name is Alton."

Since I hadn't been to the Circle for a few weeks, I wondered if he was checking on me.

"Thank you, Miss Gert."

"This is Nate," I informed when I answered.

"I hope you don't mind that I called, Nate."

The voice was immediately recognizable. Alton was quite effeminate, which had always caused problems with bullies. In the meetings, his overt mannerisms got him singled out often.

"Not at all. What can I do for you?"

He asked to meet in person, so we arranged for him to come by later that afternoon.

"I think I *might* know why Brandon freaked out," he informed after he sat in one of the chairs in front of my desk. "Or at least what might have helped push him over the edge."

Is he going to blast me for ignoring demons?

"He's...Brandon...uhm...he was...sexually involved. With Scot."

No amount of training could have prevented my reaction—an audible gasp, which I'm sure was accompanied by a horrified look on my face. When I tried to speak, I choked into a fit of coughing. "That's a very serious accusation," I said when I regained control.

"Yes, and I've debated for weeks about coming to see you. I don't wanna get no one in trouble."

"Did Brandon tell you this was happening?"

He didn't look up, but nodded in the affirmative. He mumbled something, so I reminded him that I was there to help and asked him to repeat what he'd said.

"There are others, too."

"Scot is messing around with other guys in the group?"

This can't be real.

"How do you know this, Alton?"

"Because I'm one of them."

I WAS DUMBFOUNDED. ALTON'S FACE HINTED THAT HE WAS having second thoughts about telling me.

Say something!

"You did the right thing. I'm humbled that you trusted me with this information."

What now?

"Would you be OK if I brought in my colleague? I promise he'll hold your information in the strictest confidence."

He agreed with only a blink.

Leo's door was open. "Hey, are you free to talk?"

I gave him a synopsis of what I'd just learned. Unlike me, Leo didn't react. We went to my office and listened as Alton shared his story.

"I began visiting the group after leaving Prodigal Son, which is a camp in Oklahoma run by a Mormon couple. My parents sent me there to fix me." A faraway look washed over his face.

He's not remembering singing "Kumbaya" around the campfire.

"The second night I was there, this older guy in our cabin and me kinda made out. The next night, we had sex. He told his friend, and that guy followed me on a hike and threatened to tell Elder Jacob if I didn't let him screw me. I said no, and he slapped me. Pushed me down on the ground and forced his self inside me. It tore something. Down there. I didn't know, but was bleeding when I went back to the compound. A counselor noticed. I wouldn't tell them what happened, or who was involved, so they sent me home."

"Did Scot know about this?" I asked.

"Yeah, it came up in one of our private sessions. I admitted that I liked being with older guys. A short time later was when it all started."

He said that after two or three visits, Scot implement extended hugs saying they were to show affection to another man that wasn't an attempt at sex. That transitioned to "touch therapy" to help Alton "receive the affection of a man" without it being sexual. He would massage Alton's shoulders and rub down his back. Sometimes he'd massage Alton's legs, almost brushing his crotch but never touching it. One day, he directed Alton to stand in front of a mirror and remove all his clothes. "To see your body as God sees it," he explained. Then Scot stood naked beside Alton to show they were both "made in God's image," and the body should be "celebrated." Naked mirror-gazing was combined with the touch therapy, and Scot would caress Alton's bare arms, chest, and stomach as they prayed, thanking God for his handiwork. Alton developed an emotional attachment, which Scot exploited for sexual activities and pleasure. They'd been having sex for months. He confessed to being a weak man but said that Alton was God's answer to combat the temptation to sin in a way that wouldn't compromise the ministry. "So I'll depend on you," he told Alton, "to keep our 'special friendship' a secret."

"He would pray in tongues while he fucked me."

His bluntness startled me, but had no visible effect on Leo, who then asked, "How did you find out that Scot was also involved with Brandon?"

"I accidentally saw something he…I mean, Brandon…had wrote in his notebook." Alton looked at me. "After your workshops on journaling. We were trying it."

Leo gave an approving look, which felt good right then.

"Anyway, there was stuff about what him and Scot was doing. He was pissed off that his parents wouldn't let him see his boyfriend and felt crappy that he liked the sex. After every time they *did it*, he was so ashamed. He never came out and said it was Scot, but he didn't know how to stop it."

Why didn't I see this?

After more than an hour, we let Alton go.

"I'm stunned. And clueless what to do now."

Leo was making notes and didn't respond.

Was he sickened at what he heard? And my involvement with the group?

He looked up. "This has to feel like you've been kicked in the gut, Patrón."

"Not exactly the target of the kick, but yes, it's a lot to absorb." I slid back in the chair, my hands folded on my lap. "The day you met Scot, I sensed you had *reservations*. I chose to ignore you then… and I apologize…but I'd welcome any insights."

"Yes, I had concerns, but you seemed invested in this guy and his ministry."

"Please tell me what you think."

"Some red flags. I did my undergraduate senior paper on narcissistic personality disorder, and while it's not possible to make an actual diagnosis, there were several telltale signs. In the short time we talked, he made a point of correcting me on minor matters. And regardless of the topic, he presented himself as an expert. Always precise when he talks. Doesn't use contractions. I asked him questions, and he avoided giving out too much information. Vague, but with embellishments."

Hiring Leo had clearly been a good decision!

"Have you ever caught him in a lie? Maybe about his education, his employment history, or his income. It could be white lies, or exaggerations."

That's why he asked if I trusted Scot.

I remembered the "eighty percent" success statistics he used to promote Whole-Hearted. It had nagged at me, so I spent a few hours in the storeroom at the church where the ministry's files and supplies are stored and couldn't find anything to back up that claim.

"When he talks about himself, or the ministry, does he use superlatives?"

An understatement!

"Alton says there are others," I pondered aloud. "I should try to contact folks who were once active but left." In my investigation, I'd found records of guys who'd attended the workshops but never finished. There were many who had finished but then never returned.

"Do you have access to those records?"

"No, but I bet Alton could *procure* them for me."

"You're gonna steal files?"

"We can discuss ethics later. I don't want Scot to figure out that I know what he's been doing and destroy those files."

I expected an argument. "This is going to be traumatic for those boys, but they're fortunate to have you in their corner. You...and them...will be in my prayers." He stood to leave.

"In case you're wondering, I went to the group because I had hoped they could help me." My voice trembled. "With my own same-sex attractions."

No facial reaction. "And did it help?"

Had he suspected?

"I've learned a lot about myself along with tools to make righteous choices."

"Your dedication is admirable, *mi hermano*. I admit to personal bias and doubts about the need for these programs or the efficacy of their methodology. As your friend, I love and support you."

Nineteen

"Miss Bradley called while you were out."

Finally!

Susan and I had played phone tag for weeks, leaving messages but not able to connect.

It was great hearing Susan's voice. After some catching-up conversation, she informed me she was heading into a meeting. "Whatcha doing for lunch? My treat."

"That sounds awesome. I have so much to tell you."

"Ditto."

We agreed she'd bring burgers to my office around twelve-thirty.

"What's your big news?" she asked, then before I could answer, she said, "No, wait. Let me guess. You and Trey are back together, and you're moving to San Francisco, where you'll work as strippers at a gay club and live happily ever after."

"That is *so* not funny."

"You and Cheryl are moving to San Francisco, where you'll work as a stripper—"

"No strippers, and no one is moving."

"Well, that's not exactly true."

My hand stopped on the way to my mouth. I put the French fry back down and waited.

"I've accepted a new position in Cleveland. I start the end of the month."

My news can wait.

"I...I'm not sure what to say."

"Please tell me you're happy for me."

"Of course I am, Suz. This is what you've worked so hard to accomplish."

She would be associate pastor for a large, progressive United Methodist church—the first woman in that position. "I've talked to the pastor and the board chair several times. I even flew up there three weeks ago."

"No wonder I haven't been able to reach you."

"I waited to tell 'til it was definitive."

We chatted about all the details and her timeline. When she asked about my news, I dismissed it. "It's nothing compared to this."

The reality settled in once Susan had left. I sat in my office with the door locked and cried. I had been truthful; I *was* happy for her. But from a selfish point of view, it was just another loss in my life. Combined with what I'd learned about Scot, my emotions—to use one of my mom's Southern descriptors—were being held together by spit and bubble gum.

WHEN TREY AND RICH LEFT, I MADE A COMMITMENT TO CONcentrate my energies on having a normal relationship. With Cheryl. There had been no random encounters with other men though in the evenings, I masturbated to the pictures in my magazines, which I assumed would diminish once she and I married. From all outward appearances, my life was great. I had a fulfilling job, an active social life, and the important volunteer work I did at Whole-Hearted was rewarding. I was in a relationship with a beautiful woman who had a son who adored me. I'd even grown comfortable talking about "my girlfriend" with others.

We tried to spend time together on Saturdays, taking Charlie to the mall or a movie or playing games and swimming in Joe and Rebecca's pool. At my request, we didn't discuss long-term plans to church members or staff.

When we were together, or in our phone conversations, we

talked about Charlie, plans for dinner, or what we were watching on TV. She didn't ask about my day or the work at church. On several occasions, I asked, "How was your day?" and she dismissed it with something like "same crap, different day." I stopped asking. Once she was confused about a point in Dr. Shannon's sermon, and a couple of times wanted to know the reason we did something in our worship service, but she never inquired about my faith, nor did she express what she believed. As for the Circle, she knew I worked with a support group but had never sought additional information. Likewise, I'd volunteered no details. She seemed not to notice my bleak mood after learning about Scot or the increase in my evening meetings as Leo and I worked toward a solution.

In public, Cheryl was the ideal girlfriend—poised and sociable, qualities essential to complement a minister. People would notice her beauty and comment that we made a cute couple. Of course everyone loved Charlie.

But over time, she had become more sexually aggressive in private.

It started before she got her own apartment while she was still living with Joe and Rebecca. After everyone was in bed, we did what I considered heavy petting: touching under the shirts, rubbing together while we were lying on the sofa. No nudity and no removal of clothing. I always stopped before it progressed too far. One night, while Joe and Rebecca were away visiting their daughter in college, Cheryl suggested I spend the night. Up until that moment, I'd assumed she was aware that premarital sex went against the teachings of Scripture and my ministerial ethics. I gave a cursory overview of the Bible's teachings on righteous sexual conduct.

The glaring hypocrisy of that moral conviction was lost on her.

"You haven't been with anyone since—?"

She definitely didn't want the truth to that question.

"Leigh is the only woman I've been with, and we waited until we were married before we...you know."

I couldn't tell if she was relieved or perplexed. "That's admirable. I guess it's another of those religious concepts I wasn't taught, not being a regular church-goer."

"Is that something you can accept, until we're married?"

Is it something I can do…even after we're married?

She hugged me. "You're a good guy, Nate Truett."

I noticed she had not answered my question.

When she got her own apartment, I'd go by at least one night during the week for dinner. And her sexual advances were more explicit. She wasn't content with just kissing or making out; she liked removing my shirt and twice tried to slip her hand down my pants. When I resisted, she got upset. "Nate, do you not find me attractive?"

I'm sure "I want to" would not be helpful.

This prompted an uncomfortable conversation about my unwillingness to "take our relationship to the next level." She promised it would be "our secret" and bragged about her ability to give me "the best sex" I'd ever known.

I doubt that.

I began to avoid being alone with her in her apartment or my house.

Things will be easer once we're married.

Twenty

After we learned of Scot's actions, Leo said it was imperative that I move fast but strategically. We called in Barry and Darrel since they were designated leaders and disclosed to them what we'd learned. Both were adamant that they had not been sexually involved with Scot but devastated at the news that the man they admired had failed them.

"If you two are still interested in being involved, I'd welcome your help."

They agreed, and the four of us met several times to discuss the next steps.

I invited Scot to meet with me in my office. In our last conversation—a month earlier—I said I'd let him know my decision, so I figured this wouldn't arouse undue suspicion.

When he arrived, Leo was with me, and we outlined what I'd learned. He listened but remained stoic. Leo asked if he had anything to say. For a while, Scot was silent as though he'd not heard the question. I could see his hands turn white gripping the arms of the chair. His small body stiffened and seemed to grow in stature. I looked at the seat to see if he was lifting himself out of the chair to appear taller. Or levitating.

"These are *all* lies," he declared with startling force. "From the bowels of hell, designed to damage my reputation and my ministry." He maintained a steady volume, speaking in a slow, dramatic clip. "The boys making such outrageous accusations are—"

"Scot," I interrupted. "This is not a trial. It's not a discussion. We're not here to prove these events. Our investigation has been thorough."

"It's my ministry, and I will—"

"This is about your conduct." Leo informed in his professional tone. Picking up a piece of paper from my desk, he held it out to Scot. "We've prepared this letter of resignation. It doesn't give details of the heinous things you've done, but it's effective *immediately*. All leadership will now fall under the purview of Nate, Barry, and Darrel until a board of directors can be appointed."

Scot stared at the paper, but didn't take it.

"I will *not* do it!" He crossed his arms like a petulant child, now slumping in his chair. "You have no authority to take away my ministry."

Leo took a second paper and held it up. "Your signature on this sheet gives us all rights to the ministry, including the name. Once you sign...and you *will* sign...you relinquish the ministry. Permanently! You will not visit, nor will you contact any of the members, per this agreement. If you do, you can be sued for breach of contract. Am I clear?"

The paperwork and forms were Leo's idea. His brother-in-law was an attorney and provided basic documents with lots of intimidating, legal-sounding words and phrases.

"And if I refuse?"

Leo rocked back in his chair. "Colega, you've made some bad decisions, which have hurt others. You should hear me in this: your work as leader of this ministry is over!"

Scot gave a guttural grunt.

"At this point, everyone we've interviewed...and there have been *many*...were over eighteen, but who knows what we'll find it we keep digging. Maybe boys who were younger. That's statutory rape, and we'd have to turn such information over to the police." Leo paused to let all that sink in.

I'd used the files Alton had gotten for us and had spoken with more than a hundred former members to determine why they had stopped attending. Twenty confessed to either being sexually seduced by Scot or propositioned by him. Several told me they just didn't trust him or that they found him creepy. A few hung up on me, and I received numerous profanity-laced responses. Two guys, who had met at the group, laughed and sarcastically asked me to thank him for bringing them together.

I'd found no evidence of underage guys.

Leo's bluffing.

"This is all *your* doing." Scot stabbed his skinny finger at me after signing the documents. "You have wanted this group since your first visit. Well, you got your wish, Judas, but it will come at a price. Trust me; you *will* pay for this act of rebellion. As the Word says, 'Strike the Shepherd, and the sheep will scatter.' There will be consequences for your insurrection."

"Damn," Leo exclaimed after Scot had stormed out of my office, slamming the door so hard it jarred a picture off the wall. "Definitely a narcissist. With a messianic complex. God will vindicate him? That's delusional. I imagine he sees no contradiction with what he teaches those guys and his sexual entanglements with them."

How did I not know this was going on?

"Now you have decisions to make. I mean, you have the rights to the ministry's name, and you're technically in charge."

"Oh, fuck." The words came before I realized, but Leo laughed. "Pardon my language. I had *not* thought about that."

What does this mean?

"Fuck!"

At Leo's suggestion, we agreed to cancel the next few Circle meetings, giving us time to get the new leadership in place. I drove to Woodlawn and had a private meeting with the pastor of the church that hosted the Circle and where Scot was a member. The pastor was visibly shocked and dismayed, telling me the church would rescind the use of its building. By showing him the changes we were implementing, I was able to convince him to continue its support. I also spoke in confidence with pastors whose churches financially contributed to Whole-Hearted; two of them agreed to serve on the new board of directors.

"How do we let everyone know?" I asked Barry and Darrel.

"The phone tree," Darrel suggested.

"Our list doesn't have everyone who attends," Barry explained. "Giving us their number is totally voluntary and confidential. We assure them we'll protect their privacy if we ever have to call. And some guys have phone numbers of others not on our list."

We crafted a script to use on the calls, providing the basic information: we were working on a new format and some new topics, which we'd announce in two weeks.

"I think we have every scenario covered," Barry asserted.

If only that had been true!

Twenty-One

"Hi, guys. Thank you all for being here tonight. As many of you know, I'm Nate Truett, the associate director of Whole-Hearted Ministries."

Barry was already crying, so I was sure no one was expecting angels to appear with "good news of great joy."

"This crowd is an indication that you've done an incredible job spreading the word about this important meeting."

We had to expand the "circle" with extra chairs.

"Let me begin tonight with sad news. Scot Nelson has stepped down as leader. He values his time with the ministry and wishes you the very best in pursuing your path to wholeness."

The response was mixed. There were audible gasps and spontaneous whispers of disbelief. Knowing what had happened, it shouldn't have surprised me that there were snickers, and one person laughed, in the form of a snide cackle.

"For now, I'll be working with Barry and Darrel to continue the great work here."

That got a loud, sustained round of applause.

"Let me begin our meeting by saying, 'My name is Nate, and I am a new creation in Christ.'"

Our investigation into Scot uncovered others he'd seduced and revealed an ongoing pattern of deception. Some were small, others more significant. He'd told me he was the manager of the Homewood library; he was only a clerk. The degree he claimed to have from Southeastern Bible College was a fabrication. He said

Whole-Hearted was affiliated with Exodus International, a large umbrella organization of similar ministries. When I called to tell them about the change in leadership, I was told that they had no record of Scot Nelson or Whole-Hearted.

After a while, I stopped fact-checking. "He's a pathological liar," Leo stated. "It's possible he doesn't know when he's lying. Or why he does it. But you can't believe anything he says."

It turns out there was *one* thing Scot said that I should have believed.

"I've heard a disturbing report," Dr. Shannon said in his solemn, bad-news voice, not even waiting for me to sit down in his office. The two elders who were also present at the impromptu meeting looked like they'd returned from a funeral. Of someone I'd murdered.

"Scot Nelson contacted me and says you orchestrated a takeover of his ministry by spreading rumors and baseless accusations about his behavior."

"That's not true, sir." I recounted what had happened in my office two weeks earlier. "Leo and I did our research, and everything was well-documented."

Dr. Shannon looked at the other elders, who remained somber. "Well, be that as it may, we aren't here to discuss the activities of that young man. He didn't like violating confidentiality but let us know that you were part of the group because, in his words, you struggle with homosexual tendencies, which you confessed to him. He accused you of repeatedly giving in to this sinful behavior and claims he had to rebuff advances you made toward him."

That vindictive sack of shit!

"Dr. Shannon, Scot vowed to get even with me for the actions taken against him. That's what he's doing. If you need verification, Leo was present during the entire—"

"Brother Truett, when I first asked about your involvement with this group, you said you were just a casual observer."

A few months after I began attending Circle meetings, the "holy grapevine," as Susan called it, kicked in. A church member expressed concern to an elder that I was "involved with a group of homosexuals." That information was reported to Dr. Shannon, which prompted an unexpected pastoral visit to my office. He and I talked about the purpose of Whole-Hearted, and I shared the wonderful, unique work they were doing with the guys. I tactfully mentioned that our church was a financial supporter. The pastor didn't forbid me from attending, but suggested I limit my time and visibility.

"I told you I was helping out." I intentionally kept my tone professional and respectful. "That I believed they could benefit from my training. All of that was true."

"But was it the *whole* truth?"

The pastor and elders were staring at me; it felt like an inquisition. "I've known about my attractions for many years, but my dedication to Christ, to the church, and to my ministry compelled me to surrender such temptations to the Holy Spirit for strength. I never even gave the feelings much thought until after Leigh had died. I started working with the support group and decided while I helped them, I could benefit from what they were learning. Scot fabricated the rest for his revenge."

There were no more questions, and the meeting was over.

Three days later, so was my job.

The letter from the Consistory—the full body of church elders—that I was given before being escorted to my car lauded me for my service. The elders sought to downplay my confession about having same-sex attractions, quoting from the Bible: *"There is no temptation overtaken us such that is common."* My honesty in admitting this particular "sin" was commendable. However, the elders felt it was in the church's best interest to maintain the highest of standards, with no hint of impropriety. *"We aren't sure how people would feel talking with someone who has these inclinations."*

My "resignation" date would be October fifteenth; the congregation would be informed that I'd left to pursue other opportunities. The letter told me that if I used the church as a reference, *"We will provide a respectful recommendation."* I was assured that *"this matter will be held in the strictest confidence,"* and the letter encouraged me to do likewise.

My heart wanted to sit and cry. My mind commenced pondering all the things I needed to do. My fears tried to consider every horrible scenario that might occur. Of course I should call Cheryl and give her the news.

I need to journal.

Before any of that, I had one thing to do first.

"Hey, kiddo. Miss me already?"

Understatement!

"You move away, and my life goes to shit."

Susan and I had talked once since her move. She'd found a small one-bedroom apartment near the church.

"When you use profanity, it's serious. Let me close my office door."

She listened as I relayed the conflicts that had developed with me and Scot, including the incident with Brandon's outburst. I gave her details about Alton's revelation, our investigation, and all the lies I'd uncovered. When I finished, she let out a sardonic grunt. "That asshole should be arrested. How are the guys he assaulted doing?"

"I'm keeping in touch with the ones I can find. Some of them are doing pretty well, but at least one is traumatized. But here's the kicker: when we forced him to resign, he vowed to get even. Which he did—by telling Dr. Shannon about my secret attractions."

"Oh, my God. I'm sure that uptight theocrat wasn't too sympathetic."

The tears were coming. "They fired me, Suz."

Silence.

Did the tremble in my voice obscure what I said?

Then I heard it. Muffled, like she'd covered the receiver. She was crying. Sobbing would be more accurate. Which caused my own emotions to burst forth.

"That sucks, Nathaniel." She blew her nose. "I hate what they did to you, but you must remind yourself that you did what was best for those boys. Grace and those narrow-minded elders are wrong."

"Maybe I'm naïve or just plain stupid, but I never saw this coming, Suz."

"You are *not* stupid! You are a good person, and expect others to be as well. Not everyone is."

"I showed up for work today to find two elders and a police officer. They demanded my keys and then walked with me through my office while I labeled everything that was mine so it could be boxed up and shipped to me. After that, I was escorted out with only my briefcase, which they inspected first. Miss Gert was so upset. I wasn't allowed to say more than "good-bye" to her or Leo."

"That is *completely* fucked up."

An apt summary of my life right now.

"What are you going to do? Job wise, I mean?"

"I'm thinking I'll come up there, sleep on your couch, watch bad TV all day, eat junk food, and get fat."

"That would end any chance of a future career as a stripper."

"Maybe I'll stand on Highway two-eighty with a sign that says, 'Will Counsel for Food.'"

"What about private practice? I think that would suit you."

She knows me so well.

"I've already set up a meeting next week with an agent recommended by the woman who helped me find my condo. The letter from the elders *said* I'm getting a two-month severance package plus unused vacation, so that'll help while I'm getting everything done."

Susan snorted. "The severance package sounds like hush money. What they did was wrong, so they're throwing money at you to soothe the injustice."

I had no recourse for appeal of the elders' decision, so I'd taken the money, regardless of their motive. I could be pissed off *and* pay my bills.

"Have you told Charlotte?"

"No, and I'm so dreading that one. Technically, I can leave it at 'I resigned,' but we both know she's been in church too long to believe that."

"I don't envy that conversation, but if you want my advice—hell, even if you don't want my advice—I recommend you do it sooner than later and be as honest as you are comfortable being with her."

"I DON'T KNOW WHAT TO TELL YOU."

It had been less than a week, and I was still trying to wrap my head around what had happened.

"I never expected the church to do this. I didn't think Mom would be so *upset*."

Telling Susan had been cathartic. Talking to Leo every day was therapeutic. But telling my mother had been traumatic.

"Or maybe they both responded *exactly* as I expected."

I'd followed Susan's advice and told Mom almost everything: I was working with a group of guys who struggle with their sexual attractions. I learned that the man in charge was being "inappropriate" with those under his care, and I exposed him. The elders were concerned about my participation with this group, so we mutually agreed to sever our ministerial relationship.

Mom understood what a violation of trust Scot's actions had been, asked about the boys, and was supportive of my actions to protect them. "Your father would be so proud."

I'm not so sure.

"Mom, the reason I'm working with this group is that…well, I've always had those same feelings."

"Feelings?"

"Yes, you know, toward other men." I was quick to add: "I'm not acting on these sinful desires, but the group helps me, while I help them."

"I swanny, Nathaniel. You say the silliest things."

"Why is it silly, Mom?"

She launched into a random monologue about the guy at the salon who did her hair. "He's charming, and witty, and everyone loves him. But he's so girly. You are not like that. You're just suffering from grief and confusion. You were *married*. Put that idea right out of your head, son." She then shifted the conversation. "How are you *financially*?"

"I have my savings." For as long as I could remember, my parents required me to tithe ten percent to the church. They also suggested that I put at least that much into savings, a discipline I'd maintained since my first job. I didn't tell her about the church's severance money. "It should tide me over until I get my own practice set up."

"That's good, dear." She'd slipped back into her protective mom-voice. "Now, I want you to stop with that group. You could soil your reputation." Our conversation ended bluntly because she had a showing.

"I do wish she'd been more receptive to what I'm feeling."

I knelt and brushed away some mud that had splashed up on Leigh's headstone.

"Leo believes she'll come around. In time. You'd like him. He's been so helpful."

I sat on the bench.

"I'm OK. You don't have to worry."

She knows I'm not okay.

"Arms of Grace was our dream. It was where I thought I'd spend my life. Where *we'd* spend our lives. You've been gone for two years, and now it's gone too. I have no idea what I'm going to do."

I remembered a verse my mom always quoted: "All things work together for good."

Yeah, not helpful, God!

Twenty-Two

"You won't believe what I got in the mail today."

"I'm guessing it's not an Employee of the Month certificate from the church," Leo answered.

The weeks after my termination, I experienced everything from despair to relief to depression to excitement. In addition to the hours crying into my pillow, I spent hours writing in my journal. Leo, who was helping me sort through what had happened, reminded me to treat the firing like grief and express "everything and anything" I was feeling. He was even supportive when he came by one evening to find me drunk.

"I got a note from Scot."

"Oh, *mierda*!"

Shit, indeed.

It came in a plain white envelope with my name and address printed by hand, with precision.

"Well, what did it say? Did he gush and repent and thank you for helping him confront his sin?"

Leo could always make me laugh.

I removed the single small sheet of notebook paper, cut to fit the envelope, and read Scot's unexpected message, also printed in precise penmanship:

> *You were warned!*
> *As God promised: what you sow, you reap.*
> *Or to put it another way: payback is a bitch.*

And so am I.
Fuck you!

"I'm sure deep…deep…*deep* down, what he meant was he's grateful for your loving intervention."

"I'll need my sociopath decoder ring to find that hidden message."

The note was another glaring reminder that Scot was not the person I thought I knew.

I didn't tell Leo that another card had also arrived the same day as Scot's. It was *exactly* what I'd expect, from someone I *did* know.

I'm truly sorry about what they did to you.
You deserved better.
Call if you need to talk. I'm always here for you.
Please take care of yourself.
Love, Trey.

Two messages, from two *different* people. Both brought tears but for different reasons. I knew better than to respond to either.

It was strange not having a scheduled routine. There were no staff meetings, counseling sessions, administrative tasks, board meetings, calls to return, or reports to write. Other than my bi-monthly visits to my therapist, my calendar was now empty. When I lost my job, I also lost my social life.

Worse, I no longer had a church home. With the exception of a few times I was too sick, or on vacation, I'd never *not* gone to church on Sundays. I felt untethered. Disconnected. The first Sunday after being walked out of my office, I tried watching the Grace worship service on TV, but that amplified my loneliness. And my anger. I turned it off about five minutes into Dr. Shannon's sermon.

The following Sunday, I went to a movie and then to the gym.

With no church family and Susan gone, that left Cheryl and Charlie.

"So you're gay?" Cheryl shouted. "Now it all makes sense."

The elders pledged confidentiality. That lasted for about three weeks. Apparently, someone leaked it to our minister of music, who told his wife, who told her sister. My girlfriend.

"No, I'm not gay. At various times in my life, I've experienced same-sex attractions, but I'm working to overcome them."

"Did you ever touch Charlie?"

The question, and such a horrific accusation, stunned me momentarily into silence.

"Nate, did you do anything to my son?" The quiver in her voice came through as she emphasized each word.

"How can you even think that? I would never do anything to hurt Charlie. I love him."

"What do you mean...*love him*?"

When she left my house, she said she would consider my explanation of what these feelings meant, how they had nothing to do with children, and all I'd done to conquer the feelings, once and for all. She promised to think about "us and our future."

I knew it was over.

Can I get a refund for an almost-paid-for engagement ring on layaway?

"What do you want first: the latest gossip from the trenches or my pep talk to get you off your melancholy introspective culo?"

Leo breezed past me, heading into the den where almost every day after work he came by to help me with the details of setting up my new practice, which would open after the holidays.

"I'll have you know my butt has gotten several things on our list accomplished!"

"Gossip it is then."

Leo wasn't a member of Grace, but seemed to be tapped in to everything going on behind the scenes. Earlier in the week, he told me Miss Gert had given her retirement notice, effective at the end of the year. She'd voiced support for me and criticized the way the church had treated me. Her loyalty was gratifying, but I wondered how Grace Center could function without her.

"It seems the sacred caca has hit the fan, mi amigo. The Grace Center board has requested a meeting with the church's board. Our board members are not happy that your *resignation*—" He used air quotes. "—and the personal details have leaked. They are demanding to know why the confidentiality you've afforded to church members and clients was not extended to you. Two of our board members have indicated to me they plan to resign once that meeting is done."

How petty am I that this makes me feel kinda vindicated?

"I also hear some in the congregation are upset as well. A bevy of longtime members met with the senior pastor, furious at the church's response. I heard a rumor that at least two families have left also because such personal matters about you got out."

"I've gotten calls this week from Grace clients. Should I even wonder how they have my home number or how they learned about my plans to set up a private practice?"

Leo grinned. "*Dios trabaja de forma misteriosa.*"

When I frowned, he informed, "God works in mysterious ways, dear brother."

"I'm thinking God might have some help from a crafty old woman and a devious Latin man."

"Did you decide what you'll call the Haven of Emotional Healing?" He asked, changing the subject. "More importantly, will this Latin guy be able to work with you?"

"First, that will *not* be the name. And why in the world would you wanna work with me? I'd think I'm radioactive these days in Christian circles."

"Since the elders of your church have decided to begin funneling the counseling back to the ministerial staff, I figure I'm on the chopping block."

This wasn't fair to Leo; he should not be suffering for the decisions made by Scot, or for my involvement in Whole-Hearted. Neither should Miss Gert.

"Stop that!" Leo said.

"What?"

He waved his hand in my direction. "You're all in your head, taking responsibility for what the elders did and for my job. Probably Miss Gert as well."

"I *am* the common denominator."

"That doesn't make you the cause. Now," he said, snapping his fingers at me, "focus and tell me the name."

"I was thinking *Embrace Counseling Center*. It says something of what we hope to provide: a place that will welcome them. It's also an invitation: we're asking them to embrace the process of counseling."

He gave it some thought. "I like it. Why did you decide against just using your name? Dr. Nate Truett, Marriage and Family Therapist?"

"Besides *not* being a doctor yet, I thought my name might be associated with Scot's actions and soil the reputation of the new practice. Is that paranoid?"

"Diagnosing paranoia is very time consuming. If you'd like to make an appointment—"

"Never mind. And I might have found a space. Dr. George Ackerman, one of Grace Center's referral doctors, owns an entire building just south of the Homewood city limits, and he's offered to lease me a small suite on the second floor. There are several medical practices there, but I'd be the only counselor, which could generate some referrals from other residents. The reception area is tiny compared to what I have...what I had...but the office is not bad. I won't have much room. Just a desk, a couple of chairs, and a small sofa. Maybe a few books. I won't even have a receptionist, but I did some research, and an answering service could work for now."

His usual poker face showed a little disappointment.

"Don't worry. Once you finish your license, we can expand and bring you onboard."

"What about a conference room, for workshops and group sessions?"

"Each floor has one, complete with table, chairs, and even some A/V equipment. It's shared by the tenants and can be scheduled through Dr. Ackerman's receptionist."

"Sounds like a good deal."

"It will be an adventure," I said to Leo, remembering those were Leigh's exact words to me when I hesitated about presenting my plans for Arms of Grace.

Until Embrace could support me, I'd taken a part-time job in the office of Dr. Carl Randall, a psychiatrist who'd served on the Grace Center advisory board. He'd been so supportive after my firing and enthusiastic about my new venture. I worked mornings, doing patient scheduling, follow-up calls, data entry, and filing, which allowed me the freedom to continue working with Whole-Hearted.

"Here's what we do," Leo said in his take-charge voice. "If you like the space, tell Ackerman to draw up the contract and ask about including a contingency on additional space. Go by tomorrow and measure the walls, make a list of the furniture you need, and then determine a spending budget. Tomorrow, I'll call my brother-in-law and have him draw up the legal paperwork for the name. On Saturday, Alison and I'll take you to used office furniture stores around town, and we'll get what you need. Oh, take note of whether the space needs to be painted, and we'll get supplies to do that as well."

He should be Patrón, and I could work for him.

"What if we do all this, and no one shows up?"

"That's a possibility, at least in the beginning. So I offer two pieces of advice: get comfortable chairs and take some good books with you to work."

"For someone who's unemployed, I'm exhausted."

"Wait until you're my age," Miss Gert responded. "We call that 'normal.'"

I'd gotten up early and gone to the gym; there weren't many people at *that* House of Worship. I did my quiet time and journaling, then worked on my to-do list for the new practice. We'd picked up the necessary furniture at our shopping marathon the day before, so I was recording the delivery dates into my day planner. I'd fixed a light lunch and was reading the Sunday *Birmingham News* when she dropped by unexpectedly.

"I found these in the workroom at Arms of Grace," she said after I'd gotten us a glass of iced tea. She handed me a manila envelope. "It *seems* they're mailing labels for all your clients, minus members of Grace. If someone were opening a new counseling center, these might be useful. They could even be used to announce the opening of that center."

As the keeper of all our records, it was apparent how she had gotten them.

"The Board of Elders had me contact all our clients, and your appointments are being redirected to the pastoral team. It's possible that some of your clients might be thrilled to know that you—the person who helped them when they were in need—are still available, in a new location."

"Miss Gert, you've done so much already."

The week after my firing, Leo brought my Rolodex with all my personal contacts and referrals that I'd collected over the years. He said before the crew came to pack up my office that Miss Gert had retrieved it and placed it on her desk, knowing the information was private. She'd asked Leo to make sure he got it to me.

"Inside, I *think* there might also be suggestions for office equipment. Stuff like a typewriter, phone system, and offset printer along with some vendors who can help out with good prices on quality used machines."

She was not great at being coy, and I loved her for it.

"If a grand opening of this hypothetical counseling center did happen, I would suggest light snacks and punch. Nothing as elaborate as one might have at an open house."

I snickered and gave her a huge hug.

"They made you leave so quickly the other day that there wasn't an opportunity to speak to you, Brother Truett."

"Hey, I'm no longer on staff, so you can call me 'Nate.'"

"I'll try...Nate." She crumpled up her face like she'd smelled a bad odor. "Anyhoo, it was rude to treat you like a criminal that way. We should have at least been given time to say a proper good-bye."

"Well, I'm glad you came by."

"Thank you for allowing me the privilege of working with you and Grace Center. I've been involved in church for nearly fifty years, and this was a highlight. Watching you, with those hurting people. I will always treasure that."

Shit, now I'm gonna cry.

"Lord knows I'm not one to criticize my church or my ministers, but they were dead wrong on this one."

"I think you are amazing, Miss Gert. I am sorry to hear you're retiring. You helped Grace Center succeed. Words cannot express how much I appreciate and respect you and enjoyed working with you."

"And your new office...and all your clients...will be blessed to have you. I suspect Arms of Grace will be phased out soon, and that breaks my heart." She stood and hugged me. "You have my number if you should need help planning any grand opening events in the near future."

Twenty-Three

I admit: I wasn't paying close attention. Darrel was sharing a Scripture lesson with the group, which was generating some discussion. Under the pretense of making notes in my notebook, I was working on a presentation for my first seminar sponsored by Embrace.

It had been three months since Scot's removal, and things were settling into a routine. The holidays were over, and people were returning to the Circle. Once we'd appointed a board, they named me the executive director. I resisted, but finally agreed, with the understanding that my role would be more advisory—less participatory and less *visible* than Scot had been. Barry and Darrel, who'd been involved for a while, and had completed the *Path to Wholeness* training, were designated as ministry co-leaders. Barry handled the meetings, and Darrel was revising the training materials for our first class. I would be there for weekly meetings, welcoming everyone and leading in the opening prayer, but they rotated facilitating.

Each week, I looked for Brandon. I'd spoken with his mother once and figured that at some point his parents would demand that he return to the group. But so far, he'd been conspicuously absent.

Until he wasn't.

I didn't hear the door open, but I heard it slam. And like everyone, I did see Brandon, his massive size filling the frame.

"Where's Scot?" he screamed.

Now, everyone was looking at me.

"Hey, Brandon. It's really good to have you back. It's been a while. Scot is not—"

"He did this to me. I want him to see what he did to me."

His left wrist was wrapped in bandages.

"Guys," I said, forcing my voice to sound relaxed. "Why don't y'all go into the kitchen and let me talk with Brandon?" When no one moved, I glared at Barry. "Take them *now*, please."

"No!" Brandon bellowed, and everyone froze at the force of his voice. From his pocket, he pulled out a small pistol with a shiny barrel.

Oh, shit.

In his huge hand, it looked like a toy. I couldn't take the chance it wasn't.

I wish Alton were here tonight. He always seems able to calm Brandon.

"Brandon, Scot is no longer part of this ministry."

"Don't lie to me. Where is he hiding?"

"Brandon, you remember me. I visited you in the hospital, and we talked. I promise: I am not lying."

With one hand behind my back, I motioned for Barry to get everyone out of the room.

I took a couple of steps closer and lowered my voice. "I know he did some bad things and behaved inappropriately. Is that why you want to see him?"

Brandon looked down and nodded.

"I'm so very sorry that happened, Brandon. It was wrong, and he has been removed because of those actions."

"Stop!" Brandon demanded, seeing the boys heading out of the fellowship hall. "You are trying to hide him from me, aren't you?"

"Brandon, I promise you: Scot is not here. I've asked everyone to give us some alone time so we can talk. Would that be OK? Then you and I can sit down. I am here to help."

He didn't respond, which I took as agreement and gave Barry a gesture to move faster. As Darrel walked past me, I whispered, "Call the police."

I'll reason with him until the police arrive.

It almost worked.

A MAN AND A WOMAN WERE TALKING ABOUT ME LIKE I WASN'T there. When I opened my eyes, I could feel motion, which didn't agree with my upset stomach.

"There you are," the woman sitting beside me said. "We didn't find a next of kin in your wallet. Is there anyone we should call? A wife? Your parents?"

Her face looked kinda fuzzy, and while I understood her words, none of it made sense.

"I'm not married. Not now. My wife died of cervical cancer. I had a girlfriend, but she broke up with me when she found out I had same-sex attractions." My words sounded funny as I said them, and my mouth tasted strange.

What did she ask?

"Mom lives in Memphis, but trust me, you do not want her here. She would freak out if she knew that I was leading a group of struggling homosexuals when this happened."

She looked at the man on the other side of me. "The pain medication is taking effect."

"Call Trey."

"What's his number?"

Trey left me.

"Never mind."

Susan.

"Call Susan, my best friend."

Didn't she move?

Somehow, I was able to rattle off her phone number without a second thought.

Each time I closed and reopened my eyes, it was like I'd fast-forwarded the movie on my VCR. We were driving out of the church's parking lot, and then they were taking me from the ambulance and, finally, lifting me off the gurney and onto a table.

"Mr. Truett, your shoulder has experienced some serious trauma. Can you try to move your fingers for me?"

No problem.

"The other hand, please."

Fine.

This is a bizarre dream, and I'm ready to wake up.

It was like those times I'd had too much to drink at night; I was groggy and disoriented. My head was hurting with a dull pain. Most conspicuous was how heavy I felt. I could sense my body—my arms and legs—but wasn't confident I could mandate them to get me out of bed.

What was I dreaming?

Trying to remember brought a sudden sense of terror, and I heard myself gasp.

"Nathaniel."

Someone's in my bedroom.

"Nathaniel, open your eyes."

Three times I heard my full first name, yet I struggled to identify the person's voice. My brain was fuzzy, uncooperative. There were other noises around me as well, including an annoyingly persistent beeping sound.

"He's coming around." A man's voice.

There are people in my bedroom.

"Sweetie, the doctor said you're doing fine. Look at me."

Doctor?

I now recognized the voice, and years of ingrained Southern upbringing caused me to obey my mother.

"That's good."

"Good" was a relative term. Though my eyes *were* open, the glaring light was painful. Squinting, I couldn't seem to focus on anything around me; everything appeared shrouded in a grayish mist. Mom was standing on my left side, and at the foot of the bed I could make out a tall figure with dark hair—*a man?*—in a white coat.

"Trey?"

That makes no sense.

"Good afternoon, Mr. Truett. I'm Doctor—"

What did he say?

Between the infernal beeping noise that sounded loud enough to warn ships in a storm and the pounding in my head, his words were garbled.

Out of the corner of my blurry vision, I saw movement. I turned my head—*damn, that hurts*—to see someone standing near a door. It was very bright behind him. Unlike the man at the end of my bed—the doctor—this person was dressed in all dark clothes. Like a mortician. Or the angel of death.

Oh, fuck. Am I dying?

"What's going on?" I asked, sounding more like a frog than myself. The soreness in my throat felt like I'd been screaming.

Susan and I went to a football game one night in college, and I was so hoarse the next day.

"What do you remember?" This was the man in dark clothes.

"Can you all give us a moment?" Doctor White Coat said. "We'll do a quick exam, then you can both talk with him. But since we just removed the endotracheal tube, he won't feel like talking for long."

I was in a hospital.

When Mom and the man in black left the room, the doctor listened to my heart, flashed a light in my eyes—*damn, that hurts too*—and touched around my chest. My sight was clearing up. I looked down and saw I wasn't wearing a shirt. My left arm was on my bare chest, secured in place with brown bandages wrapped around my body.

I was injured and in a hospital.

I need to remember.

In compliance, the fog in my brain dissipated.

Oh shit. I wish I could forget.

His badge identified him by his last name: Gentry. He stood next to my bed, and I could see his clothes were dark blue. My breathing staggered, and my heart rate increased when I saw his holstered gun. The tube in my arm and wires on my chest prevented me from running away.

"You are a very brave man," Officer Gentry said, flipping open a small notebook and taking a pen out of his pocket.

"I don't feel brave."

What I feel is sadness. And pain.

"Are you strong enough for questions?"

I figured there was only one answer he would accept.

He started with my personal information: name, age, address, and phone numbers. He asked why I was at the church that night and how often the group met. That was followed by how long I'd known Brandon and if I knew about his mental illness, or that he hadn't been taking his medication. He even asked if I'd had any prior knowledge that Brandon would show up with a gun.

"Mr. Truett, let's talk about the events on Tuesday night. At any time in your interaction with Brandon, did you touch the gun? Did you try to wrestle it from him?"

The idea would be laughable if any of this were the least bit funny. Brandon was at least six inches taller and outweighed me by at least fifty pounds.

"I *never* touched the gun. For most of our conversation, we were about four to five feet apart. I invited him to sit and talk, but he was too agitated. He paced around and around. I kept talking to him. Much of what he said didn't make sense. He thought I was the former leader of the group, in disguise."

"Did anyone antagonize him? Taunt him?"

"No."

"From other eyewitness accounts, you *were* able to calm him down."

"Yes. I convinced him that I wasn't the former director. He relaxed, and we talked. I assured him that we could get it all worked out and that he should give me the gun. I think he agreed. I mean, he nodded and extended his hand—the one holding the gun—toward me."

The cop was writing furiously, so I waited.

"But something happened? He changed his mind?"

That part was hazy; it happened so fast—I remember being stunned.

"BRANDON, IF YOU GIVE ME THE GUN, YOU AND I CAN GO TO THE hospital *together*. They'll help you feel better. You remember when I visited you in the hospital? You told me how much better you felt. Your mom is probably worried about you." I chose not to mention his father, knowing the conflict in their relationship.

His face softened. "She'll be so mad that I took her gun."

"I'll make sure she gets it back."

Nodding, he held out his hand, open with the gun flat in his palm, and took a step toward me.

"Nate, look out!" someone screamed from another room.

Brandon jumped back and was once again gripping the gun. He grabbed my extended hand and yanked. Hard! I heard a pop.

Did he fire the gun?

There was a sudden, searing pain in my shoulder.

Did he shoot me?

I stumbled with Brandon still holding my arm. I twisted my body, and he did the same but in the opposite direction.

More pain.

I glanced in the direction of the pain.

Shouldn't there be blood?

He swung around, throwing me down. I landed hard, my head hitting the floor. He let go of my arm but held tight to the gun. Through the tears from the intense pain, I could see a look of panic.

"Brandon, I'm fine. I know you didn't mean to do that. Just don't hurt anyone. Please."

"He shouldn't have done it," Brandon repeated his refrain. "Why did he make me do it?"

I was having trouble seeing; a dark, cloudy frame surrounded everything.

Is someone turning the lights on and off?

The room was spinning, and my stomach was not enjoying the ride. I was about to heave.

Maybe if I stand up, he'll see that I'm OK.

When I tried, my legs were wobbly. The next choice was to push myself up with my hands, but my left arm wouldn't move. It was hanging there beside me but ignored any directives my brain gave about movement. I reached around with my other arm and tried to lift it.

Mind-numbing, stomach-churning pain.

An acrid taste coated my mouth. The threat of vomit became a reality as my dinner came forth. I managed to turn my head to avoid getting it all over me and him.

The last thing I want to do is vomit on the guy pointing a gun at me!

"I'm sorry," he whimpered.

I wiped the tears to see him better. His arm was flailing. "Brandon, it's—"

Pain and nausea and screaming and confusion and sirens converged around me.

Then…darkness.

"YOU DON'T THINK HE MEANT TO HURT YOU?" OFFICER GENTRY inquired after I gave my account of the events.

He was so angry. At Scot, for what he'd done. At his parents, too, for making him come to the group in the first place and that they wouldn't let him see his boyfriend. And off his meds. From my vantage point—on the floor, eyes filled with tears from intense pain, fighting to remain conscious—it appeared to be an accident. All his emotions, adrenalin, and confusion converged. I just happened to get tangled up in all of it.

I shook my head, which caused me to wince in pain. "He's so large and awkward. He doesn't know his own strength. He kept apologizing to me."

I tried not to imagine what might have happened if Scot had been there instead of me.

"It could have been...your injuries could have been much worse."

It's bad enough.

While Mom and the cop were in the hall, Doctor Jacobs—I'd been able to read his name badge—explained that he had performed extensive surgery on my left shoulder to repair a torn rotator cuff and tendons and to set fractures in my clavicle, scapula, and humerus. I had two metal pins holding some of the fixes in place. There would be weeks in the sling, followed by extended physical therapy, but the doctor was optimistic it would all heal in time. He also said I had a concussion and a huge knot on the back of my head from when I had hit the linoleum floor.

My voice had deteriorated to a squeak, so the cop and I ended our conversation.

"Most folks don't handle a crisis the way you did, Mr. Truett. You probably saved the lives of all those boys."

Not all the boys.

Officer Gentry used his finger to illustrate how the bullet had struck Brandon just under his ear and entered his skull.

I preferred to believe it was a fluke—that he had not come there with plans to die. He was unstable, waving the gun around, and his huge finger mistakenly squeezed the trigger. I seemed to recall, for that brief interval before I blacked out, his total surprise when the gun fired.

It's what I needed to tell myself.

Twenty-Four

The first thing Mom asked, after my debriefing with the police, was how to contact my pastor. "He can come by, pray with us, and get you on the church's prayer list."

"I don't have a church, Mom. Or a pastor." My deep scratchy voice sounded like I'd spent years smoking. "They fired me, remember?"

It's not like I'd completely stopped going to church. Since taking over as executive director of Whole-Hearted, I had visited the churches that financially supported the ministry. Several were Charismatic or Pentecostal, where compared with my Presbyterian background, the services seemed emotional, even chaotic. There were a couple of Independent Baptist churches, with lively singing and loud, serious sermons containing long appeals to accept Jesus, be baptized, and join the church. I also attended a few nondenominational churches and one small Methodist congregation. My attendance wasn't about my comfort level with different styles of worship. I'd been baptized as a child and definitely wasn't interested in joining. My visits were about visibility and building good relationships with these pastors. Occasionally, they would introduce me, even allowing me to "share my testimony" with the church.

Mom launched into a lecture about the importance of a "fellowship of faith," reminding me of how I'd been raised to be in church and reiterating that attending was an expression of my devotion and obedience to my calling. There were unending questions about the new practice, my finances, and why I was no longer dating Cheryl. The same Cheryl she had adamantly disapproved of me dating.

Smothering her interactions were undertones of disapproval about my continued involvement with "those" people and the always-unspoken "I told you so."

The first few days, my hospital room should have been equipped with a revolving door, considering all the visitors. My nurse said she checked my chart to see if I was some incognito celebrity. I was heavily medicated, and drifting in and out of sleep, so many of them were vague and jumbled together. One time I was talking with Leo, blinked, and there were two Arms of Grace board members. "What happened to Leo?" I asked. Mom informed me that he had left six hours earlier. I woke up once in the night convinced Scot had been standing beside me, laughing. I was comforted when I learned he'd never been there.

Miss Gert brought me a beautiful pineapple upside-down cake, which we gave to the nurses. Claire Shannon came by. She was gracious, as usual, telling me that Dr. Shannon was out of town but sent his love and prayers. I wasn't sure I believed her but was relieved at not seeing him.

I was coming out of one of my dozed-off intervals and could hear Mom whispering across the room. The beep of my heart monitor relentlessly proclaimed that I was still alive. Or at the very least, my heart was still beating. I couldn't imagine how anyone could sleep with that hellish noise without heavy sedation. Now that I was awake, the clattering monitor was interfering with hearing what Mom was saying and to whom. I chose not to open my eyes.

"He had a bad night. Moaned in pain, and I think he had a nightmare. Probably reliving that nasty incident."

Was that true?

"What has the doctor said about his recovery? Will he have full use of his arm?"

I knew that voice, so I opened one eye.

Susan!

"Hey, you." My still-squeaky voice made my enthusiasm sound like I was sucking helium.

"Sorry I wasn't here sooner. I was stuck in the woods, helping lead a singles' retreat." She leaned down to kiss me on the cheek. "I came as soon as we finished."

"When I'm strong enough to get up from this bed," I assured her in a whisper, "I *will* get even with you for calling my mother."

"Love you," she said, offering a loud smooching sound.

"Look at all the flowers," Mom remarked to Susan. My mother was convinced that a person's influence could be measured by how many flowers showed up in the hospital or at the funeral. "I'll be sure to keep all the cards so you can send thank-you notes when you get home."

At least if this *was* my funeral, I wouldn't have to adhere to this never-to-be-ignored Southern protocol instilled...grilled...into me by my mother.

"There's one from the staff at Grace and the elders," she beamed. "Isn't that nice?"

I imagined an accompanying card with something like: "*The Board of Elders voted, and the majority decided to pray for a speedy recovery.*"

"You got a pretty arrangement from your nice friends Leo and Allison."

Pretty was Mom-code for "small."

She pointed at an arrangement near the window. "That's from my office." Of course it was huge and ostentatious. She would be mortified if hers were not the largest in the room.

"Mom, can you ask the nurse if I can have some Jell-O? Or fruit?"

"You slept through breakfast, so I reckon you must be hungry," she acknowledged as she walked to the door before turning back to me. "But if you wanted me to leave, you could've just told me."

Susan and I waited until the door had closed before we burst out laughing. It made me cringe in pain, but being with Susan was almost worth it.

"Get used to it," Susan said once Mom was gone. "She's staying with you while you recover."

"Can I get morphine with that Jell-O?"

Susan teared up. "You scared the shit outta me, kiddo. Tell me what happened."

I gave her a quick recap, avoiding the graphic details. Her facial response would go from sympathy to anger to fear to disbelief, all accompanied by tears. When Mom returned, Susan volunteered to stay with me for the afternoon.

"Mom, you look so tired." I used my most concerned-son voice. "Go get some rest. The guest bedroom has everything you need."

Even pushing seventy, my mom still drove herself, but not long distances, so she'd rented a car when she'd flown in from Memphis.

"When you come back tonight, can you bring me some T-shirts and shorts?" I instructed her where to find them.

"Is there anyone...*anyone*...you want me to call?" Susan asked when we were alone.

Did she mean Trey?

I did a sweep with my one arm. "I don't even know how all these folks found out?"

She seemed stunned. "I assume they learned by reading the newspaper article."

I gave her a blank stare.

"You made the news, kiddo." She walked to the small cabinet by the bathroom and pulled a *Birmingham News* from inside. "Charlotte showed it to me this morning."

The article, on page five, had a small picture of Brandon that looked like it was from his high school yearbook, superimposed on a picture of the church where the Circle held meetings. Next to it was a larger picture of me, holding a Bible in one hand, looking at the camera with a big say-cheese-for-the-camera smile. It was one originally taken for the staff page of the Grace Church member directory.

How the hell did the paper get that photo?

In the context of this tragedy, it was inappropriate.

The story took up almost the entire bottom section of the page.

The headline read: *Local minister saves thirteen lives at Christian ministry*. Underneath was included a smaller headline: *Disturbed boy with gun threatens support group, kills self.*

Bethanne Greenfield, the religion reporter, explained the work of Whole-Hearted Ministries as "encouraging homosexuals to reject the sinful lifestyle and live normal heterosexual lives." Two board members detailed the circumstances that had led to my taking over as executive director, without using Scot's name. "We wanted someone who knew these struggles but who walked in victory over the desires." Both praised my credentials, my leadership, and expressed gratitude for my bravery and courage. Several of the boys who were there recounted what had happened and how I had tried "valiantly" to help Brandon. The reporter also interviewed the pastor of the Assembly of God where the Circle met. "We are blessed to partner with this important organization. They're doing God's work, and these attempts by the devil—this horrible death and the abominable actions of the former director with those under his care—will not keep them from proclaiming the Gospel message of healing and transformation." Of course the reporter got the pastor to expound on Scot's "abominable actions." Brandon's parents had been unwilling to comment, asking that their privacy be respected as they grieved the death of their son.

The sigh I released caused pain in my chest and came out sounding more like a moan.

The reporter had obtained background information about me: where I attended college, my marriage to Leigh, her death, and my ministry with Grace. Dr. Shannon was kind, expressing condolences for the "troubled boy" and a speedy recovery for me. There were quotes from several *unnamed* staff members who were not surprised by my "brave actions." One Grace minister—also unnamed—made a point to emphasize that "the church doesn't condone the sin of homosexuality" and commended my work to "put these men on God's righteous path."

At least there's no mention of my new practice.

I folded the newspaper and tossed it to the foot of my bed. "Mom must be so embarrassed that my involvement with this ministry, and with *that* sin, is so public."

I did a slow look around the room at the flowers and cards.

"There's not one from Trey," she said.

"I wasn't...OK, I was," I admitted, not hiding my disappointment. "He probably doesn't even know I'm here."

"There is a lovely card from your board. Says they're praying for you and suspended all activities until you're ready to resume your position."

"I don't think that's such a good idea."

"What do you mean?"

"I've been doin' lots of thinking, and this article helps clarify some things for me. I mean, I'm not thrilled at how I was portrayed—"

"I thought you came off as—"

"Don't say 'brave' or 'courageous.' I wasn't, and I'm not. I am grateful I was there for the boys who *could have* been injured, but it doesn't change the fact that I never wanted to be the leader. Still don't. While I appreciate the tools I've received from the ministry... even what I learned from Scot...there are other resources available. It's time to move on."

"Your mother will be *very* supportive of this decision."

I ignored her snark. "I'll arrange grief counseling for anyone who wants it; I'm sure this has been traumatic, especially for those present that night. But once that's done, *I'm* done."

"Who will take over for you?"

"I hope...no one. I'm going to suggest to the board that we shut it down."

To her credit, Susan didn't applaud my decision, but her face beamed approval.

"After all, this bad publicity will destroy the group. I mean, the former director was sexually abusing members, leading one of them to burst into a meeting with a gun and kill himself. Who the hell would want anything to do with a ministry as fucked up as this one?"

Turns out I would make a *terrible* psychic!

SUSAN OPENED THE FRONT DOOR, AND WE ALL WALKED INTO my house. After six days in the hospital, I was ready for the familiarity of home where I could relax.

"I wish you'd reconsider staying in the guest bedroom, Sweetie. I worry about you going up and down those stairs."

"Mom, the surgery was on my shoulder, not my legs."

So much for relaxing.

"I'll take your bag up to your bedroom," Susan offered. She'd be heading back to Cleveland later in the afternoon; Mom would take her to the airport.

I saw a small stack of mail on the credenza, which I'd tackle later. I hated to admit how tired I was.

Susan and Mom took my car to get us lunch from Green's. The quiet of my house—no noisy monitors or announcements in the hallway—brought an instant tranquility. I secured the mail under my good arm and climbed the stairs to my study. The answering machine was blinking, and just as I reached to push the playback button, the phone rang. The unexpected noise startled me, sending a knife-like pain through my shoulder when I jumped. All the mail dropped onto the floor.

"Is this Nate Truett?" the unknown female voice asked.

I have no interest in switching long distance services!

"I'm Vivian O'Neal. I'm a news segment producer for the *700 Club*, and we'd like to schedule a time for you to come on our show to be interviewed by Reverend Robertson."

"Why?" I was so stunned, and confused, it was the only thing I could think to say.

"We read about your heroic actions and the incredible work you're doing with boys living the sinful homosexual lifestyle. We want our viewers to hear your story."

"How did you…who told you about this?"

I heard her rustling through papers. "Oh, here it is. An intern read it on the newswire and alerted us. Apparently, Associated Press picked it up from your local newspaper and broadcast it to their national subscribers."

National?

I explained that I'd just gotten out of the hospital and promised to call her soon with my answer.

Sitting at my desk, I listened to my *twelve* messages. Vivian was there. Twice. Bethanne Greenfield, the *Birmingham News* reporter who had written the original story, also called, wanting to do a follow-up interview. There were interview requests from *Christianity Today*, *Moody Monthly*, and *The Advocate*, a magazine I'd never heard of. Two of our local TV stations had also left messages, wanting to send a camera crew. Even more surprising, I had a message from a woman with *Good Morning America* and someone from *The Phil Donahue Show*.

If all of that weren't bizarre enough, as I played the messages, *his* voice came on. "Nathaniel. I just heard what happened." There was a quiver in Trey's words.

Dammit!

"I knew showing up at the hospital would be...I didn't know if they'd let me see you. Hell, I'm not even sure you'd want to see me. I *am* worried and can't find out anything from the nurses or information desk. I need to know you're all right. Please call me. In fact, if you think it'd be OK—"

The message time limit cut him off. I pushed the button to save his...to save all...the messages.

I heard Susan and Mom come in downstairs.

"HOLY SHIT. YOU'RE A CELEBRITY."

When we finished lunch, just before Susan had to leave to catch her flight, she and I went to my study—using the excuse of privacy to say good-bye—and I'd played her the messages.

"I'm not interested in being a celebrity. How do I politely, but firmly, tell these folks to leave me the hell alone?"

"Nathaniel Truett, on national TV, talking about his work with homosexuals. Your. Mother. Will. Freak. Out."

"Freaking out my mother is always fun, but I'm looking for reasons *not* to do these interviews!"

"I know someone who's very familiar with handling the media."

Without a conscious decision, like some instinct long buried inside me, my gaze went to the stained-glass sculpture on the bookcase.

"No way!" I protested, though knowing she was right.

So while Mom took Susan to the airport, I called Trey, using the number he'd included in the card when I was fired.

When I heard his voice, I almost hung up. I was dizzy, and my stomach rolled in response.

Barfing would not be a great way to begin our conversation.

"Trey, it's Nate—"

"Oh my God, Nathaniel, I've been so worried. How are you?"

Hearing his concern alleviated my trepidation about calling him. I touched the Library Lion he'd given me as a housewarming gift.

"I think bench presses are off my exercise card for a while. I'll have to wait for the surgery to heal up, then the doctor says with months of physical therapy, I should be fine."

"It's such a tragic story," he noted. "I am very sorry you went through that."

"Let's just hope I don't get fat again while I'm recuperating."

"You were *never* fat. The important thing is that you rest and heal."

We chatted, staying on safe subjects like his job and my new practice. I asked him about living in Montgomery, and he gave polite answers. In spite of my curiosity, I didn't ask if he was dating anyone.

"I have a favor, and feel free to reject it outright."

I couldn't...wouldn't blame him if he did.

When he didn't hang up on me, I gave him the details about the media calls. "I know that you…well, this group is not something you support, so I'm kinda embarrassed to even call, but Susan thought you could help. After the way I treated you, you'd be within your rights to just tell me to fuck off—"

"I told you I would be there if you needed me, and I meant that."

"I'm not looking for publicity, or to perpetuate this hero nonsense. A troubled boy is dead, and I didn't do anything noble. I need advice from someone like you about whether I should call these reporters back or not."

The long pause made me uncomfortable. "Why not do it? Or at least some of them. I can't help with any messaging, 'cause I…well, you know…but you *did* save those boys' lives, and that's inspiring. Besides, if you don't do the interviews, they could do the story anyway. Without you. This way, at least you have input. It's known as 'controlling the narrative.'"

"That makes sense."

"And you shouldn't downplay your bravery. What you did was incredible."

I was too tired to protest. "Thank you. This was helpful."

"You can always count on me, Oraios."

Dammit!

Taking his advice, I returned the calls from *Christianity Today* and *Moody Monthly* and agreed to phone interviews. They wanted a good headshot, so I sent a photo I'd had done for an Arms of Grace brochure. It was professional, and I didn't think it looked self-righteous. I requested the young woman at the *700 Club* give me time to recover, though in fact I wasn't sure about being on that show. I called Bethanne Greenfield; she asked me lots of questions for a follow-up article. I also sent her the same headshot. I was a call-in guest on our FM Christian radio station, which would also be broadcast on twenty other stations owned by the parent company.

On-camera interviews were a little trickier since wearing a shirt was difficult. A local TV station offered to come to my house, so

Leo went to the thrift store and found me an extra-large shirt that I could wear over my upper body like a poncho. I agreed to be on *Good Morning America* in two weeks, once my arm was in a sling. Call it vanity, but I refused to be on national television in a shirt big enough for an entire boy band.

Mom was not happy about any of the interviews. I knew she'd prefer I didn't talk about the shooting, or the ministry to homosexuals. She masked it by saying, "You should be resting."

Doing the interviews was exhausting, not just because I was physically tired but also because having to rehash the story over and over took an emotional toll. I was glad when they were all done.

My elation was premature.

Mom had magnanimously agreed to stay with me for at least a month. "Longer if you need me," she said in her mom-tone. After a week, I was exasperated. Every time I'd make a noise—moving my shoulder *did* hurt—she'd launch into a barrage of questions about pain level, my need for Tylenol, whether I was overdoing it, or if I should take a nap. She didn't like it if I watched TV, even when I did it in the privacy of my own room. When Alton, Barry, Darrell, and other guys from the Circle visited, she was downright rude.

"She has to go," I told Leo. "If she stays much longer, you'll have to check me into Hill Crest."

Leo was working at the psychiatric hospital as he finished his licensing requirements. He didn't stay at Grace very long after my firing; he said he would not work for a place that was so disloyal to faithful people. He vehemently disagreed with the "untenable" position of firing someone because he had a particular temptation. "That's *jodidos*," which he explained translated loosely as "fucked up."

Convincing Mom to go back to Memphis was as arduous as I expected. She was hurt that I asked and played all her maternal manipulation tactics, including tearful stories of how I was given to her by God after so many years of prayers.

I felt like crap but remained adamant nonetheless.

"I'll take care of him." Leo promised to come by every day.

It took some convincing before she agreed. She'd gotten to know Leo from my time in the hospital and liked him. Nevertheless, she gave him detailed instructions, my medication schedule, my favorite foods, and a list of "important" phone numbers: my doctor, the surgeon, the emergency room, and her home and office.

I'd miss her cooking, which I couldn't do with one arm, but we stocked up on convenience food, frozen dinners, and an ample supply of junk food, which would carry me over until I recovered some range of motion in my shoulder. I resigned myself to the reality that I'd gain weight but chose to apply my Scarlett O'Hara approach and think about that later.

"GOOD EVENING, *MIJO*," LEO SAID IN A HIGH-PITCHED VOICE when he came by after work. "Are we resting? Did you take your medicine? Do we need a bath?"

"You only *think* you're funny."

"Seriously though. How are you feeling?"

"Not bad. My chest is itchy, and I'm going stir crazy."

"So basically the same as yesterday."

"Got an interesting phone call earlier."

"More requests for interviews?"

"Goodness, no. I'll be glad when those are over. This was from a member at Grace. Said he was concerned about me and that the Lord placed it on his heart to call."

"That sounds nice."

"Yeah, you'd think. I don't really know the guy; I mean, we spoke in church, but it's not like we were friends. Anyway, we chit-chatted for a few minutes, then he asked how I'd be supporting myself since leaving the church. I mentioned Embrace, and he proceeded to give me this very polished presentation to sign me up into his

Amway group. Went on and on about what a wonderful Christian organization it is and all the money I could make."

"Multilevel marketing for Jesus. Gotta love that."

"He wanted to come by to demonstrate the products. I couldn't convince him I wasn't interested, so I pretended it was time for my nap."

"You shudda told him you'd settled with the insurance company for an exorbitant amount of money."

One article mentioned that I could file a civil suit against Brandon's parents for the negligence that led to my extensive injuries. They probably had the money, but I didn't want to add to their grief. Without asking though, they had voluntarily agreed to pay all my medical expenses.

"Hey," Leo said, his head buried in the refrigerator. "Where'd this leftover salad come from? Tell me you didn't go get it."

"Looking like this?" I waved my hand up and down my still-naked torso. "No way."

He got distracted making my dinner and didn't press the question. Telling him how the salad got there would be awkward; I was still reflecting on it myself.

GETTING MYSELF READY WAS A SLOW AND TEDIOUS PROCESS; simple tasks like brushing my teeth or shaving took longer. I couldn't take a shower, so I had to use a wash cloth and soap. I'd not mastered the art of putting on a shirt with just one mobile arm. Breakfast was cereal or Pop Tarts. Mornings included activities that didn't require much effort: reading my Bible, watching TV, making notes on my presentation to the Whole-Hearted board about closing the ministry.

Around eleven, I answered the doorbell, and there was Trey, standing on the small front porch. As soon as he saw me, his face showed his shock, and his eyes filled with tears. For several seconds, neither of us spoke.

"I was in town for a meeting with my old firm," he offered, "and thought I'd stop in to see how you're doing."

I was embarrassed for him to see me so disheveled. I was in ratty sweat pants, I still couldn't wear a shirt, and my hair probably looked like I'd been bobbing for apples in an oil drum.

"Do you...uhm...wanna come in?"

"Are you feeling up to company?"

"If you can stand how bad I look." I opened the door wider. "Besides, you are *not* company." As he walked by, I noticed a near-negligible movement, maybe the impulse to give me a hug. He did get close enough for me to catch his scent, which flooded me with memories.

"The doctor says it's healing nicely," I said, pointing to my shoulder when I noticed he couldn't stop staring at the bandages. "I should be out of this binding soon, and then it'll be a sling and physical therapy."

He looked around as we headed to the den. "Isn't your mom staying with you?"

"She left a few days ago...wait, how did you know that?"

"Susan. We've talked a couple of times since...you know. She's kept me up-to-date about your recovery."

Sneaky.

Once we were seated in the den, the awkward silence settled in again, allowing me too much time to gaze at him: stunning in dark blue slacks and a form-fitting, light blue knit shirt that highlighted his dark complexion. Black-rimmed glasses had replaced his contacts, making him look smart and sexy as hell. He noticed that I was looking at him, and a sheepish grin appeared.

That smile!

I asked about work, and he raved about his new life. "Montgomery is very different, and I'm still adjusting." He told me that Southern Poverty was consulting with Birmingham Center for Legal Services on a project, and since he knew both organizations, he'd been asked to be the liaison.

"Where are my manners? Can I get you something to drink? I can't make my own meals yet, but there are snacks in the fridge."

Instead, he went to the deli and got us salads and fruit. As we ate, we talked about movies and racquetball and laughed about my mom's over-attentiveness. It all felt familiar, comfortable.

We were...*us.*

For a moment, I imagined what might happen if I weren't bandaged up like a mummy.

My name is Nate, and I'm a new creation in Christ.

I'd made a vow to God and to myself: my actions would never compromise the core values and message of the ministry like Scot had done.

Trey is the past, I reminded myself. To bolster my resolve, I mentally quoted the Apostle Paul's admonition to the Philippians: *forgetting what lies behind and reaching forward to what lies ahead, press on toward the goal for the prize of the upward call of God in Christ Jesus.*

"I'm sorry this happened to you," he said as we shook hands at the front door.

Would he recoil if I hugged him?

"It scares the hell out of me to think—" He stopped and shook his head. "We aren't...well, even though we're a hundred miles apart, I like knowing you're OK."

But I'm not.

I couldn't say that to him. I struggled to admit it to myself.

Twenty-Five

During my recovery, Leo helped with clients who couldn't, or wouldn't, reschedule. Dr. Randall told me to take the time needed to heal and not to worry about my job. I stayed in touch with Barry and Darrel, planning the resumption of the Circle meetings in March. The publicity I'd received, which highlighted the work of Whole-Hearted, sidetracked my intention to close the ministry. I was still determined to step down.

As soon as all this attention fades.

Beyond that, my days were filled with boredom. Accentuated with occasional bouts of nebulous sadness about everything from Brandon's death to my injuries to my firing to my uncertainties about my recovery.

And of course, Trey.

To fill my time, I read more books by former-gay authors, relating their personal testimonies of change and the disciplines they credited with the transformation. I studied literature from other organizations that helped people leave homosexuality, taking notes about their methodology. They were all so different, so I was attempting to cobble together what I saw as the best parts into techniques we could use. At least when I left, the ministry would have the potential of achieving *actual* success, closer to reality than Scot's made-up rate of eighty percent.

The last week of February, we were able to remove the elastic bandages that secured my arm to my body though I had to keep using the sling until cleared by the orthopedic surgeon. The doctor instructed me to limit movement, especially up and down, as much as possible. "Let the PTs help you with exercises to increase your range of motion," he said as he wrote a prescription for pain and signed the authorization for the physical therapy. "They'll also monitor the progress and pain to prevent post-operative damage."

I think I was most excited that I'd be able to shower and put a shirt on that didn't fit me like a tent.

On the night we planned to have our first meeting, Barry agreed to drive me to the church. We arrived to a chaotic scene of protesters carrying signs and chanting, "Gay is OK" and "We won't go away."

How did they know we were meeting tonight?

When I stepped out of the car, I became the center of their attention, lighted up like someone about to perform the opening number on stage. The folks with signs also crowded in on me. I heard yelling: "Murderer" and "Why do you hate gay people?" A woman came up to me and announced, "I love my gay son." Somebody reached for me, got my sling, and pulled. The pain almost put me on my knees.

Filming all of it were several camera crews.

A well-dressed woman shoved a microphone in my face. "How does it feel to come back to the place where your courageous actions saved so many lives?" A different woman with a mic asked if I had any responses to the protesters present. A man's voice—I couldn't see his face because of the bright lights in my face—offered to go in with me to talk to some of "the survivors."

I stopped and addressed the crowd in a loud voice. "Thank you all for coming tonight. I know it's your job to cover this story, and I'm happy to cooperate. However, I cannot allow you to come inside. Please respect the privacy of our group and turn off the cameras."

That didn't happen, and only five of our regulars walked past the media to come in for the Circle.

For weeks, at least one reporter, often with a camera, would show up for our meetings. One tenacious guy found out where I lived and had the audacity to knock on my door. He even followed me to visit Leigh's grave. Her parents were there, and they were not pleased with me or the intrusion. But most persistent were the protesters; they were always there, marching in front of the church.

AFTER THE SHOOTING, MY TRAVEL SCHEDULE BECAME INSANE. I received invitations to speak at conferences, workshops, retreats, revivals, seminars, evangelistic crusades, chapel services at several Christian colleges, and denominational meetings. Regardless of my planned topic, they always introduced me as the guy who saved all those kids, and I had to include a synopsis of *that* story. To Leo and Susan, I referred to myself as "The Most Famous Unintentional Ex-Gay Leader in the Country."

I had gotten back into town from a pastors' conference in Little Rock and almost decided not to attend the Circle. Barry had invited a guest speaker—a radio preacher with a strong message about the dangers of the country's growing acceptance of homosexuals. I'd never heard him, but Barry was a fan. So I picked up my car and drove the short distance to the church.

I arrived a few minutes past seven, so I knew the sharing had begun. Even after all this time, a small group of protesters were outside, and for some reason, I walked over to a woman I'd seen there many times. I introduced myself and asked if she'd be willing to tell me her story.

"My son came out to us three years ago. His father and I were fine 'cause we already knew. But our church was so cruel. They said he had to leave the congregation. When we stood up for him, we were all disfellowshipped. Our son, who is a wonderful, devout young man, tried to end his life, thinking it would make *our* lives easier. He survived, thank God. I am a Christian mother, and I love my gay son."

What can I say to her?

Since Brandon's death, I'd heard more and more stories about young people ending their lives because of rejection for being gay.

She asked about my shoulder and even expressed her condolences for the death of Leigh. "I read about you in an article after the tragic suicide of that young man here. You've been through so much. Could I pray for you?"

"Yes, please," I said through my tears.

I'd expected her to be condemning and confrontational, praying down divine wrath on me. Instead, she held both my hands and thanked God that I'd been able to protect those who were in the building the night of the shooting. She asked for healing of my body, and my heart, and prayed that God would comfort my grief, grant me peace in ministry, and show me His love. When she finished, we hugged. She said she would continue to pray for me, and I went inside.

Barry was introducing Pastor Danny Nolan who had a small Pentecostal Church of God in Gardendale, a community just north of Birmingham. He also owned a successful machine parts business, which gave him the income to purchase advertising slots on Birmingham's popular Christian radio station along with a Sunday afternoon broadcast of his church's service.

The man, probably in his sixties, was as serious as he was obese. His face was puffy and red, looking as though his somber attitude had permanently imprinted itself on his appearance. He congratulated the group for its diligence in resisting the work of the devil. Opening his large black Bible, he read from First Corinthians, chapter six, emphasizing the passage about those who would *not* inherit the Kingdom of God. "Heaven is a place for the righteous; God will not allow sexual deviants to pass through those Gates of Pearl, nor will He permit perversion to defile those Streets of Gold."

Pastor Dan, as he liked to be called, turned the worn pages of his Bible to Leviticus, chapter eighteen, and read the verse that calls homosexuality an abomination. He then went to chapter twenty and read, "If a man lies with a male as with a woman, both of them have committed an abomination; they shall surely be put to death; their blood is upon them."

It was nothing we hadn't heard, though not with the severity... and profuse sweating...he brought to the subject. "They want to be known as 'gay,' which is saying they're happy. But I refuse to surrender that wonderful word to those who are *not* happy. How could they be, living in such debauchery? Let's call them what God calls them: sodomites. Even normal society has a better vocabulary: they're fairies, queers, and faggots."

His crude language stunned me, so I looked around the room to gage reactions. Such words were powerful triggers and could bring up strong memories of being bullied. We didn't allow that kind of terminology during our share-times.

He chastised our national leaders for "kowtowing" to the liberal homosexual agenda, driven by Satan's principalities of darkness. He went on to state that the crime of homosexuality should be punishable by death "because everyone knows it's a sickness that will destroy our nation."

I thought of the loving mother outside.

"Sorry to interrupt," I said. "Are you suggesting we kill homosexuals?"

"Not me." He held up his Bible. "God."

Is this the kind of message that drove her son to try and end his life?

Keeping my tone and volume in check, I asked: "How do you propose we do that?"

"The Bible is clear that homosexuals are worthy of death. We need laws, but thankfully God often intervenes. This homosexual disease that's risen up among the queers is His judgment on their wickedness. God will not be mocked. And it's why so many who are trapped in that depravity are suicidal; they're acting on an internal sense of divine order."

What?

"Again, not to be disruptive, but are you saying that homosexuals who kill themselves are doing God's will?"

He paused, and I hoped he was thinking and would say something that let me know I had misunderstood. "Our God is loving and long-suffering, drawing us to repentance. But when we refuse, there are consequences. The Apostle John tells us it's Satan who comes to kill and destroy. We learn in the story of Job that sometimes Satan does God's bidding. When we act outside of God's intentions, we move out of God's protection, and Satan is allowed to carry out God's will."

"So Brandon died because God wanted him to?" Alton's words were halting, full of emotion.

"It's easy to feel the loss at anyone's death, but don't lose sight of the lesson here. You can be sure that that young man will have all eternity in the fires of hell to regret his choices."

He can't be that callous.

Several guys were crying, and Alton stormed out, slamming the door.

"Study Scripture," he said, unfazed by the reactions around him. "You'll find there's a direct correlation between sins in the Bible that carried a death penalty and suicide."

"I'm sorry, but as a therapist, I can say there are a number of reasons people take their own lives. Including mental illness."

"What godless humanism labels 'mental illness,' the Word of God says is demon possession. We aren't called to coddle the unclean spirits but to cast them out."

This is a crock of shit!

I took my place next to him. "We've heard some...*interesting*... food for thought tonight, but to be good stewards of our schedule, let's close in prayer."

"You don't do these boys any service by lying to them," he said to me as I locked up the building.

"First, you've never been to one of our meetings, so you have no idea *what* we tell our members. And maybe you disagree with our approach, but I'll take it any day over using their grief, and fear, to traumatize them. That's not evangelism; it's intimidation."

I SAT DOWN AT THE TABLE WHERE LEO AND I WERE MEETING for dinner. I searched the small dining room of the Silvertron Cafe to see if I recognized anyone.

"I took the liberty of ordering you a rum and Coke," he said. "In a *regular* glass."

"That's why I love hanging out with you."

I still had concerns about drinking in public, which he understood. He raised his tumbler. "Here's to being a liberal Methodist."

Not long after I was fired from Grace, the pastor at Leo's Baptist church gave a scathing sermon about homosexuality. Following the service, Leo told the minister about his lesbian sister and respectfully suggested the man do some more studying on the subject so he wouldn't come across as such a Pharisee. Leo and Allison never returned to the church.

"How was Cleveland?"

"The wedding was lavish. Susan looked so beautiful. I've never heard of a man of honor, but she wanted me at her side. I knew it was pointless to argue since…well, since it's Susan. We had a great few days before I flew to Chicago for a Christian Woman's Leadership Conference."

We ordered our meal, and I gave him the details about Susan and Russell's wedding. He was the manager of a branch bank and a deacon at a Methodist church in Cleveland. They met at a conference and had been dating for a year. He was nice, but seemed shy, though most people seemed that way when compared with Susan. Most important, he loved her, so I approved.

I'd finished my disguised cocktail by the time our food arrived, so I ordered a Diet Sprite.

"You're awfully quiet, Nate. What's going on?"

Oh, the joys of having a best friend who's also a perceptive therapist.

"I'm feeling a little *introspective*."

"Yeah, weddings'll do that."

"I got called into a meeting of the board last week, just before I left for the wedding."

He put his fork down and folded both arms on the table.

"They're *concerned*. Apparently, they've received reports that I'm—in their words—less than enthusiastic these days. I come across as, quoting them again, 'soft on the sin of homosexuality.' They want to see me more *definitive* about God's disposition toward this sin and the promise of real and lasting change. You know: repent and change, or face hell and eternal damnation."

"Are they right?"

"About the hell fire and damnation?"

"You're deflecting."

I related the incident with the radio preacher. Barry thought I was rude for abruptly ending his presentation. "I guess they might have a point. I mean, since Brandon's death, I've chosen to direct our discussions to topics such as navigating interpersonal relationships, prayer, handling grief, and understanding God's will. We do talk about our struggles, but I've made it a point to be encouraging, not condemning. I don't want anything like what happened with Brandon to ever happen again."

At the board meeting, rather than deny or debate the allegations, I highlighted all I did for the organization, even bringing out my day planner to detail my travels and media appearances for the past seven months at which I promoted, or at least referenced, Whole-Hearted. I shamelessly reminded them that I'd been on *Good Morning America*, *The 700 Club*, *Oprah*, and the cover of *Newsweek* magazine. I admitted to fatigue from the hectic schedule and promised to rest and bring a renewed, energetic presence to the meetings. I stopped short of agreeing to the board's specified message.

"You have a lot going on. You had a serious injury, and surgery, then worked your ass off with physical therapy, and continue to work out on your own. You spend so much time traveling. Cut yourself some slack."

"You remember Alton, don't you? He's the kid who came forward about Scot's sexual activities."

Leo nodded.

"Several months ago, I learned that he'd been diagnosed with AIDS."

"Oh, Nate. I'm very sorry."

Ever since Brandon's death, Alton had confessed to several moral relapses. Nonetheless, he continued to attend, and we encouraged him in his wholeness journey.

"When I found out, I called his house, but his mother went off on this horrible tirade about God's curse on her son. Said that God was punishing him now with this disease and then for all eternity for the sin that caused it. I attempted to reason with her, but to no avail. I asked if I could come by and pray with him. 'It's too late. God has forsaken him,' she told me. Saturday, I had a message that Alton died. I can't believe his last days were filled with such vile rhetoric and thinking he deserved what happened to him."

"That's *morboso*. And *sádico*."

Let's go with fucked up!

Her words might be shocking because it was her son, but they weren't much different from the messages I was hearing as I traveled to Christian conferences and churches. Or from people like the radio preacher who came to the Circle.

"Nate, what's going on? You can talk to me."

No, I can't!

"Chalk it up to jet lag." For now, that answer would have to be sufficient.

"*Si tú lo dices.*" It was Leo's way of saying he knew there was more but wasn't going to push.

I had a conference of ex-gay ministry leaders coming up. I hoped that would help me put things back into perspective.

Or shove it all back down.

JUST BEFORE LUNCH, WITH MY BRIEFCASE IN HAND, I HEADED to the auditorium where I'd be speaking. It would have been polite to attend the morning sessions, to hear the other speakers, but after being on the road for two full weeks, I relished being alone. I ordered breakfast in my room and reread my presentation one last time. Or several last times.

When the elevator doors opened on the second floor, I took one step, then froze. There was Trey, like he'd been waiting on me. He was wearing a pair of khaki pants and a T-shirt with SPLC, for Southern Poverty Law Center, emblazoned in gold on the front. It was difficult not to notice the letters of the organization once I'd stopped looking at his body underneath. When the doors squashed in on me, I hopped into the hall.

He smiled.

Dammit!

We hugged, giving me a whiff of that familiar Trey-Aroma.

"Are you here for my presentation?" I joked as I pulled away rather than linger in the embrace.

I was one of the keynote speakers at the annual meeting of The Christian Citizens Coalition, an organization working to lobby politicians about issues important to mainstream Christians.

"Well, no." He stared above my head. "Folks from Southern Poverty are outside, handing out brochures in opposition to this organization and this conference."

Got it.

"Well, it was nice to see you." I turned to leave.

"Nathaniel." He grasped my arm, causing me to wince in pain. "Please think about what you're doing. I know we disagree about many things, but I also know *you*. These people...you are not like them." His concerned look was tender, even persuasive. More than that, it was like he saw the questions and doubts already swirling in my head. He always did have a sixth-sense ability to see inside me.

"It's been a year since we've spoken." I regretted how terse my words sounded. "How do you know—"

"Seven months to be exact." He handed me a folded piece of paper. "That's my home number. I'd like us to get together before you leave town. Talk and catch up."

No way that's gonna happen!

When I finished my presentation, I planned to jump in my car and drive back to Birmingham, knowing my schedule was clear for the foreseeable future.

It'll give me time to put Trey out of my mind. Again.

A cute young man walked up, whispered in his ear, and they left together. Arm in arm.

I did my speech, but Trey's words were in my head—distracting me, causing me to rethink what I'd written. I left out entire paragraphs of what I'd written, probably making the speech come across as stilted and disjointed.

I headed back to my room, and he was again waiting by the elevator. I wanted to blame him for the horrible speech that I hoped he hadn't heard. "Let me drop off my briefcase, and we can go somewhere to get some coffee."

He joined me in the elevator but stood on the opposite wall. No words, just a gaze and his smile. The temperature in the cramped space seemed to rise.

Dammit!

Twenty-Six

"Good morning, Delia."

"Welcome back, Nate."

It had been almost three weeks since I'd been to my office or had any client appointments. With no upcoming speaking engagements, and no interest in accepting any, I was ready to get back to my clients and into a routine.

"Is Leo here yet?"

"He's in his office." She handed me my schedule. "Your first appointment is not for an hour."

Delia had recently graduated from Jeff State Community College, with an associate degree in office administration. She was only part time for now, but was exceptional and had been essential once I had brought Leo on as my partner.

"Sorry to be blunt, brother," he said after giving me a welcome-back hug, "but you look like...*el infierno*."

"Yeah, I feel that way too."

"How was the conference?"

I'd actually been to two conferences since I'd seen Leo, one in Colorado Springs and then one in Montgomery. Both had been emotionally taxing, which I was sorting out.

"*Bien*."

"I will not be deterred by your gratuitous use of my language. I don't believe you're fine. Might as well spill it."

It's like he's a mind reader.

"I was at a leadership conference. For...uhm..."

"Ex-gay stuff," he inserted with a wave of his hand. "Yeah, yeah. Go on."

"I attended all these workshops and listened to all the keynote speakers. A panel of mothers of gay and lesbian kids, a pastor who'd been fired from his church in Denver, a middle-aged woman who realized she had same-sex feelings after more than twenty years of marriage, a seminary student who wrote his master's thesis on the early church's rejection of Roman homosexual morality, and a former actor who now runs a ministry in Los Angeles. They all had amazing testimonies of how God worked in their life, or in the lives of their children, but none of them had formal training in psychology or counseling. And yet, they are *experts*." My air quotes showed my disdain. "In many cases, they run their own ministries. I find that somewhat *unnerving*."

Leo's ever-intact professional demeanor didn't change as he repeated my last word.

I continued. "I had similar concerns after attending an Exodus conference last year. I'd hoped this one would be different."

"You never mentioned this."

Because I didn't want to give voice to my ever-increasing uncertainties.

"Everyone is *convinced* that homosexuality is wrong, but no one agrees on what causes a person to become a homosexual. They talk about bad parenting, sexual abuse, generational sin, demons...the list is endless. Since they disagree on the cause, they differ on how to cure it. These groups are all over the spectrum, from Catholic to Pentecostal. The methodologies to treat homosexuals are just so random. Some seem based in valid principles of therapy though applied and carried out by those who have no formal training in counseling. Others are downright strange. Each ministry is independent, so their leaders can say and do whatever they want; there are no professional standards of practice. Exodus is the national umbrella organization, but they don't provide actual oversight." I looked up from the notepad I'd been doodling on while I rambled. "Makes me wonder if any of them have a clue about what they're doing."

He placed one hand to the side of his cheek, widened his eyes and, with his other hand, pointed at his face. "This is my surprised look."

Yeah, very professional.

"I kinda assumed Scot was an anomaly, but at both conferences, folks would talk about prominent leaders who'd been forced to resign in disgrace because they'd been caught in a gay bar, visiting gay theaters, or having sex with their clients." I glanced down at my scribbling. Brandon's name was in the swirls of meaningless line and circles. I'd also written ABS3.

Alexander Bastien Stavros, the third.

"Is this about them, or you?"

"Can't it be both? I asked without looking up.

Trey.

"It's just a lot right now. I'm frustrated and discouraged. I'm thirty-one years old and alone. And if I'm honest, lonely. I reckon I thought my life would be, you know, *different* by now."

"Straight, married, white picket fence...all that?"

I rocked my head back and forth in response. He wasn't being snide, but at some level was challenging my thinking. Again.

"No dating prospects?"

I laughed. "I see attendees at conferences, clients here, and other men who are also working to overcome their own sexual orientation. When do I have time to meet anyone, much less date?"

"It's good that you're at least open to it."

"Even if I decided to end this ex-gay pursuit, none of *those* guys would interest me."

"Are you considering that?" There was enough excitement in his voice for me to know he would support such a decision.

"I was in Montgomery last week, and I ran into an old...uhm... friend."

His eyebrows arched in an unasked question.

"It was awkward and uncomfortable. Then, it wasn't. We talked and laughed, and...well, I can't stop thinking about it. I can't stop thinking about *him*."

Leo and I'd had numerous discussions about theories of cause of homosexuality, both biblical and psychological. However, I'd never talked about my actual sexual experiences. Today I told him everything about Trey. He asked a few questions, but mostly he listened.

"I know it's crazy after all this time. I mean, we've been apart much longer than we were together."

Together?

I'd never spoken about us in *that* way.

"Then I saw him, and everything came rushing back. It's a bad analogy, but he's like a wound. Every time I think it's healed, I see him or talk to him…and the pain is fresh again."

"If I were a therapist, I'd say it sounds like your feelings for him are unresolved. Oh, wait. I *am* a therapist."

"And an asshole." I laughed when Leo stuck his tongue out at me.

"We were going for coffee, so I needed to drop off my briefcase in the room and change into casual clothes to be ready for the drive home later. He went with me." My audible exhale was both the pleasure of the memory and the frustration that I'd allowed it to happen.

"Did you two…*dormir juntos*?"

My limited Spanish must have registered my confusion.

He used his index finger and other hand in an obscene illustration. "Did you two have sex?"

"No. Not technically."

"I'm not an expert in these matters, but if sex between you and this guy is technical, you might be doing it wrong."

"It started out innocent, and then…"

When Trey and I got into my room, I went into the bathroom to change into casual clothes. Even though he'd seen my body—*Don't think about that!*—I wasn't about to let him see the ugly scar on my shoulder. While I was changing, he said he'd leave a message at the front desk in case any of his team needed to find him.

"Won't they see this as fraternizing with the enemy?" I asked from the bathroom.

"You could never be my enemy."

When I walked out, he was smiling. "But I do like the idea of some good old-fashioned *fraternizing*."

"Where should we go?" I asked, redirecting the conversation rather than dwell on the possibility. "You know, to talk."

"I called room service and ordered a fruit and cheese plate along with diet sodas. Hope that's OK. Here is more private and comfortable than *fraternizing* at a restaurant, wouldn't you say?" He motioned for me to sit on the sofa next to him.

Damn!

"Why Mr. Stavros, are you trying to seduce me?"

"It crossed my mind, but that would be counter to both of our roles here at this conference, wouldn't it, Reverend Truett?"

While we waited for the food to arrive, he asked about everything from my shoulder to my practice to Miss Gert. As soon as the waiter left after delivering our food, he got serious. "What do you know about these people? This organization?"

"I know they're looking to be part of the political conversation in government, making sure politicians know what issues are important to the Christian community."

"Oh, that's merely their shiny exterior. When we dig deeper, I think it's more nefarious." He slipped a file folder from his backpack: newsletters and fundraising letters from the group to its members and donors. "We've been monitoring this group for years." He pointed out that the organization had been around since the sixties, originally started to oppose forced desegregation in schools. "Even today, the group still has deep-seated racism that's evident in their materials," he said, handing me an article.

He showed me that they favored criminalizing homosexuality, forcing schools to teach the Bible, with lessons that instilled a Judeo-Christian view of homosexuality as perverted and unnatural, and penalizing mental health professionals who didn't comply with the historic understanding of homosexual behavior. "They promote family values, but it's more like something from a dystopian version of *Ozzie and Harriet*."

"Please believe me. I never knew any of this. When they invited me to speak, they included a brochure with the contract, which said their mission was to be a moral influence on government leaders. Now I'm embarrassed that I agreed to be associated with this conference."

He patted my knee. "I know. That's why I wanted us to talk. Plus, I always enjoy your company."

"I owe you an apology, Trey." The statement came without much thought.

There was no reply.

"I didn't respect you. Or us. I know I hurt you, and that breaks my heart because you were so good to me. I was messed up, but you were my stability. I shouldn't have…" I was unsure how to continue. Or even if I could. Many old emotions that I did *not* want to deal with in front of him were pushing up.

"I won't lie: it hurt, but time and distance gives perspective. Maybe wisdom. I forgive you."

"Is it OK to say that I miss you?"

"Same here." He slid closer and we hugged. Then I kissed him. I intended it to be casual, from one friend to another.

I forgot how much I enjoy kissing him.

There was more kissing. Intense kissing. My hands moved across his chest like they were mindlessly following a homing device. In that moment, the feel of his skin clouded my will.

I pulled back. "I'm sorry. I can't do this." I explained as best I could, knowing his aversion to the confines of religious beliefs, that I took my role as executive director seriously. "I believe in what God is doing in my life and in our group."

I don't want to be like Scot!

"I understand that as well." He stood and buttoned his shirt. "We're on different paths. Your ministry and my job are at odds.

We're a gay version of Romeo and Juliet."

"I won't even ask which of us is Juliet," I joked, though I didn't feel jovial.

"And I hope we'll avoid that tragic ending."

"So you didn't...?" Leo asked with a disappointed look, combined with an exaggerated pout.

"Just because your wife is pregnant, you are not allowed to live vicariously through my life."

"Anything else?" he asked when I didn't continue.

Experience had taught that if I didn't open up to Leo, or tell him to back off, he'd keep asking questions to draw me out. Forced interrogation, disguised as therapy.

"I'm lonely, I'm tired, my board of directors thinks I'm not committed, and I'm having feelings for someone I can't have. Isn't that enough?"

"Not to add to your burden, but hear me out, *mi hermano*. I've known you for while now, and you're disciplined, diligent, and dedicated. I doubt anyone wants to be straight more than you or has tried harder than you to make that happen. You read books on this subject and attend all those conferences. You pray, you memorize Scripture, you go to therapy, and you're active in that support group."

"I've always believed that in time these feelings would go away. Or dissipate. I never wavered in that belief, holding on to the hope that one day, a light would turn on in my heart and that final piece of the puzzle would be revealed."

"But it hasn't, has it?" His question came with a soft, gentle tone.

"I honestly thought I'd made such progress. Then I saw Trey..." A long, slow release of air came from deep inside me. "I hear these glowing testimonies, and I wonder: why doesn't it work for me? I beat myself up, thinking there's something wrong with me. I'm conflicted about everything I've been taught and everything I've been doing for the past few years."

My name is Nate, and I'm so confused.

"Perhaps the foundational premise is *flawed*."

Leo didn't believe homosexuality was a sin; he thought the verses used to promote that idea were too obscure for such dogmatism.

"I'm beginning to think I may *never* change. Which scares the crap outta me, Leo. I have no theological framework to process that possibility."

"It pains me to see you this, uhm...*desconsolada*." The word was unfamiliar, but the meaning, and his concern, was clear as his hands twisted back and forth in front of his chest.

"My brain is messed up right now. Seeing Trey. What *almost* happened between us. I refuse to be one of *those* leaders who's one person in public and someone else in secret. I have all these questions about what I'm doing at Whole-Hearted."

"What are you saying?"

"I'm thinking of stepping down. Maybe I shudda done it a while back. How can I help them when I haven't been able to help myself?"

He paused, then laughed. "I'll gladly write you a letter of resignation, with minimal Spanish profanities."

"I'll take that into consideration."

"Did you talk to Susan about this?"

"No, but I do need to let her know. I just hate to bother her; she's been busy with her church." Susan had achieved her lifelong goal: she was the senior pastor of a small church in a Cleveland suburb. I was thrilled for her! "But if I decide to move ahead with this, she'd help you write the letter—with English translations for the profanities!"

THERE WERE VOICES IN THE RECEPTION AREA. I IGNORED THEM to finish up my notes from the day's clients, but when I heard Leo's loud laughter, I had to check it out.

"Look who dropped by for a visit." He hugged Miss Gert, who was sitting next to him.

She stood and greeted me with a hug as well. "It's good to see you, Brot…uhm, Nate."

"How are you?" Leo asked.

"Gooder'n some, older than dirt."

Dang, I love this woman.

"I brought homemade cinnamon rolls." She pointed at the aluminum-wrapped package on Delia's desk. "An early Thanksgiving treat. And I wanted to give y'all my new address. I sold our house, and I'm moving into that old-folks home down in Pelham."

She was downplaying it. I knew the place—an upscale senior adult retirement center.

"You got a minute?" she asked me.

"For you, all the time in the world." We walked into my office. "It's much smaller than our old place, but I love it here, and working with Leo." Once I had secured enough business for two therapists, we rented the space next to me, tore out some walls, and now had an office suite.

"It's perfect, and I'm proud of you. I hope you don't take that in the wrong way. I'm just being motherly."

I wish my own mother was proud. Since the shooting, she and I had not been on the best of terms.

"Did you know I had a son?"

"No, you never mentioned him."

"He died about twenty years ago in a car crash." She was staring into nowhere, perhaps reminiscing about him, or reliving his death. "He was *special*. Like you. And your friend, Trey."

What?

"You knew about him. About us?"

"I'm an old woman; I ain't a dead woman. Yet." She smiled at me. "I saw how he looked at you. Arthur—that's my son—had that same look after he'd met Curtis when they were in college at Auburn. I knew about him. And them. A mother always knows. But Artie's father didn't approve, so they moved away to a place without so much rejection and ignorance. I talked to him every week and even visited them twice in San Francisco. Artie and Curtis were happy together. I wish I'd been stronger so I could have seen him more often. But I'm glad he had someone who was there for him. I'm thankful they found a place where they could thrive and be who they were created to be."

"You never told...you surprise me, Miss Gert."

"I consider myself a devout Christian woman, but I'm also a curious old lady. I like to read books that tell me stories I haven't heard by folks who are different from me. I read *Time* magazine and *Christianity Today*, and I also read *People*. The world is a big place, with so much to learn. My son taught me that." She took both my hands and squeezed them in her own; the wrinkles were evidence of her advanced age, but at that moment, I viewed them as displays of her vast experience and acquired wisdom. "Don't be discouraged, dear boy. God formed us to love and be loved. Doin' the work you do—hearing people when they hurt and helping them in some of the worst times of their lives, it takes a heavy toll on a body, soul, and heart. To have someone you love...who loves you... at home is a Gilead's balm. You are not a better Christian when you resist the love your heart wants, even when it's something others don't understand. Love makes you a better person. My son taught me that as well."

She stood. "Thank you for letting me visit, Nate. The new space is lovely."

Maybe I should bring Miss Gert on staff as a counselor.

I was speechless as I walked her out.

Be who they were created to be.

That night, I wrote out my resignation to the Whole-Hearted Board of Directors. It was tactful and superficial, thanking the members for the confidence they'd put in me. I provided nebulous reasons for my decision: the prompting of the Spirit on my heart, needing to spend more time with my clients, and a conviction that the ministry needed fresh leadership. I wished them all the best in the future.

I didn't include any profanities, Spanish or English.

As I read and reread it, I kept coming back to the real reason: I no longer believed in the mission, the message, or the methods of the organization.

They won't be open to that kind of honesty, any more than I would have just a few months earlier.

Once the letter was sealed, ready to be addressed, and mailed, I walked into my bedroom with a sense of peace—*Maybe it's just relief*—at my decision. I knew Susan would be thrilled.

I picked up the phone.

"Hey, sorry to call so late. You got time to talk?"

Part III

An Escaped Remnant

Twenty-Seven

"Are you sure?"

I lowered the book I was reading. The concern was touching, even after our heated exchange earlier in which I'd lashed out, insisting I did *not* want to discuss it.

"I heard you when you said to drop the subject, but can you at least tell me why?"

I'd made my decision, and this conversation needed to end. I wanted to read my book. To be more accurate, I wanted to deflect the discussion by pretending to read my book. Nonetheless, I yielded to the inevitable. "Her parents could be there, and I can't see them."

"But you always go on the…on *that* day. It's…it has been ten years since her death."

As if I didn't know!

The year after Leigh died, I was at the cemetery every Saturday. That changed to regularly and then periodically. Over time, it was down to occasionally. Or rarely. But I always went on October 28th.

"After I was fired from Grace, and the reason for my termination became public, they were so cruel. Told me I was sick and depraved. That I didn't deserve Leigh, and accused me of deceiving her. Even when I explained my involvement with the ex-gay ministry—my commitment to overcome the desires—her father said he would rather see her dead than married to me. I won't run the risk of seeing them."

"What horrible things to say to anyone."

"But it's true: I wasn't honest with her."

"As I see it, you were as honest as you could be. You didn't know then. You tried to be what your parents and religion expected."

"I'm not the same man she fell in love with and married. Hell, I doubt if we met today she'd even be friends with me."

"Oh, I disagree. I've known you for a long time, Nathaniel. You are...you have *always* been a kind, generous, funny, loving, and compassionate person. That's the man she fell in love with, and it has nothing to do with your sexual orientation."

"I did love her." Tears were now running down my face. "I wasn't pretending. It was real."

"I know."

"She was my first love. Her death...her absence...left a void that's still there after all these years."

"Of course," Trey said, taking a seat next to me.

"She will always have a place in my heart, but I hope you know that *you* are the love of my life."

"Yes, I know that too," he replied, pulling me close under his strong arm. "I feel the same about you. Always have, always will. And it's in love that I repeat: you should go to the cemetery." He didn't continue until I glanced up at him. "And I'd like to go with you."

I had not expected that. "Really? You would do that?"

He placed his hand on mine, his finger fiddling with the black onyx ring he'd given me for my last birthday. "Every year I've waited here as you drove up to pay your respects. I've always admired your love and loyalty. This is important to you, and I want to be there to honor Leigh Anne, and to support you, especially if *those* nasty people are there."

The night I called Trey, more than six years ago, I'd just resigned from Whole-Hearted, and little in my life made sense.

"Do you have time to talk?" I'd asked.

"I can be there in less than two hours," he responded without hesitation.

Instead, I drove down to Montgomery, figuring the ninety-minute drive would help clear my head. It was well after midnight when I arrived. He'd made coffee and even had some healthy snacks. "I figured you hadn't eaten."

He was right of course. He was always right about me.

We hugged when I arrived, and he didn't even asked why I was there.

"I know it's strange showing up in the middle of the night, but thank you."

I had no idea what to expect when I drove down to Montgomery that first night. He could have been seeing someone or in love with someone. He had a life, and for several years, it had not included me. I just needed to talk to him. In all my confusion, I remembered him as *stability*.

He shrugged. "It wasn't how I pictured my day going this morning, but it's always good seeing you."

So gracious.

"I lied to you," I blurted out.

"You didn't like the store-bought veggie and cheese plate?"

And he knows how to make me smile.

"At my hotel, after we…uhm…kissed. I said I was doing fine. That I was living my Truth. That's the line I use when people ask, but it's a lie. My whole life is a lie."

I stirred the ice in my empty glass. "I tried for so long to not be gay. It didn't work!" I cut my eyes up to him. "But you knew it wouldn't." It sounded accusatory, like this were somehow his fault. "I wish I'd listened to you back then."

If I'd expected him to lecture me, or slam my faith, or say, "I told you so," I was mistaken.

"It hurt seeing you in so much conflict. I guess you had to try."

"Perhaps. I'm not objective enough to know anymore. I wish I'd made different choices."

"So being straight is no longer what you want?"

"It's taken me years to admit this—and you are the first person to hear me say it aloud—but no, it's not. I feel like I've wasted so much time trying to be something I can't, and I don't wanna waste any more."

"What *do* you want?"

"I want *you*." I didn't care that it sounded like a corny movie line. "I love you. I know I never said it to you, and I should've, but I couldn't allow myself to admit something like that back then. I'm saying it now. Maybe it's too late, and you may not even—"

His kiss interrupted my rambling. "I love you too, Oraios."

We talked until after two. I took off my shirt and showed him my shoulder, concerned he'd be repulsed. When he touched the scar, it was comforting and familiar. I placed my hand over his and held it there.

He made up the sofa for me; we agreed to take things slow.

That lasted for about half a day.

For that first year, we'd see each other on weekends; I went to Montgomery, or he came to Birmingham. Once, I accompanied him to an event in Philadelphia, sponsored by the Southern Poverty Law Center where he was now the director of communications and media relations. We even went on a vacation together to Fort Lauderdale, staying at a clothing-optional gay resort. My conservative Presbyterian upbringing wouldn't permit me to opt for no clothing, but it was fun watching guys gawk at my boyfriend.

As I worked to maintain my practice, I also struggled to do that with my faith. So much of what I believed—the things I'd always been taught—didn't make sense now. I gave up trying to confront all my doubts or answer all my questions. I finished my doctoral work and proudly added PhD to my name. That motivated me to make other changes in my life. Leo took over Embrace Counseling, I sold my townhouse, and moved to Montgomery. Trey and I bought a condo, I got a part-time position teaching at a small, private liberal arts college, and I started a new counseling practice.

I was ready to live a quiet life with the man I loved.

I'd been in Montgomery for about eight months when Mom died. I always felt bad that the spotlight on me had shone on her as well. She would get calls from reporters, or Christian leaders, asking her what she thought of my ministry or something I'd said in the media. She was hostile to those who called and resentful of me. After I confessed that I'd abandoned the process of trying to change—a process she continued to deny I needed—and "came out" to her as gay, our relationship deteriorated even further.

We had polite phone calls and exchanged birthday cards. She didn't come to the ceremony when I received my PhD; I told myself it was because of her declining health. She never got to meet Trey though she knew about him; we'd invited her to visit several times. When she got sick, I went home. In her hospital room, I begged her to talk to me about my life, but she refused.

I wasn't there when she died.

Trey, Susan, Russell, Leo, and Alison stood with me by her grave in Memphis, next to the church where I'd been raised. There were lots of flowers, which would make Mom happy.

At the graveside service, Susan, dressed in her robe and wearing her clerical collar, read a passage from Psalms and then offered a prayer of gratitude for Mom's dedication and service to the Lord. Trey had his arm around my waist through the entire service, which got more than a few curious stares. I had nothing to say. Just tears of regret.

"*Mi más sentido pésame*," Leo said with a hug. "My heartfelt condolences, brother." He took a step toward the grave and said softly, "*Solo pido a Dios que te dé fortaleza para sobrellevar esta pérdida.*" Alison explained it was a prayer asking God to give me strength to handle my loss.

"She loved you," Susan said, taking my hand.

"I know. Just not *this* me."

Twenty-Eight

"Hey, I have something to talk to you about when you get home."

I'd finished my last class and was grading papers when Trey called. "If you're going to break up with me, can we do it after dinner? I'm hungry."

He kept me in suspense until we were seated, with our food.

"We're hosting a conference in June in New York City, talking about AIDS and discrimination. We'll be doing workshops, and we've secured some heavy-hitter keynote speakers."

"And you want me to go with you so we can take in a Broadway show. Or a carriage ride through Central Park?"

"We can definitely do that, but actually, we were hoping...that is...I'm hoping that *you'll* be one of our speakers."

"You need a therapist's perspective on AIDS?"

"No, we want to hear from someone who was involved in ex-gay leadership."

My chest tightened; I felt ill and pushed my plate aside. "How does that relate to the conference theme?"

"We're spotlighting the ways that society ostracizes and oppresses gay and lesbian people. And let's face it: the church is one of the biggest offenders." He added, "You know that all too well."

Since the night I drove to Montgomery, I'd chosen not to talk about my ministry at Grace and especially my time at Whole-Hearted. After numerous unpleasant conversations, Trey and I had come to an "understanding" that such discussions were triggers for me. "The Nate I was when we met," I'd explained to him, "The *me* back then...he drove you away because of who I was and what I believed. We should leave that *me* in the past."

My therapist was the only person I opened up to about the lingering shame and guilt that plagued me from my involvement in the "ex-gay" movement. To her I expressed my often overwhelming sense of failure as a Christian, as a minister, and as a son. Dr. Cawdell listened as I excavated the theological programming that had motivated me to want to change, had made me believe I *should* change. I talked to her about the guilt surrounding my actions while I was involved. She was helping me accept personal responsibility for past actions, balanced by a forgiveness of myself.

Who wants to hear that shit from a conference speaker?

At the end of one emotional session, Dr. Cawdell offered her perspective. "You made mistakes. You said things that hurt others. But you didn't do it with intent or malice. You acted on what you knew...what you believed...at the time. Then you learned new information. That's how we grow. New knowledge replaces old knowledge. We all have things in our past that we wish we'd done differently. But we didn't know what we didn't know until we knew it. It's unproductive and unhealthy to beat ourselves up *now* for what we didn't know *then*."

My initial instinct was to tell Trey no. I wasn't sure I had anything of value to offer those in attendance. Besides, I'd had my time on the stage, in the spotlight. I could do without the exposure. Or the heat.

In the eight years we'd been together, Trey had been more than patient with me as I recovered from all that harsh programming, little by little shedding the rigid armor of dogma I'd accumulated. He encouraged me during my bouts of depression and held me after the night terrors. And while he'd been skeptical, even a little belligerent, he'd been supportive when I began to rediscover some semblance of faith and attend a small United Church of Christ near the college campus. I had not been to church since moving to Montgomery, not counting Mom's funeral. The pastor, Dr. Katherine Wilson, was a kind, middle-aged woman who made me feel welcomed and comfortable. Her sermons were casual, funny, thoughtful, and inspiring. One day, Pastor Katy invited me to coffee, and I found myself telling her about my past. She was patient as I fought with my emotions to describe my upbringing, my marriage, my secret struggles, and how I got involved with the ex-gay ministry. I hadn't planned to, but I also told her about Brandon's death and my life since then.

"I *do* remember reading about that incident, and I can't fathom the horror and trauma you experienced. As I listened, it occurred to me that the faith of your childhood tried to make you into someone you weren't created to be. But I suspect there were elements of that faith that got you through the tragedy of what happened and gave you strength for all the positive decisions you've made to become the person you were intended to be. As the Apostle Paul tells us in First Corinthians thirteen: 'When I was a child, I spoke like a child, I thought like a child, I reasoned like a child; when I became a man, I gave up childish ways.'"

These days, I was learning to live with the prevailing uncertainty of persistent doubts and unanswered questions when it came to religion. This was the first time in almost a decade that a verse from the Bible had brought me comfort.

"I can tell it's painful, Nate" Pastor Katy said. "But it's a great story, and I hope at some point you'll find a way to talk about it more freely. One of the things I've learned is that a great story is meant to be shared. It speaks to others. That's why Jesus used parables so often. Maybe your story can prevent others from having to endure years of painful struggle of denying who God created them to be."

"If you're not interested," Trey told me, "we will understand. But with your background, your training, and your incredible speaking ability, you're the perfect choice."

Flattery?

I wanted to resent him for asking me to dredge all that up, but such a sinister motive was not in his nature. The counsel of Dr. Cawdell and the exhortation of Pastor Katy swirled around in my head.

It's just one presentation.

As usual, my psychic abilities proved useless.

THE APPLAUSE AFTER MY INTRODUCTION HAD BEEN COURTEOUS, but then Trey had been sparse with details, telling the audience about my position at the university and as a therapist. In the program, the title of my address was "Recovering from Religious Abuse."

There was lots of murmuring noise when I walked on stage, and some were leaving. It made sense. A professor talking about religion screamed *Boring!* The fact that I came after a charismatic, articulate TV celebrity talking about his father who had died of AIDS didn't help. Throughout his short testimony, cameras were flashing.

I retrieved a large black King James Bible from the shelf in the podium. The people I could see in the first rows looked surprised. Or curious.

"I was raised in a conservative church. My father was a pastor and leader in our denomination." I held the Bible high over my head. "This was the very Bible he used in the pulpit, at my home church in Memphis, Tennessee." A smattering of folks—apparently residents—clapped.

"In my world, this was God's authoritative Truth." I hugged it to my chest. "I was taught to cherish it, to study it, to memorize it and, most of all, to *believe* it. I went to a Christian college founded on teaching the principles of the Bible. I dedicated my life to being obedient to what's in here, and I chose a career in ministry so I could help others do the same."

I placed the Bible on the podium. Standing to the side, I gazed at it as I counted in silence the seconds I'd rehearsed. "So when people quoted...from the Bible...that I was 'an abomination' because of my secret sexual desires, of course I believed it. They said my attractions were unnatural, immoral, depraved. And I believed them."

I turned to the auditorium. "For a young boy who loved God and wanted to serve the church, I was devastated. And terrified.

Then I heard someone say this Bible—" I pointed to my left, "—also offered the path to conquer my attractions. Clinging to that promise, I got involved with a small ministry that promised I could change my sexual orientation. That was blessed good news because I was on staff at a conservative Church, and I *desperately* needed to be *not* gay. If anyone found out I had these hidden feelings, I would lose my position.

"For three years, I did everything I was instructed to do—what I was supposed to do—to overcome what that Book calls *sin.* I even began dating a lovely woman. In these groups, we were told to claim God's promise *as if* it were already reality. Say it, and you will see it. Repeat it to believe it and receive it. 'My name is Nate, and I'm…straight.'" There were giggles and some muttering. "I was dedicated and determined. Folks around me assumed it was working, and I couldn't tell them it wasn't because…well, 'I'm Nate, and I'm struggling' wasn't a positive confession of faith."

I noticed movement and glanced toward the wings. The young actor who'd spoken before me and several of Southern Poverty's staff were standing next to Trey. Listening to *me.*

"When the leader of our ex-gay ministry was removed because of impropriety, I was appointed executive director. Now I was in charge and had to stand before struggling young men, insisting they do something I could not do—change who they were."

The murmuring was louder this time. And angrier. It rattled me, and I'd lost my place in my speech.

"The internal turmoil was wrecking my life—emotionally, spiritually, and physically. Many nights, I drank myself to sleep, and I had trouble keeping food down. But what could I do? Could I admit that after all my rigorous efforts, it wasn't working? Absolutely not. I mean, I was the leader. How would that look? So like a good Christian soldier, I pushed down the doubts and persevered. I kept trying, kept praying, and kept repeating my mantra. 'My name is Nate, and I'm *not gay*?'" I reached over and patted the Bible. "After all, this book says, 'With God, nothing is impossible' so the problem had to be me.

"Not long after I took over in the role of leader, an unstable young man in our group showed up angry, confused, off his medication. And with a gun. You might have heard the story; it was all over the news. I convinced him to allow the other boys to go into another room so he and I could talk. I desperately wanted to help him. I tried to help, but he committed suicide—right in front of me."

I heard gasps.

It had been so long since that awful night, but right then, on that stage, the feelings surged up like it had happened last week. Brandon's face was vivid. So was his anguish. My shoulder twinged. I got dizzy. And queasy. It was all so real. The sound of the gun echoed in my head. The taste and smell of his splattered blood. With each memory, I walked back and forth on the stage and told the story, tears rolling down my face. Some who'd been leaving were now standing against the back wall. The auditorium was so quiet that I could hear folks in the hallway.

I was off script. This was not part of what I'd intended to say.

I hope Trey won't be upset.

"The Christian media called me a hero and a righteous success story of someone who'd changed his sexual orientation." I paused to push the accompanying emotions back down and prevent breaking into sobs in view of an audience. "Afterward, I was invited to share my *story of transformation*—" I used air quotes. "—with churches and groups around the country. I was on radio and TV and in Christian magazines. But notoriety couldn't silence the questions inside, growing louder and more persistent.

"Then another member of our ministry died. Of AIDS. A gentle, sweet, and brave young man. As he became sicker, his own mother told him that his disease was divine judgment and that he'd spend eternity in hell because of his sinful choices. He spent his final days on earth hearing that hate, disguised as religion. My heart broke, and with it, my ex-gay house of cards imploded. God...the Bible... as a weapon to hurt people. What the hell was wrong with us? How did we get to that kind of merciless mentality? This was not the

Gospel—the Good News—my father had taught us in church. This was not the Jesus I had learned about in Sunday school."

Picking up the Bible again, I held it out with extended arms. "At one time, *this* was where I went for answers; now I don't know what I believe about what's here. But there is one verse I remember." I opened to the passage. "Don't worry, I won't be preaching a sermon or having an altar call." That got some laughs, which helped me relax. "In James, chapter one, verse eight, we read: '*A double minded man is unstable in all his ways.*' You know what? I do believe that...because I lived it. I wanted to be straight, said I was straight, and pretended to be straight. I was living a lie. I *was* that double-minded man, and my life was an unstable mess. I lost a job I loved, and it almost cost me the man I loved."

When I put the Bible back on the podium, it made a noise louder than I'd intended.

"It's been years since I've talked about any of this. As you can probably tell, it's not an easy topic for me. I spent a lot of time trying to forget it, throwing myself into my career, and self-medicating with alcohol. I hoped I'd put it away in some secret shoebox, in a dark corner of my mind's attic. Thankfully, I have a wonderful, patient partner who was there with me and for me. I learned in AA that we are only as sick as our secrets. So once again, I find myself coming out...of a different closet. My name is Nate, and I used to be an ex-gay leader."

A camera flash startled me, and I saw a young man crouched in front of the stage.

"Let me conclude with this: I was wrong, and I'm sorry." My tears returned with full force. "I deeply regret my role in adding to the pain and suffering of those already being condemned and rejected by their parents and their churches. I apologize to all the young men who were part of my ministry and to those who looked up to me as some kind of example or role model. I am neither. There is no way to undo the damage done, to restore what was taken away from us. I can't give grieving parents back their dead son. So tonight, with single-mindedness and my whole heart, you have my promise that I will spend the rest of my life working to expose the deception and the dangers of those folks who, as I did, lie about sexual orientation and make false promises that it can…that it *should*…be changed."

I gathered the sheets of paper that contained my intended speech and picked up Dad's Bible. "Thank you."

The applause was sparse and scattered through the auditorium. When I reached Trey, he hugged me so tight. "God, I never knew all that," he whispered in my ear. "I love you."

The actor who'd spoken before me put his arm around my waist. "Hear that out there?" He pointed to the stage. It was loud, and I assumed they'd introduced the next speaker. "It's for you, Nate. You should go back out there. In my world, that's a *curtain call*."

Trey took my hand, and together we walked to center stage. The applause increased, accentuated by more camera flashes.

WHEN THE PHONE RANG, I UNTWINED FROM TREY ON THE SOFA where we were watching *The West Wing*.

"Holy headlines, Batman," Susan said as soon as I answered. "How do you always manage to get your name in the paper?"

"She read the article," I whispered to him.

A reporter from *The New York Times* was covering the SPLC event, heard my speech, and asked if we could talk afterward. In addition to coverage about the conference, a separate story about me ran called, "Confessions of a Double-Minded Man."

Once again, I was the man who saved those kids, but now I was denouncing the kinds of programs with which I'd once been involved. "They make claims they can't substantiate and promises they can't keep," I was quoted. "They lied to me, and I believed their lies. Worse, I perpetrated those lies to others. In my own deception, I deceived others." The article included my apology about my involvement and concluded with the scandalous detail that I was now openly gay and living in a "homosexual relationship."

The story was picked up by a national newswire; newspapers, magazines, and TV stations were calling for interviews. A few groups were requesting speaking engagements. I felt bad I'd overshadowed the conference message though Trey was unfazed, noting that SPLC was mentioned in almost every article about me.

Christian media outlets that had once sought me out to be a guest, or spokesperson, condemned me. They vilified me for abandoning my faith and for the lives I was leading astray. They warned about my eternal destiny, saying I should repent of my rebellion. Of course, this prompted a flood of harsh, hateful mail sent to my home, my office, the college, and to Southern Poverty. A couple of the letters were threatening enough to be handed over to the Montgomery police.

My story was also covered in several national gay and lesbian magazines, which then circulated in many gay and lesbian local publications. Most reported the events of Brandon's suicide; fewer included my apology. Some portrayed me as intentionally harming unsuspecting kids and questioned the sincerity of my apology. They hadn't bothered to interview me, but their coverage resulted in nasty mail from the gay and lesbian community as well.

In the midst of it all, there were affirming, encouraging messages that kept me from total despair. Miss Gert sent a note saying how much she loved and missed me. The youth minister from Grace Presbyterian, now the senior pastor of his own congregation, said he appreciated my integrity. "I know that our denomination's teaching about homosexuality is tenuous at best. But my church is just not ready to hear that message."

One day, Darrel, who'd been active while I was the leader, called in tears. "Thank you, Nate. I left the group six years ago, came out, and have an amazing boyfriend. But I've lived in fear that you'd find out and be disappointed." He told me Barry had taken over as director of Whole-Hearted. "He's been in the local news a lot since your very public coming out." He read me an article in which Barry had the gall to insist I'd never really been *that* involved. "Our ministry is about living in holiness," Barry explained. "The success we offer is not based on misleading statistics but on God's promise to lead us on the path of righteousness, for His Name sake."

"I'm proud of you, Nathaniel," Susan gushed, then proceeded to offer her opinions about which of the speaking engagements I would accept.

So much for my quiet life!

Epilogue

"I missed you."

I toss my bag in the back seat and lean across the center console to kiss him.

"How did it go at the conference?"

I'd been a featured presenter at a national marriage and family therapists' symposium in Chicago. My presentation focused on the deceit of those who promised a change in sexual orientation, highlighting the spurious methodology often used by untrained leaders. Of course, I shared my own story of "ex-gay" involvement. I chose to skip the final-night gala to fly back to Montgomery and avoid spending another night in a hotel.

"You know those counselors—party animals and rabble-rousers."

I don't travel as much as I did after Brandon's death, and I'm not the national sensation I'd once been, which is fine with me. However, I made that promise at the SPLC conference, so I welcome the opportunities. I've written articles for national publications and made myself available for media interviews. After an appearance on *Politically Incorrect*, a publisher contacted me to write a book about "ex-gay" treatments, citing my credentials as a one who was part of that world, a licensed therapist, and professor of counseling. In the book, I critiqued the conservative religious presuppositions of homosexual origins, the fraudulent claims by groups that promise that sexual orientation can be changed, the spurious methodologies they use, and the vague criteria of success often cited. My book primarily targeted parents with gay or lesbian kids, but included anyone thinking about enrolling in one of these programs. It was only a minor success in the general population, but I'm told it's a regular topic of conversation at "ex-gay" conferences.

I take a small amount of pleasure in that.

One surprise that came with this round of notoriety was reconnecting with some of the ministry leaders who used to cause me such *Why is it working for them and not me?* consternation. Turns out, they were having the same internal conflicts and doubts I was. And eventually, they'd also made the decision to abandon that mindset. It's exciting to join my voice with others.

In my travels, I've also met many men and women who were once part of an "ex-gay" group or program. The stories they tell, the hurt they endured, serve to renew my dedication to speaking out. We are the "escaped remnant," as one of the former leaders described us, using a term from the Old Testament book of Ezra.

"Mom and dad called while you were gone. We're uncles again. They want us to come up soon and meet baby Caroline."

"That's wonderful. When I talked to Alena last week, she was miserable and so ready for this baby to arrive. Yes, let's do it. Leo has been bugging me for weeks, and I told Darrell that we'd meet his boyfriend."

I recline the seat as Trey drives.

At home, I undress and head to the hot tub on our patio while he gets us some wine. I close my eyes and relax.

Let me be honest: there *are* still times when I think about being straight, even though I'm convinced such a change is not possible. Certainly not necessary. I reckon it's those old tapes in my head—embedded religious messages of condemnation and judgment—that aren't easy to erase. Sometimes they can be loud and incessant, telling me: You're not *really* gay. You can change.

I feel movement and look up at the stunningly gorgeous man who captured my heart. His arms flex as he slowly lowers himself into the water. His toned, sculpted physique draws my gaze, causing my own body to respond.

Nope!

"My name is Nate, and I *am* a gay man."

Afterword

My name is Bill, and I'm the *actual* author of this book. (*Sorry, Nate.*)

For years, folks encouraged me to write my autobiography. Instead, I decided to filter my memories through the lens of a fictional life. Nate is both me, and not me. What you just read is a fictionalized amalgamation that includes actual experiences from real events, people, practices, and (sadly) theological beliefs. I'm drawing from my own personal life along with thirty-plus years of research.

Like our not-always-valiant protagonist, I'm from Birmingham, and I served as a minister in a conservative church. I too spent years trying to change, or at least suppress, my sexual orientation. Over time, I received invitations to speak to churches, at conferences, and in the media about my efforts to change, which many took as a "successful transformation." A ministry grew up with those who sought me out, and I served as the executive director.

After nearly eight years, I knew it wasn't working. I was burned out and depressed. Once I could admit that, I walked away rather than knowingly perpetuating the lies. My ministry was over, my faith was crippled, my marriage ended, and my family was fractured. I was a failure. The emotional and spiritual toll led me to the point of suicide. It took years of hard work, therapy, and many loving, patient people to help me put my life back together. For the past three decades, it's been my passion to protect others from the harm inflicted by these people and groups.

I hope I've provided a detached objectivity in the narration while presenting the appalling realities of these "ex-gay" programs. I often wanted to interject my own feelings, my own perspective, based on hindsight. But Nate had to learn these lessons in his own time, as I did.

That said, I confess: I didn't do justice to these ministries and individuals. I knew it would be impossible to accurately convey the heinous messages they proclaimed or include the legion of extreme methods employed by various groups in their quest for "success." (*It would be a horror novel!*) This story centers on the struggles of one man, caught up in that insidious mindset.

Please don't be too hard on Nate. He's a "double-minded man," an example of what we now call "cognitive dissonance." So was I. If something or someone didn't align with our ingrained, unquestionable theology, we ignored, denied, or discounted it in favor of what we believed. Faith over facts. We couldn't embrace or act on our "same-sex attractions." The Bible said it was wrong. End of discussion!

Because I'm vocal, and appear regularly in the media, I hear from those who are appalled at my participation and my leadership in an "ex-gay" ministry.

How could you teach that?

How could you believe that?

The words used by Nate's therapist are the ones I live by and what I tell others: I didn't know what I didn't know...until I knew it. It doesn't reverse the damage that was done to me and by me, but it's how I've been able to cope.

Writing this book was cathartic for me. I pray it offers hope to other survivors and serves as a cautionary tale to anyone considering these treatments.

Thank you for going along with me...and Nate...on our pilgrimage.

~ *Bill Prickett, 2019*

About the Author

Bill Prickett grew up in Birmingham, Alabama. He served more than five years in youth ministry, eleven years as pastor of a Southern Baptist Church, and four years as pastor of an independent, evangelical congregation. He has a bachelor's degree in religion, with a double minor in English and psychology. His seminary training included advanced theological studies and biblical languages.

To comply with the teachings of his conservative Christian faith, he spent more than eight years trying to change his sexual orientation. Eventually, he became executive director of an "ex-gay" ministry, working with others who also struggled with homosexuality. He wrote curriculum for the group, spoke at churches and conferences around the country, was interviewed by national and local media, and became a go-to consultant for evangelical organizations and Christian counselors.

Since abandoning those futile efforts, he's spent decades speaking out about the deception and dangers of programs now known as conversion therapy. Numerous publications have featured his survivor story or sought out his personal insights on this subject.

After leaving the ministry, he built a successful career in public relations and communications. Now retired, he lives outside Dallas with his husband and their rescue mutt, Brody.

CPSIA information can be obtained
at www.ICGtesting.com
Printed in the USA
LVHW040059011019
632709LV00003B/163/P